Read, Write, LOVE

The Remingtons, Book Five

Love in Bloom Series

Melissa Foster

ISBN-13: 978-0-9910468-8-1
ISBN-10: 0991046889

This is a work of fiction. The events and characters described herein are imaginary and are not intended to refer to specific places or living persons. The opinions expressed in this manuscript are solely the opinions of the author and do not represent the opinions or thoughts of the publisher. The author has represented and warranted full ownership and/or legal right to publish all the materials in this book.

READ, WRITE, LOVE
All Rights Reserved.
Copyright © 2014 Melissa Foster
V1.0

This book may not be reproduced, transmitted, or stored in whole or in part by any means, including graphic, electronic, or mechanical without the express written consent of the publisher except in the case of brief quotations embodied in critical articles and reviews.

Cover Design: Natasha Brown

WORLD LITERARY PRESS
PRINTED IN THE UNITED STATES OF AMERICA

A Note to Readers

What a joy it was to write about an author who rarely steps out of his writing cave. Talk about being able to relate! Kurt needed a very special woman to drag him into the real world, and the moment I met Leanna Bray, I knew she was the perfect soul mate for him. This book is set on Cape Cod, and in it you'll meet four of the characters from the Seaside Summers series. I hope you enjoy them all as much as I do.

In the back of this book you'll find recipes for the Luscious Leanna's Sweet Treat jams mentioned in this book. Luscious Leanna's Sweet Treats are also available on Amazon, through my website, and also through Al's Backwoods Berries website.

Read, Write, Love is the fifth book of The Remingtons and the fourteenth book in the Love in Bloom series. While it may be read as a stand-alone novel, for even more enjoyment, you may want to read the rest of the Love in Bloom novels (the *Snow Sisters*, *The Bradens*, and *The Remingtons*).

Melissa Foster

For Les, who totally gets me

PRAISE FOR MELISSA FOSTER

"Contemporary romance at its hottest. Each Braden sibling left me craving the next. Sensual, sexy, and satisfying, the Braden series is a captivating blend of the dance between lust, love, and life."
—*Bestselling author Keri Nola, LMHC*
(on The Bradens)

"[LOVERS AT HEART] Foster's tale of stubborn yet persistent love takes us on a heartbreaking and soul-searing journey."
—*Reader's Favorite*

"Smart, uplifting, and beautifully layered. I couldn't put it down!"
—*National bestselling author Jane Porter*
(on SISTERS IN LOVE*)*

"Steamy love scenes, emotionally charged drama, and a family-driven story make this the perfect story for any romance reader."
—*Midwest Book Review (on* SISTERS IN BLOOM*)*

"HAVE NO SHAME is a powerful testimony to love and the progressive, logical evolution of social consciousness, with an outcome that readers will find engrossing, unexpected, and ultimately eye-opening."
—*Midwest Book Review*

"TRACES OF KARA is psychological suspense at its best, weaving a tight-knit plot, unrelenting action, and tense moments that don't let up and ending in a fiery, unpredictable revelation."
—*Midwest Book Review*

"[MEGAN'S WAY] A wonderful, warm, and thought-provoking story...a deep and moving book that speaks to men as well as women, and I urge you all to put it on your reading list."
—*Mensa Bulletin*

"[CHASING AMANDA] Secrets make this tale outstanding."
—*Hagerstown* magazine

"COME BACK TO ME is a hauntingly beautiful love story set against the backdrop of betrayal in a broken world."
—*Bestselling author Sue Harrison*

Chapter One

THE TIDE LAPPED at the sandy shore beyond the deck of the cedar-shingled bungalow where Kurt Remington sat on the deck of his cottage, fingers to keyboard, working on his latest manuscript. *Dark Times* was due to his agent at the end of the month, and Kurt came to his cottage in Wellfleet, Massachusetts, to hunker down for the summer and complete the project. He lived just outside of New York City and he wrote daily, sometimes for ten or twelve hours straight. In the summers, he liked the change of scenery the Cape offered and was inspired by the Cape's fresh air and the sounds of the sea.

He'd bought the estate of a local painter a few years earlier with the intent of renovating the artist's studio that sat nestled among a grouping of trees on the far side of the property. Initially, Kurt thought he might use the studio as a writing retreat separate from where he lived, with the idea that leaving the cottage to work might give him a chance to actually have a life and not feel pressure to write twenty-four-seven. What he found was that the studio was too far removed from the sights and sounds that inspired him, and it made him feel like even more of a recluse than he already was. He realized that it wasn't the location of his computer that pressured him. It was his internal drive and his love of writing that propelled his fingers to the keyboard every waking second. The idea of making the studio into a guest cottage crossed his mind, but that would indicate his desire to have guests, which would mean giving up his coveted writing time to entertain. So there it sat, awaiting...something. Though he had no idea what.

The cottage was built down a private road at the top of a dune, with a private beach below. A curtain of dense air settled around him. Kurt lifted his eyes long enough to scan the graying clouds and ponder the imminence of rain. It was seven twenty in the evening, and he'd been writing since nine o'clock that morning, as was his daily habit, right after his three-mile run, two cups of coffee, and a quick breeze through the newspaper and email. Once Kurt got into his writing zone each day, other than getting up to eat, he rarely changed his surroundings. The idea of moving inside and breaking his train of thought was unsettling.

He set his hands back on the keyboard and reread the last few sentences of what would become his thirteenth thriller novel. A dog barked in the distance, and Kurt drew his thick, dark brows together without breaking the stride of his keystrokes. Kurt hadn't risen to the ranks of Patterson, King, and Grisham by being easily distracted.

"Pepper! Come on, boy!" A female voice sliced through his concentration. "Come on, Pepper. Where are you?"

Kurt's fingers hesitated for only a moment as she hollered; then he went right back to the killer lurking outside the window in his story.

"Pepper!" the woman yelled again. "Oh God, Pepper, really?"

Kurt closed his eyes for a beat as the wind picked up. The woman's voice *was* distracting him. She was too close to ignore. *Get your mutt and move on.* He let out a breath and went back to work. Kurt craved silence. The quieter things were, the better he could hear his characters and think through their issues. He tried to ignore the sounds of splashing and continued writing.

"Pepper! No, Pepper!"

Great. He was hoping to squeeze in a few more hours of writing on the deck before taking a walk on the beach, but if that woman kept up her racket, he'd be forced to work inside—and if there was one thing Kurt hated, it was changing his surroundings while he was in the zone. Writing was an art that took total focus. He'd honed his craft with the efficiency of a drill sergeant, which was only fitting since his father was a four-star general.

More splashing.

"Oh no! Pepper? Pepper!"

The woman's panicked voice split his focus right down the center. He thought of his sister, Siena, and for a second he considered getting up to see if the woman's concern was valid. Then he remembered that his sister often overreacted. Women often overreacted.

"Pepper! Oh no!"

Being an older brother came with responsibilities that Kurt took seriously, as had been ingrained in him at a young age. That loud woman was someone's daughter. His conscience won over the battle for focus, and with a sigh, he pushed away from the table and went to the railing. He caught sight of the woman wading waist deep in the rough ocean waves.

"Pepper! Oh, God. Pepper, please come back!" she cried.

Kurt followed her gaze into deeper water, which was becoming rougher by the second as the clouds darkened and the wind picked up a notch. He didn't see a dog anywhere in the water. He scanned the empty beach—no dog there, either.

"Pepper! Please, Pep! Come on, boy!" She tumbled back with the next wave and fell on her ass, then struggled to find her footing.

Christ Almighty. Really? This, he didn't need. He watched her push through the crashing waves. She was shoulder deep. Kurt knew about the dangers of riptides and storms and wondered why the hell she didn't. She had no business being out in the water with a storm brewing.

Drops of water dampened Kurt's arms. He swatted them away with a grimace, still watching the woman.

"Please come back, Pepper!"

The rain came in a heavy drizzle now. *Damn it to hell.* Kurt spun around, gathered his computer and notes and brought them inside. He checked to see that he'd saved his file before pushing the laptop safely back from the edge of the counter, then turned back to the French doors. *I could close the doors and go right back to work.* He eyed his laptop.

"Pepper!"

She sounded farther away now. Maybe she'd moved on. He went back out on the deck to see if she'd come to her senses.

"Pep—" Another wave toppled her over. She was deeper now and seemed to be pulled by the current.

"Hey!" Kurt hollered in an effort to dissuade her from going out any deeper. She must not have heard him. He scanned the water again and saw a flash of something about thirty feet away from her. *Your damn dog.* Dogs were smelly, they shed, and they needed time and attention. All reasons why Kurt was not a fan of the creatures.

The rain picked up with the gusty wind. *Damn it.* He grabbed a towel from inside and stomped down the steps, *Dark Times* begrudgingly pushed aside.

LEANNA BRAY WAS wet, cold, and floundering. Literally. She'd been floundering for twenty-eight years, so this was nothing new, but being pummeled by rain, wind, and waves, chasing a dog that never listened? That was new.

"Pepp—" A wave knocked her off her feet and she went under the water, taking a mouthful of saltwater along with her. She tumbled head down beneath the surface.

Now Pepper and I will both drown. Freaking

perfect.

Something grabbed her arm, and she reflexively fought against it, sucking in another mouthful of salty water as she broke through the surface, arms flailing, choking, and pushing against the powerful hand that yanked her to her feet.

"You okay?" A deep, annoyed voice carried over the din of the crashing waves.

Cough. Cough. "Yeah. I—" *Cough. Cough.* "My dog." She blinked and blinked, trying to clear the saltwater and rain from her eyes. The man's mop of wet, dark hair came into focus. He held tightly to her arm while scanning the water in the direction of where she'd last seen Pepper. His clothes stuck to his body like a second skin, riding the ripples of his impressive chest and arms as he held her above the surface with one arm around her ribs.

"Come on." She coughed as he plowed through the pounding surf with her clutched against his side. She slid down his body, and he lifted her easily into his arms, carrying her like he might carry a child, pressing her to his chest as he fought against the waves.

She pushed against his chest, feeling ridiculous and helpless…and maybe a little thankful, but she was ignoring that emotion in order to save Pepper.

"My dog! I need to get my dog!" she hollered.

Mr. Big, Tall, and Stoic didn't say a word. He set her on the wet sand and tossed her a rain-soaked towel. "It was dry." He pointed behind her to a wooden staircase. "Go up to the deck."

She dropped the towel and plowed past him toward the water. "I gotta get my dog."

He snagged her by the arm and glared at her with the brightest blue eyes she'd ever seen—and a stare so dark she swallowed her voice.

"Go." He pointed to those damn stairs again. "I'll get your dog." He took a step toward the water, and she pushed past him again.

"You don't have t—"

He scooped her into his arms again and carried her to the stairs. "If you fight me, your dog will drown. He won't last in this much longer."

She pushed at his chest again. "Let me go!"

He set her down on the stairs. "The waves will pull you under. I'll get your dog. Please stay here."

Her heart thundered against her ribs as she watched him stalk off and plow through the waves as if he were indestructible. She stood in the rain on the bottom stair, huddled beneath the wet towel, squinting to see him through the driving rain. She finally spotted him deep in the sea, wrapping his arms around Pepper—the dog who never let anyone carry him. He rounded his shoulders, shielding Pepper as he made his way back through the wild waves.

She ran to the edge of the water, shivering, tears in her eyes. "Thank you!" She reached for Pepper and the dog whined, pressing his trembling body closer to the guy.

"You have a leash?"

She shook her head. Her wet hair whipped across her cheek, and she turned her back to the wind. "He doesn't like them."

He took her by the arm again. "Come on." He led her up the stairs to a wooden deck, opened a French door, and leaned in close, talking over the sheeting rain.

"Go on in."

She stepped onto pristine hardwood. The warm cottage smelled of coffee and something sweet and masculine, like a campfire. She reached for Pepper. Pepper whined again and pressed against the man's chest.

"He..." Her teeth chattered from the cold. "He must be scared."

"I'll get you a towel." He eyed the dog in his arms and shook his head before disappearing up a stairwell.

Leanna scoped out the open floor plan of the cozy cottage, looking for signs of *crazy*. How crazy could he be? He'd just rescued her and Pepper, and Pepper already seemed to be quite attached to him. *He went into the water in a storm without an ounce of fear. Damn crazy.* It dawned on her that she'd done the same thing, but she knew *she* wasn't crazy. She'd had no choice. To her right was a small kitchen with expensive-looking light wood cabinets and fancy molding. A laptop sat open beside two neatly stacked notebooks on the shiny marble countertop. The screen was dark, and she had an urge to touch a button and bring the laptop to life, but she didn't really want to know if there was something awful on there. He could have been watching porn, for all she knew, although he hadn't checked her out once, even with her wet T-shirt and shorter-than-short jeans shorts. She couldn't decide if that was gentlemanly or creepy.

She shifted her thoughts away from the computer to the quaint breakfast nook to her left. Her eyes traveled past a little alcove with two closed doors and a set of stairs by the kitchen to the white-walled living room. There was not a speck of clutter anywhere. A pair of flip-flops sat by the front door, perfectly lined up against the wall beside a pair of running shoes. She located the source of the campfire smell. A gorgeous two-story stone fireplace covered most of the wall adjacent to an oversized brown couch. There was a small stack of firewood in a metal holder beside the hearth. The cottage was surprisingly warm considering there wasn't a fire in the fireplace. Dark wood bookshelves ran the length of the far wall, from floor to ceiling, complete with a rolling ladder. The room was full of textures—a chenille blanket was folded neatly across the back of the couch, a thick, brown shag rug sat before the stone fireplace, and an intricately carved wooden table was placed before the couch. Leanna had a thing for textures, and right now she was texturing the beautiful hardwood with drops of water. She snagged a dishtowel from the kitchen counter as the man came back downstairs with Pepper cradled in his arms like a baby and wrapped in a big fluffy towel.

The possibility of him being crazy went out the door. *Crazy people don't carry dogs like babies.*

He shifted Pepper to one arm and handed her a fresh towel. "Here. I'm Kurt, by the way."

Pepper sat up in his arms, panting happily. *Show-off.*

"Thank you. I'm Leanna. That's Pepper." She tried to mop up the floor around her. Every swipe of the towel brought more drips from her sopping-wet clothing. "I'm sorry about this. For the mess. And my dog. And…" She frantically wiped the floor with the dishrag in one hand, using the fisted towel in the other to scrub her clothes, trying desperately to stop the river that ran from her clothes to his no-longer-pristine floor. She lifted her gaze. He had a slightly amused smile on his very handsome face. She rose to her feet with a defeated sigh.

"I'm so sorry, and thank you for rescuing Pepper."

He glanced at his laptop, and that amused look quickly turned to pinched annoyance. His lips pressed into a tight line, and when he glanced at her again, it was with a brooding look, before stepping forward and closing his laptop.

"You should have"—Pepper barked in his ear; he closed his eyes and exhaled—"had the dog on a leash."

The dog.

"He hates it. He hates listening, leashes, lots of things." Pepper licked Kurt's cheek. "Except you, I guess."

Kurt winced and set Pepper on the floor. "Sit," he said in a deep, stern voice.

Pepper sat at his feet.

"How did you do that? He never listens."

He dried Pepper's feet with the towel, apparently ignoring the question.

"Labradoodle?"

You know dogs? She was intrigued by the dichotomy of him. He was sharp, brooding, and maybe even a little cold, yet Pepper followed him to the fireplace as if he were handing out doggy biscuits. Leanna couldn't help but notice the way Kurt's wet jeans hugged his ass. *His very hot ass.* He crouched before the fireplace, his shirt clinging tightly to his broad back, his sleeves hitched up above his bulging biceps, and she made out the outline of a tattoo on his upper arm.

"Yeah, Labradoodle. How'd you know? He looks like a wet mutt right now."

He shrugged, expertly fashioning a teepee of kindling, then starting a small fire. "Where's your place?" He slid an annoyed look at Pepper and shook his head.

"Um, my place?" she said, distracted as much by Pepper's obedience as by Kurt's tattoo. *What is that? A snake? Dragon?*

He looked at her with that amused glint in his eyes again. "House? Cottage? Campsite?"

"Oh, cottage. Sorry." She felt her cheeks flush. "It's about a mile and a half from here. Seaside? Do you know it? My parents own it. I'm just staying for the summer. I've known the other people in the community forever, and Pepper likes it there."

He looked back at the fireplace, the amusement in his expression replaced with seriousness. "Come over by the fire. Warm up."

She tossed the towels on the counter and joined him by the fire, shivering as she warmed her hands.

He kept his eyes trained on the fire.

"Did you drive here?" He picked up a log in one big hand and settled it on the fire.

"No. I biked."

"Biked?"

"I bike here a couple times each week with

Pepper, but we usually go the other way down the beach. Pepper just took off this time. I left my bike by the public beach entrance."

His eyes slid to Pepper, then back to the fire. "I don't know Seaside, but let me change and I'll drive you home." He headed toward the stairs with Pepper on his heels. Kurt stopped and stared at the dog. Pepper panted for all he was worth. Kurt looked at Leanna, as if she could control the dog.

Fat chance. "He's not really an obedient pet." She shrugged.

Kurt picked up Pepper and brought him to Leanna. "Hold his collar."

Okay, then. She looped her finger in Pepper's collar and watched Kurt go into the kitchen and wipe the floor with the towel he'd given her. Then he wiped the counter with a sponge before disappearing into the alcove by the kitchen. He returned with a laundry basket, tossed the dirty towels in, and then returned the basket to where he'd found it and climbed the stairs.

"Guess he doesn't really like dirt...or dogs after all," she said to Pepper.

Pepper broke free and ran up the stairs after Kurt.

Leanna closed her eyes with a loud sigh.

Just shoot me now.

Chapter Two

KURT STOOD IN the bright bathroom in a fresh pair of black Calvin Klein briefs, drying the remaining dampness from his arms and legs. His night of writing was shot to hell. How was he supposed to concentrate on writing a dark thriller with a wet dog and an insanely sexy woman in the room? Her clothes clung to every curve of her womanly body, and it had taken all his focus to look away. And she was cute, too. Damn cute, the way she fought him to save that damn dog. *Pepper. Pepper?* The dog was white, not an ounce of black on the thing anywhere. Pepper? How about Salty or Sugar? He shook his head, thinking about the way she looked up at him with those almond-shaped hazel eyes of hers, all flustered as she tried to wipe up the floor.

He ran his hand through his wet hair, tossed his wet clothing into the rattan hamper, and went into the bedroom to get dressed.

"Are you freaking kidding me?" Pepper was sprawled across his white comforter. "Get off there." Pepper sat up and panted eagerly.

Great. Wet dog smell. Kurt tucked Pepper under one arm and tugged the blanket off the bed with the other, bundled it under his arm, and carried both downstairs.

"Here." He handed the dog to Leanna and took the blanket to the laundry room, mumbling under his breath about his muse running away as he filled the washer and tossed the blanket in. He was about to head upstairs when Leanna's dead stare stopped him cold.

"What?"

"Um. Nothing." She crinkled her nose, dropped her eyes, and trapped her lower lip between her teeth.

Too damn cute.

He followed her gaze south to his briefs and realized he'd forgotten to finish dressing.

"Christ." He shook his head. "Thank Pepper for that." He went back upstairs to dress and swore he heard her whispering *thank you* to the damn dog.

Kurt returned with a Duke sweatshirt and another dry towel. "Here." He handed the sweatshirt to Leanna. "I don't want you to freeze. You can change in the bathroom."

"Thank you, but I only live a few minutes away. I don't want to take your stuff."

"Really, it's fine." He walked to the door and slipped his feet into his flip-flops. When he turned around, her bare back was to him, the thin pink line of her bra barely visible beneath her wet, dark hair.

Kurt's eyes followed her smooth, tanned skin down the graceful curve of her back to the flare of her hips in her low-rise shorts. A second later the pink, lacy bra fell to the ground and his sweatshirt slipped over her head, covering that beautiful back—and leaving him hot all over.

She turned around with a sweet smile and a sigh. "That's so much better."

He shook his head again to knock himself out of his gawking stupor. "I'm sorry. I thought..." He looked toward the alcove by the stairs. "The bathroom is right over there."

"Oh, I'm not shy." She swatted the air. "Besides, I had my back to you, so it's not like you saw me naked. Thank you, by the way. This is so much comfier than my wet shirt and that awful bra." She shivered.

Awful bra? "Are...?" He cleared his throat in an effort to clear the image of her bare back from his mind. It didn't work. "Are you ready to go?"

"Sure. Thanks again." She joined him by the door.

He looked down at her bare feet. "Shoes?"

"Oh gosh. I didn't even notice. I think I lost them in the water. It's okay. I have more." She went out the door with a bounce in her step and ran through the rain to the passenger side of his liquid-silver Mercedes SL convertible.

Kurt carried Pepper to the car to keep his paws from getting muddy again. After Leanna settled into the passenger seat, he set the towel at her feet and placed Pepper on top of it.

"Stay," he commanded. By the time he started the car, Pepper had inched his way across Leanna's lap to the center console, where he put his fluffy white face on his front paws and breathed through his nose, blinking his big, dark eyes at Kurt.

"I'm really sorry, but even if I wrestle with him, he won't listen. He never has." Leanna petted Pepper's back.

Kurt bit his tongue about the dog dirtying up his car. Apparently, it wouldn't do any good anyway, according to little Miss Adorably Sexy Not Shy Leanna. She gave Kurt directions to Seaside, and he drove the main drag, trying not to worry about the dog on the leather or the lacy pink bra in Leanna's hand.

In an effort to distract himself, he asked, "How long have you had him?"

"Pepper? I don't know. A year, maybe?" She kissed his damp white fur.

"And he still doesn't listen?" Kurt glanced at the dog, who had fallen fast asleep and was snoring.

"I try, but..." She shrugged. "He's kind of a free spirit, like me, I guess." She rolled up the sleeves of Kurt's sweatshirt and swiped at the half-wet, half-dry hair hanging unkempt around her pretty face.

Free spirit. He thought about her bare back and felt his body warm again.

She looked down, tugging at the bottom of his sweatshirt. "Did you go to Duke?"

"Yes, I did."

Pepper sighed in his sleep.

"I went to UVA. Business major."

She lowered her cheek to Pepper's back, and all Kurt could think about was the smell of wet dog—and how he'd really like to be that wet dog. *Christ. Stop it.*

He needed a talkative free spirit like he needed writer's block. He trained his eyes on the road and begged his mind to follow. The rain eased to a drizzle as he pulled into Seaside Cottages.

"I really appreciate you driving me home. I could have walked if it wasn't raining." She pointed to the right. "Follow the road this way, but go slow. There are chipmunks around here."

"Chipmunks?"

"Yeah. I see them in the mornings. I don't know if they come out in the rain or not, but I wouldn't want you to run one over."

Chipmunks. He couldn't remember the last time he'd even noticed a chipmunk. He followed the narrow gravel road up an incline to a fork and went around to the right, as she directed him. Pitch pine trees lined the road and filled the tight spaces between the small, one-story shingled cottages.

"That's me. Right there." She pointed to a driveway paved with seashells.

As he pulled in, he asked, "Do you have a car?" It was common to bike on the Cape, but most people had vehicles, even if they opted not to use them. The seashells crunched beneath his tires. Crushed seashell driveways were common on Cape Cod, and every time Kurt drove onto them, he silently hoped they didn't slit his tires.

"Uh-huh. It's so big that it blocks my view of my friend's cottage when I'm on my deck." She shrugged. "So I park it over at the laundry room." She tucked her hair behind her ear and stroked Pepper's back.

The cottage couldn't have been more than twenty

feet wide, with lavender shutters and a weathered fence around a deck on the side. The front garden was a mishmash of flowers and bushes, which reminded Kurt of Leanna—a little unkempt, a little wild, and incredibly pretty. He parked and went around to open her door, pondering the idea of a separate laundry room.

"Thanks. I could have done that." Pepper jumped across her lap and circled Kurt's feet. "Pepper thanks you, too. Did I tell you that I found him near a dumpster? He was so skinny I thought he was going to die. You'd think he'd listen to me since I saved his life, but no such luck. He's kind of like the worst best friend you ever had." She stepped from the car and touched Kurt's chest to steady herself as she tugged at her wet shorts, without missing a beat of her solo conversation. "He only listens to me when he feels like it." She shrugged. "But I love him, so..."

Kurt barely registered her explanation past the feel of her hand on his chest. It had been months since he'd been close to a woman. He'd been on constant deadlines, and women had been the farthest things from his mind.

Until now.

"Come on in and have a drink. Hey. The rain stopped. That's lucky." She opened the gate to the deck. "Come on, Pepper."

Before he could comprehend her offer, she had disappeared. He was about to close the passenger door when he noticed her bra and T-shirt on the floor. He groaned and picked them up, wrapping her T-shirt over her bra so she didn't think he was a pervert fingering her lingerie, although that's exactly what he'd like to do. If it were still on her.

Two towels, a bathing suit, and a T-shirt hung over the deck railing, drenched from the rain. The deck was fairly large for such a small cottage, with a grill and patio table and chairs. There was a back gate to the deck, and beyond that, a grassy area and a few more cottages, each with brightly colored shutters. The word *quaint* came to mind. Kurt knocked on the wooden edge of the screen door.

Leanna came out of a room holding the bottom of his sweatshirt between her teeth and zipping up a pair of jeans—but not before Kurt got an eyeful of bare skin where panties should have been.

She waved him in as she released the bottom of the sweatshirt. "Come in."

He stepped inside and quickly cataloged his surroundings. The kitchen and narrow living space spanned the width of the cottage, and was devoid of any seating besides a small table with three chairs pushed against the wall to his right. Pepper was sacked out beneath the table. Kurt's neck muscles tightened as he glanced at the line of green cabinets along the left wall, beneath which was a sink full of dishes. Every square inch of table and countertop was covered with jam and jelly jars, big metal pots, spoons, and other dishes streaked with dried red goo. An enormous mound of sneakers, flip-flops, and rain boots were piled on the floor to his left beside Pepper's food and water bowls. Directly across from where he stood was a slightly open door. He caught a glimpse of a sink just beyond. *Bathroom.*

Holy. Shit.

"This is...cute."

She smiled as she reached for the refrigerator door. "Thanks. There's a really cute loft through there." She pointed toward the door to Kurt's right. "Old-fashioned pull-down stairs, too. My brothers and sister and I used to fight over who got to sleep up there. You can't even stand up there, the ceiling's so low, but we loved it. And there's a pull-out couch in that room and a television, but I never use them." She shrugged and stared into the nearly empty fridge. A second later she pulled out two bottles of beer and used the inside of his Duke sweatshirt to cover the tops as she twisted them off.

"Here." She handed a bottle to Kurt and dropped her gaze to her shirt and bra, still in his hand.

"Oh gosh," she said with another cute crinkle of her nose. She took them from him in exchange for the beer. "I swear I wouldn't remember my head if it weren't screwed on." She opened the door of the room she'd come out of earlier and literally tossed the wet clothes into it. Kurt assumed that was her bedroom. Then she picked up a stack of clothes from a chair and carried it into the same room. "Sit down. Let's chat a bit."

Chat a bit? Just being around such chaos made his nerves tighten. "Thanks, but I really can't stay."

"Really? You can't stay for a while? Bummer." She came out of the bedroom and trapped her lip between her teeth, cocked her head to the side, and used her fingers to untangle the knots from her damp hair. She seemed completely unaware of her actions—and how hot she looked—as she leaned her head to the other side and began freeing the knots there, too.

Kurt, on the other hand, was all too aware of everything about her. She released her lip, and her tongue swept across it, leaving it slick and alluring.

The cottage door swung open, and a tall blond woman wearing a colorful summer cover-up over a bathing suit stepped inside. "Holy crap, it's funky out there tonight."

Kurt stepped to the side to give her room.

The blonde put her hands on her hips and exhaled loudly, raking her eyes down Kurt's body. "I came to see whose sweet ride was outside." She shoved her hand toward Kurt. "Bella Abbascia. Nice to meet you. I'm Leanna's neighbor."

He shook her hand. "Kurt Remington."

"No way." Bella looked at Leanna. "No effing way."

Leanna's eyes darted between them. "What?"

Kurt looked down, readying himself for what he always hoped to avoid. Attention.

Bella stepped closer, and Kurt leaned back a little.

"You are him. Holy crap. Leanna Bray, you sneaky little minx. Why didn't you tell me you knew him? Jeez. I'm a huge fan of yours. You write the scariest crap I've ever read." Bella shook her head, and her thick blond hair swept across her shoulders.

"Crap?" Kurt could tell by her wide-eyed stare and smile that she enjoyed his work and *crap* wasn't meant in a derogatory fashion.

"You know what I mean." Bella grabbed his arm and pulled him over to the empty chair. "Sit, please. I would love to talk to you."

"Actually, I was just leaving." He turned toward the door. "I've got some writing to do."

"Wait. You're a writer?" Leanna asked.

"Jesus, Lea. Look at this place." Bella began gathering dishes. "He's not just a writer. He's one of the hottest thriller writers out there." She ran her eyes over him again. "No pun intended."

"Bella." Leanna swatted her arm. "I was late this morning and didn't have time to clean up after I made the last batch." Leanna looked at Kurt. "I'm sorry. I'm so used to this. I never even notice the mess."

"No worries. I'll be going."

"Kurt, wait, please." Bella put her hands on her hips again. "Actually, you know what? I can see why you'd want to bolt. It's like a typhoon hit in here or something. I'd tell you she's not usually like this, but our jam girl is always a little like this."

"Jam girl?"

"She makes jams and jellies and sells them at the flea market." Bella looked between the two of them. "Wait. How do you know each other? You guys don't even know what the other does for a living? Did you just hook up tonight or something?"

Flea market?

"No, no, no." Leanna pushed Kurt toward the door. "I'm sorry. Bella knows no boundaries."

Her hands were on his chest again, and she was gazing at him with a look of something—embarrassment, maybe—in her gorgeous hazel eyes. *Typhoon* might just have been the accurate word for her. She was a hot mess. A hot, incredibly sexy mess, and she made him a little dizzy.

And surprisingly, he liked it.

"Thank you for helping me and for driving us home." She glared at Bella.

You're pushing me out? Why does that make me want to stay?

"Sure. Be careful next time you're out there. You could have really been hurt in the current."

Pepper jumped off his bed and clawed at Kurt's legs. Leanna reached down to pick him up, and Pepper escaped her reach, running circles around Kurt.

"See? I told you he has no manners." Leanna blew a wayward hair from her eyes. It fell right back in front of them.

Between the dog barking and circling his feet and Leanna touching his chest, Kurt was having trouble thinking straight.

Leanna blew at the lock of hair again. It flitted up, then fell back in her eyes again. Pepper added whining to his reverie.

Kurt shot a look at the dog. "Hush," he said sternly.

Pepper sat at his feet with a whimper, his tongue lolling from his mouth.

Leanna blew at her hair again, and Kurt reached out and tucked the offending lock of hair gently behind her ear.

"Wow." Bella opened the refrigerator door and grabbed a beer. "You got Pepper to listen. You can write and you're magical? Impressive."

Weirdest night ever.

Kurt held up his beer. "Thank you for the drink." *Christ. Leanna's bike.* Had she made his mind completely nonfunctional? How'd he forget that?

"Your bike? Should I put it in my garage?"

"Yeah, sure. I'll come by and get it."

He nodded, stifling the urge to ask when. Of course, first he'd have to waste time looking for her bike, and for some strange reason, that didn't bother him one bit.

"Have a nice night, ladies." He drove out of the complex completely perplexed—and intrigued—by the messy free spirit that was Leanna Bray.

Chapter Three

IT WAS THREE forty-five Saturday afternoon, and even beneath the awning above her booth at the flea market, it was a scorcher. The flea market was held in the parking lot of the Wellfleet Drive-In, and it was where she'd met Al Black when she was a little girl. He was an elderly jam maker from Plymouth, and over the years they'd become trusted friends. When Al became ill last year, he'd contacted Leanna, shared his recipes, and when he passed away a few months later, at the ripe old age of eighty-two, the idea for Luscious Leanna's was born. In honor of her friendship with Al, and with the support of her most trusted friends, she'd set out for the Cape, hoping to make a go of the business.

Normally, Leanna wasn't anxious for the flea market to close. She enjoyed the constant influx of people and loved knowing they enjoyed her products. But today she planned on taking a basket of goodies to

Kurt to thank him for rescuing Pepper the evening before. Bella had given her hell for pushing him out of the cottage, and she'd given her more hell for not trying to hook up with him. But Leanna wasn't in Wellfleet to pick up a brooding writer; she was there to figure out her career. If she'd learned one thing about Kurt Remington in the short time they were together, it was that he might be brave, hot, and successful, but he was the epitome of organized and—the thing she could never even hope to be—neat. Bordering on tragically so, from what Leanna could tell. And for a girl who sniffed her tank top to see if she could toss it on over her bathing suit for the second day in a row, that was a scary thought. She was brought up right, however, and showing gratitude was important. Even if she sometimes pushed handsome guys out of her cottage so her hot and aggressive girlfriend didn't start hitting on them.

She'd arrived late again that morning and missed the first rush of customers. Leanna had brought a few of her new jam flavors to the flea market—apricot-lime and strawberry-apricot—and they'd caught the attention of some of the regulars. She wondered how much business being late had cost her. It didn't matter how hard she tried or how early she got up; she was always late. For everything. She was even born a week late. Her mother should have nipped it in the bud when she was younger. Punished her more or something. Anything. But Gina Bray would never have done anything so regimented—or expected. *I don't want my kids to be cookie-cutter clones of other children.* How many times had she heard her mother say that to her teachers when they'd complain that Leanna wasn't focused or that she was too talkative or too loud? And her father, Colonel Will Bray, who should have been more regimented and stern, given his military career, was equally as forgiving of his children's faults. It was a wonder that she and her siblings ever got anywhere on time or completed a darn thing in their lives. But they all had. At least each of her siblings had. Her older brothers, Colby and Wade, had found their calling. Colby was a Navy SEAL, and Wade was an artificial intelligence guru. Even her younger siblings had found their groove. Bailey was a musician, and Dae, who her parents adopted from Korea when he was a baby, was a demolition expert. Only Leanna seemed to still be floundering, and at twenty-eight, she wondered if she'd ever find anything that didn't leave her longing for more.

Pepper whined at her feet where she'd tethered him to the leg of the table with a long leash. She hated leashing him to the table, but they didn't allow unleashed pets at the flea market. Leanna thought about Kurt. She probably should have had Pepper on a leash last night, but she was glad she hadn't.

"We're leaving in a few minutes. Can you please wait?" Leanna patted his head. The flea market closed at four, and she had disassembling her booth down to a science. She could do it in fifteen minutes flat. Most of the time. Today she hoped she could, as she was anxious to bring the basket to Kurt.

Pepper looked at her with pleading, big, round eyes and barked. He had already wrapped himself around the table leg a bazillion times and she'd had to untangle the unhappy pup. He wanted to roam free—and she didn't blame him, as she had that gypsy urge running through her blood, too.

Leanna had sold one hundred and forty-two jars of jam and jelly today, and at four dollars a jar, it wasn't exactly a killing, but it was good enough. She loved working at the flea market. Vendors changed often, and there was always an influx of new and interesting people to watch or to chat with. She kept a little radio on beneath the table, and when it wasn't too busy, she would dance by herself. Leanna had become friends with the neighboring vendors, and she was trusting by nature, so she never thought twice about having them watch her booth if she had to walk Pepper or use the ladies' room.

Pepper whined again.

There were only a handful of customers left on the flea market grounds, and Pepper was wrapping his leash around the table leg again.

"Hey, Carey," she called to the lanky twenty-four-year-old vendor in the next booth. He, like Leanna, had maintained his booth for the entire summer, and they'd become friends. They'd gone to the beach a handful of times, went out for drinks, and generally hung out. "Would you mind watching my stuff for a few minutes so I can walk Pepper?"

"No prob." Carey sat with his feet propped up on a plastic milk crate full of vinyl records, wearing the same style cargo shorts and tank he'd worn all summer. He had a deep tan and longish, light brown sun-streaked hair, and because they'd gone swimming together, Leanna knew he had a six-pack beneath his tank top and looked amazing in his board shorts.

"Thank you. Poor Pepper hates this, but you know I hate to leave him home alone. I worry he'd be lonely."

Pepper heard his name and barked, pulling against his leash as Leanna untied it from the table leg. His white fur was now brown with dirt on his belly and paws.

"Pepper, calm down. Please."

Pepper pulled and pulled, and the jars on the table clanked together. When she finally freed the leash from the table leg, he took off running.

Leanna ran her hand through her hair and sighed. Her shoulders slumped forward. She loved the little curly-haired brat, but he sure tried her patience.

Carey laughed.

She held her palms up with a shake of her head. "Off I go."

Leanna headed toward the snack bar, Pepper's destination of choice. Vendor tents were set up in lines of twelve, with wide paths between them for customers. Each vendor had their own setup of tables or clothing racks. Some even set their products on blankets on the blacktop. One of the things Leanna loved most about the flea market was the diversity of what was offered. There were booths with antiques, and booths with what looked to be garage sale items. Hippie clothing, leather products, jewelry, and books were also sold. As she passed by a clothing vendor and neared the snack bar, the scent of popcorn and hot dogs filled the air, reminding her of when she'd come to the drive-in with her parents and siblings as a child.

She smiled at the memory, enjoying the brief walk in search of her dog.

On one side of the snack bar was a patio with picnic tables and bleachers beneath a small awning. She found Pepper on the other side of the snack bar, at the little sandy playground, running circles around a group of children, jumping playfully into the air, slowing down just long enough to pant. The children, who looked to be six or seven years old, giggled with delight while the parents stood close by with mildly concerned eyes, obviously wondering if this jumping, happy dog posed a danger as he licked the toes of one of the little girls.

Leanna loved Pepper so much it made her heart ache, everything about him, from his crazy barking to his running away, and she knew he was about as harmful as a baby. He'd kill them with cuteness before he'd bite anyone.

"He won't bite. Do you mind if he plays with them?" she asked a twenty-something couple. With their consent, she leaned on the split-rail fence surrounding the park and watched for a minute or two before saving the children from enjoying themselves too much.

"Aww, please can he stay?" asked a wide-eyed girl with pigtails.

"Please? Please?" asked another little boy.

Leanna looked toward her booth, where a group of women were perusing her products. Carey hadn't moved from his laid-back perch. *What's another few bucks?*

Thinking of Pepper and the way he'd taken off into

the ocean, she snagged his leash and sat on the ground with him while the kids petted him. *This is what life is about.* Living in the moment was something Leanna was very good at, and this moment filled her with joy—but joy didn't pay the bills. Leanna had a trust fund, passed down from her great-grandfather, but other than dipping into it to pay for college, she'd made a decision a few years earlier not to touch that money if she could help it. She wanted to find something that made her feel whole and fulfilled, and if she relied on her trust fund, she'd never experience enough on her own to fill that need. She lived simply, and even though she'd begun worrying about if she'd ever find a fulfilling career, she liked knowing that if or when she did, she'd have found it on her own, and she hadn't simply sat back and used her great-grandfather's hard-earned money.

After the children had played for a few more minutes, Leanna returned to take down her booth for the afternoon. Carey finished taking down his display and loading up his 1979 Dodge van. He smacked the door of his rust-orange-colored van, as he did every day. *Good luck, you know?*

"If you had a van like mine, you wouldn't need luck." Leanna glanced at her hand-painted 1968 Volkswagen Bus, which her father had given her as a college graduation gift. She wiped sweat from her forehead with her forearm, then placed the last insulated container of jam into the back of the van.

Carey leaned against his van. He was easy on the eyes, six feet of lean muscle, with angular features, full lips, and green eyes.

"Maybe you're right. Your *happy mobile* doesn't break down like my van does. Wanna hit the beach?" he asked.

She looked at Pepper sprawled out in the back of the van and debated going with Carey. They had fun hanging out together. Carey was nice and he was definitely hot, but Leanna wasn't attracted to him as anything more than a friend. That had surprised her at first, given their close proximity the last two months and the good times they'd shared, but when she looked at him, she saw a nice guy. A friend. And it stopped there. Now her mind drifted to Kurt—in his Calvin Klein briefs—and a shiver ran up her spine, sending a tingling to the parts of her that hadn't felt anything for months. She had more important things on her mind than finding a man, but she was still female.

"Can't today. I've got a few things to do, but thanks anyway."

She told herself she owed Kurt a thank-you basket. That was her story, and she was sticking to it.

THE SUN BEAT down on Kurt's bare back as his fingers danced over the keyboard. He was in the zone. The killer was a breath away from his unsuspecting victim. Kurt's heart slammed against his chest; sweat dripped from his torso and beaded his forehead. His hand perspired with every determined keystroke. This was what he lived for. The moment he became so engrossed in his writing that he was right there with both the victim and the villain, holding his breath in the space in between.

He heard tires in the driveway and blinked the noise away, hoping whoever it was had lost their way and was just turning around. He went back to the villain, who closed his eyes as he caught the victim's scent, spurring on his deviant desires.

Knocking drew his focus toward the cottage.

"Damn it," he muttered and turned back to his writing.

The knocking continued. Kurt clenched his teeth and continued hammering out the scene that played in his mind like a movie.

"Hello?"

Kurt's fingers froze. *Leanna.* The thought of her in his arms, her wet body pressed against his chest, sent a wave of heat through him. He stared at his laptop, calculating his writing time. He'd written five thousand words and hoped for another three thousand before the day's end. Once Leanna started talking, he'd have no hope of writing a word. She talked more than his fictional victims when pleading for their lives.

And for some unknown reason, she intrigued him. He wanted to hear what she had to say.

He heard scratching on the deck stairs, and then Pepper was clawing his bare legs and barking at his feet.

Holy Christ.

He shoved away from the table and, ignoring Pepper, descended the stairs and went toward the front of the house. He stopped cold at the sight of a rainbow-colored Volkswagen Bus. A colorful starburst surrounded a spare tire hooked to the front of the old van. He took a step around the gaudy, hand-painted vehicle. Yellow flowers covered half of the side, running from front to back, and a gigantic blue dragonfly covered the driver's door. An ocean scene of fish, red mushrooms, and bikini-clad women covered the center of the van. A half-moon with a face, *of course*, covered the rear panel, and the expanded top of the van was painted blue with white clouds and stars.

Holy hell, she was not only messy, but a hippie to boot?

He looked down at Pepper, panting beside him.

"Hey there." Leanna came around the side of the house with a basket under one lean, tanned arm and flashed a smile that nearly knocked him off his feet. "I brought you something."

"Hi," was all he could manage. Her body glistened with sweat, making her light blue tank top stick to her stomach and chest. She wore another pair of cutoffs, and when she bent over to pet Pepper, she flashed a curve of bronze skin where her ass met her thighs. Kurt swallowed hard.

She popped back up and handed him the basket. Her eyes took a slow roll down his body.

Kurt arched a brow, amused by the once-over, but apparently, she didn't realize she'd done it, or hadn't cared that he'd noticed, because she never missed a beat.

"I wanted to say thank you. I was kinda rude last night, pushing you out of the cottage and all, but I'm not a total ass. I hope I'm not interrupting anything." She didn't give him time to answer, as she followed the slate path toward the back of the house. "You were on the deck?"

He couldn't do much more than watch and follow. Leanna befuddled him. No one befuddled Kurt Remington. He was unflappable. Or at least he'd always thought he was.

"Oh, gosh, you were working." She leaned over his computer screen.

Kurt closed the laptop. "Writing."

Her eyes grew serious. "You don't like people to read as you write? No worries. I get that, I guess. In case you want to change something? You don't want that person to know you changed what you'd written?"

What? No. Or at least I don't think that's why I do it. Holy cow. Now she had him questioning his writing practices in ways he never had.

"I have beta readers and editors who read my work before publication."

She flopped down on a chair with another stomach-rattling smile. "What's a beta reader?"

Distracted by Leanna and by her dog, who had made himself at home on Kurt's chair, he answered cryptically. "A beta reader. Test reader before publication." He glared at Pepper and pointed to the deck. "Off."

Pepper jumped down.

"You need to teach me that," Leanna said.

"What?"

"*That.* Off. Sit. The way you get him to listen to you." She leaned her head back and dropped her arms to the sides of the chair. "It's so nice out here. You have the breeze from the ocean, the sunshine, privacy..."

Privacy? Kurt could think of a hundred things to do when a woman was in that position—and he'd never once thought about doing them on his deck. Until now. The thought of Leanna naked in the chair aroused him. He brushed the sand Pepper had so kindly left behind from his chair and sat down before she could notice. Not that she seemed to notice much. She made herself right at home.

He eyed the basket to keep his mind off of the way a bead of sweat was heading south between her breasts.

"Thanks for the basket, but you didn't have to bring me anything." He grabbed a jar of jam and read the label. "Luscious Leanna's Sweet Treats?" *Luscious Leanna?* Holy hell, he was in big trouble.

She sat up and leaned toward him. "I wanted to. You were nice enough to go into the ocean in the middle of a rainstorm and save me and Pepper. Now I know you were probably writing some crazy thriller, so that means I *really* interrupted you."

As opposed to fake interrupted me? He had to work hard to pull himself from his writer's mind-set. She'd crinkled her nose as she'd said *really,* and she was so damn cute he couldn't do more than watch as she stood and leaned over the railing. He noticed jam handprints across the back pockets of her shorts. Kurt wished they'd been from his hands. She threw her hands up in the air and exhaled loudly, before turning back to him with that glorious smile again.

"You're so lucky. I mean, this is what you *do.* You write with the ocean in your backyard." She glanced into the French doors and winced. "I hope your floors survived us."

She touched his shoulder as she flitted past and sat down on another chair. He liked that warm touch, and she'd done it with a sense of familiarity. *Weird.* He'd never met anyone who was so comfortable in her own skin. Pepper licked the perspiration from Leanna's legs. Kurt was a little jealous of the pesty little dog. He smiled despite the interruption to his writing—and despite wondering if that jam on her butt was still wet and would ruin his chair.

"They survived just fine." *But I'm not sure I will.* She stirred all sorts of desires in Kurt that he usually kept under wraps—and drew upon only when his projects were sufficiently complete or when he was ahead of schedule and could spare a few hours to burn off steam. His stomach was doing something strange and unfamiliar, too. *What is that? A flutter? Pang? Ache?* He ran through a plethora of words that might or might not be accurate.

"What are you thinking about?" Leanna asked.

"What?"

"Your eyebrows are all pinched together, and you were staring at the table like you were deep in thought." She looked at his computer. "Oh gosh. I interrupted you. I'm so sorry." She rose to her feet.

Pepper crawled under Kurt's chair and whined.

He needed to get back to writing. He should just let her go, thank her for the jams and bid her farewell so she could go flit about on some other guy's deck. Damn if his hand didn't reach out and land on top of hers.

"Stay." The word came without thought, surprising him as much as her.

Her eyes widened. "Stay?"

He nodded. "I'm going to write, but you can relax in the sun if you'd like, or take a walk on the beach."

She looked around. "You don't mind?"

He shrugged, knowing he was probably making a huge mistake, but something in his crazy gut wanted her around, and he'd never felt that way before. What was an hour or two? She'd get bored and move on, and he would have enjoyed the view of her.

"Sure." He pulled the laptop closer to him and opened it. "There's a beach blanket and towels in the linen closet by the laundry room."

She crinkled her nose and smiled again. Pepper crept out from under his chair and began pawing at his lap.

Kurt narrowed his eyes at him. "No."

Pepper lay back down.

"Okay, but if we drive you crazy, just say the word and we'll leave." She reached for the door handle. "Are you sure? Actually, I have a towel and blanket in my van. I can get it."

Kurt shook his head and went inside, where he retrieved a blanket and a towel and filled a thermos with ice water. When he returned, Leanna was standing in the center of the deck in a charcoal-gray string bikini, struggling to put her hair up in a ponytail.

Kurt stopped cold. Every sexy curve was on display, from her rounded hips to her full breasts, which were pushed together by barely there swatches of dark material. Two thin lines of fabric ran from her hips to another tiny triangle of gray covering her promised land. He swallowed hard, trying to regain control of his limbs. She wasn't a rail-thin model; nor was she overly plump. Beneath the tank tops and cutoffs, Leanna Bray was one hundred percent hot, sexy woman, and she stole any chance Kurt had at rational thought.

After securing her hair, she took the towel from his hands. "Thanks so much. I really appreciate it. I was going to take Pepper to the water later, so this saves us time." She traced a finger over the tattoo on his chest. "I never would have guessed you to be a tattoo guy."

It was all he could do to shift his eyes from her rounded breasts to her finger working its way across his bare chest.

"And the one on your arm?" She touched that one, too, and he could tell by the unchanged inflection of her voice that she wasn't trying to be sexy or flirtatious. She was just being Leanna—curious, sweet.

And he was getting hard. He cleared his throat and stepped away.

"Thanks. They were a..." Still in shock over everything about Leanna, he was at a loss for words. He was used to being in control, and Leanna was stealing that from him one hot breath at a time.

She cocked her head and looked up at him.

"A whim," he managed. *Whim?* He'd never done a thing in his life based on a whim.

She smiled. "Really? You don't strike me as a whim

guy. Hm." She turned and tossed the blanket and towel over her shoulder. "I guess I'll hit the beach, then. Come on, Pep." She headed for the beach with a bounce in her step.

Kurt let out a breath and ran his hand through his hair. He watched her spread out the towel and lie down on her back, her hands tapping to some silent beat, her lips slightly parted, and Pepper running circles around her. She was *so* not what he needed. *What am I doing?* How was he supposed to think of killing and darkness with that beautiful, touchy-feely, all-too-comfortable-and-happy woman a few feet away?

He nearly jumped out of his skin when his cell phone rang. He needed the distraction.

"Hi, Jackie," he answered. Jackie Tolson had been his literary agent for six years. She was five feet tall on a good day, weighed about a hundred pounds soaking wet, with stick-straight black hair cut severely above her shoulders, and she was as aggressive as a trapped cobra.

"Kurt. How's life at the Cape?"

He pictured her leaning back in her pristine Manhattan office furnished top to bottom in leather, mahogany, and white, wearing her Manolo Blahnik strappy heels and designer suit, a pen sticking out between her perfect teeth and her perfectly applied makeup softening her sharp features. The thought brought a smile to his lips. He liked Jackie, and he loved her meticulous nature and her bulldog determination. Professionally, they were a great match.

"The Cape is…" He glanced down at the beach, where Leanna was on her hands and knees, rolling around with Pepper in the sand. "Interesting."

"Interesting as in *inspiring*, or interesting as in *we're going to be late with our submission?*"

He watched Leanna chase Pepper into the water. "Have I ever missed a deadline?"

"No, and I'm just waiting for the day you do. I'm not sure if I'll celebrate that you finally have a life or I'll hate you for making us look bad."

"If I ever miss a deadline I think you'll be second in line to shoot me."

"Yeah, yeah. You'll shoot yourself first. I've heard it from the best of them. Everyone misses a deadline at some point. Did you hear from Layton?"

Layton was Kurt's editor at his publishing house, Partner Press. "Yes. He's ready and waiting, and we'll have revisions back sixty days after he receives the manuscript."

"Good. And I know timely revisions are a piece of cake for you. I wish you could teach your dedication and work habits to the rest of my clients."

Leanna turned and waved.

"Mm-hmm." *God, she's sexy.* He lifted his hand in a semi wave.

"Kurt?"

He wanted to run his hands over every inch of Leanna's glistening skin and hear her soft voice calling out his name. "Hm?"

"You sound distracted. Is something going on with your family?"

"Family? Uh, yeah. Jack's getting married at the

end of the summer, but everyone's good. Why?"

"I can't think of anything else that would distract you. What are you doing right this second?"

She knew him too well. "Going inside to grab some grapes." Which he did. "Now I'm sitting back down at my computer to nail this scene."

"Fair enough. What were you doing?"

"Watching a hot chick run through the ocean."

"Yeah, right." She laughed. "Okay. Let me know if you run into any issues."

He ended the call, bothered by her disbelief of him watching Leanna. Was he that boring? It had been weeks since he'd been out on a real date. Before he came to the Cape, his sister, Siena, had set him up with an attractive friend of hers. He'd spent the whole night revising a chapter in his head. Kurt wasn't a *dater*. He didn't enjoy small talk, and he had yet to find a woman he preferred over writing. Hell, he had yet to find anything he preferred over being in front of his keyboard and creating heart-pumping literature. Sure, there were women in his life who were available when he had the urge to spend a few hours in the arms of a soft, willing woman, but those nights were on his terms and his schedule. Like everything in Kurt's life, he believed to do it well, he had to be determined and focused and give it his all. He'd much rather focus on writing.

He sat down at his computer and spent the next two hours trying to concentrate on something other than thoughts of Leanna. He'd just gotten himself centered when Pepper bounded onto the deck, barking.

He slid him a stare. "Hush."

Pepper whined, then flopped on Kurt's feet. Kurt kicked him off and Pepper crept right back. *Christ.*

Leanna came up the deck with her hair a tangled mess, sandy from hip to toe, and dragging the sandy blanket and towel behind her.

"That was so much fun. You should have come. How can you sit there and not want to go in the water?" She ran her fingers through her tangles.

How can you not realize how goddamn sexy you are? "Salt water makes my skin sticky."

She laughed and flopped into the chair beside him, leaving a sandy path in her wake. When she leaned forward and touched his thigh, he felt a sear of heat blaze a path to his groin. Again. He couldn't tear his eyes from the droplets of water slipping down her cleavage if his life depended on it.

"It's supposed to. It's salt water," she said as if he were being silly. She leaned back and put one foot on his lap.

He stared at the tan, pretty appendage.

"How'd the writing go? Did you kill someone off?"

"Not yet." He picked up her foot and held it away from his lap; then he snagged the towel from her lap and gently wiped the sand from her foot, and her ankle, and her knee. Sand piled up beneath her.

She popped a grape into her mouth and lifted her brows. "You planning on removing all the sand from me? Because I think I have some in my butt crack, too."

He froze.

She laughed. "I'm kidding. Thank you for wiping me off. I guess you don't like dirt too much, huh?"

He handed her the towel and became hyperfocused on her foot resting too close to his crotch. "I like things to be neat, I guess. But I'm not a neat freak."

"Uh-huh." She laughed.

"Why is that funny?" He grabbed a handful of grapes and popped one in his mouth to distract himself from her inviting, sandy thigh.

"Because you are a total neat freak. I think it's cute." She brushed the sand from her thighs.

He pressed his lips together. "Cute? I'm anything but cute. And I'm not a neat freak."

She lowered her foot from his lap and leaned in close again. "Let's see how long you can go without sweeping the sand from the deck."

She smelled sweet and salty, and Kurt couldn't help but wonder if she might taste that way, too.

"You, luscious—" *Shit. How did I let that slip?* "Leanna, you don't even know me." *But for some strange reason, I want you to.*

They rose at the same time and bumped chests. She grabbed his arm to keep from falling over. Her warm, sun-kissed skin felt so damn good against him that he didn't back away. Couldn't back away. His hands found her hips, the ridge of her bikini bottom barely noticeable beneath his palms. The way she looked up at him, eyes full of wonder—and surprise—caught him off guard.

"Sorry." He dropped his hands and stepped back.

She closed the gap between them and dropped her eyes to his chest, which was rising and falling with each embarrassingly heavy breath.

"So, big thriller writer, you're not used to having a mouthy girl around, are you?"

"I have a mouthy sister." *Jesus. Sister? At a time like this?* She had him too befuddled to think straight.

"Does she make you breathe like this?" She pressed her hands to his chest again.

The little voices in his head told him to walk away. Get writing. Run like hell. But his hands didn't listen as they found her hips again and pulled her against him so she could feel what she was doing to him. The glint in her eyes, the way she slowly and sensually licked her lips, and the way her fingers slid down his chest told him that she had to know.

"No one makes me breathe like that," he admitted.

Pepper barked at them, and this time Kurt didn't give him a harsh stare or a command for quiet. Kurt lowered his mouth toward Leanna's lips as she pushed away from him.

"I'd worry if your sister made you breathe like that," she said as if she had no idea that she'd just driven him out of his mind *or* that he'd been about to kiss her. She picked up the towel and draped it over her shoulder. "I'll help you clean up."

He couldn't move. Besides the fact that he was hard as a rock, he could barely breathe. She went inside, and he heard her opening and closing doors. He tried to force his legs to function and cringed thinking about the sand trail she was leaving on his floors. She returned a few minutes later with a broom and a dustpan.

"Finally found them hanging up behind the laundry room door. You are so organized." She stood on her tiptoes and swept the broom back and forth fast and undirected, sending sand all over the deck. "If you didn't kill someone, what did you write?" *Sweep, sweep.* Sand flew into the air and landed on his chair.

He took the broom from her hands and began sweeping to keep from taking her in his arms and kissing that never-quiet mouth of hers.

"My villain was making his way to the victim, mentally obsessing over her." *Like me at this very moment.*

"Look how pretty the sky is over there." Leanna pointed over the ocean. "I love the way it goes all purply pink."

All purply pink. He smiled. "It's pretty, all right." He noticed that while she sometimes spoke simply, her eyes held knowledge. She didn't come across as a ditzy brunette. Cute, yes. Ditzy? No way. Smart and happy, though simple, were perfect words to describe Leanna.

She knelt and held the dustpan while he swept the sandy mess into it. When she stood, she turned and knocked into the table, dumping the sand all over his chair and the deck again. "I'm such a klutz. I'm sorry." She reached for the broom and Kurt reached for her.

Okay, maybe klutzy, but not ditzy—and adorably attractive.

They were chest to chest again, and he wanted to feel her lips against his more than he wanted to write his next chapter, but he didn't need distractions. He was behind on his word count, and he had a deadline looming. He reluctantly guided her into a chair and swept the mess off the deck, buying himself time to figure out what the hell he should do. When he was done, he leaned against the table, crossed his arms, and looked at Leanna.

She drew her feet up on the chair, knees to chest, and smiled up at him. She was always smiling. "Sorry."

Pepper barked at him again, and he glared at the dog. "Hush."

Pepper plopped onto his butt, and Kurt wished he could command himself to do the right thing as easily.

"I need to write."

"I know. I really just came to bring you the basket." Worry flashed in her eyes.

He picked up the basket and rifled through it. There were two jars of jam, a loaf of homemade bread, and dried flowers.

"Did you make all of this?"

"Mm-hm." She traced her kneecap with her index finger.

He'd noticed that she did that often and wondered if she was nervous or bored. He couldn't be sure, but it endeared her to him even more.

"That was really sweet. You're really sweet, Leanna." *And sexy and wickedly distracting.*

She pushed to her feet and stood between his legs. "I'm nice, but I'm not sweet."

Leanna's lips were a breath away, close enough that an inch would bring them together, but the determined tone of her voice and the feisty look in her beautiful eyes told Kurt that she was stating a fact. Defending her strength. And that made him want her even more.

"And I've overstayed my welcome." She traced his

tattoo again. "Go write. I'm really glad you let me stay. I had fun."

"You did?" Kurt considered himself anything *but* fun.

"Are you kidding? Playing with Pepper on the beach and then having the added bonus of seeing you all flustered and shirtless...and sexy? Priceless." She stepped back. "Do you want me to take the towel and blanket inside?"

He was still hung up on *shirtless and sexy. No, but I'd like to take you inside.*

"I've got it. Thanks. And thanks for the basket."

She swatted the air. "Pfft. Have fun writing, but you should really get out sometime. There's a world of temptation out there that you might enjoy. I mean, sand between your toes? Come on."

"I walk on the beach every night, and I enjoy plenty of *temptations*." He walked her to her van with Pepper at their heels, thinking about the temptation that was less than a foot away.

She narrowed her gaze. "Somehow I think your idea of temptation and mine are a little different."

Which is exactly why you have to leave. He eyed her colorful van. "Nice wheels."

"My dad refurbished it for me when I graduated from college, and I can't imagine driving anything but my happy mobile."

"Happy mobile?"

"Yeah." She opened the door and Pepper jumped in; then she climbed into the driver's seat. "I mean, look at the thing. Can you really look at it and not smile?"

He couldn't look at *her* without smiling. "No, I guess I can't."

Chapter Four

SEASIDE WAS A small community of one-, two-, and three-bedroom cottages, most of which had been owned by the same families for decades. Leanna's grandfather had purchased their cottage before she was born. Her family had spent a few weeks each summer at the cottage, and during their visits, her parents kept them on the go. Between afternoons at the beach, walking through quaint nearby towns, and evening family-oriented concerts, it left little downtime, and the downtime they'd enjoyed had been spent at Seaside. She was glad for the friendships she'd fostered in the community and even more pleased that they'd lasted this long. She couldn't imagine her summers without her Seaside friends.

Leanna was cooking hamburgers on the grill when she heard Bella talking with their friend Amy Maples in the area behind her cottage. A minute later Bella peered over the gate.

"Hey, chicky. Is Mr. Sexy here?"

Leanna laughed. "No. Mr. Sexy isn't here."

Bella and Amy joined her on the deck in their typical summer outfits, sundresses worn over their bathing suits. Amy had straight, short blond hair and was about as big around as a pencil, with expressive green eyes and a big heart. Pepper ran circles around them, barking at Amy, his favorite female human. Leanna sometimes wondered if Pepper was more attached to Amy than to her. Amy crouched, and Pepper rolled onto his back so Amy could rub his belly.

"How's my favorite boy?" she crooned. "Did you get to see Mr. Sexy, too? Am I the only one who didn't get to meet the handsome writer?"

"Um, no." Jenna Ward lived in the cottage next to Bella, and she'd inherited her one-bedroom cottage from her mother. She walked through the front gate wearing a one-piece bathing suit and a colorful sarong wrapped around her waist. She wore her pin-straight dark hair in a short blunt cut just below her ears, and she had a wide smile on her face. She threw an arm around Leanna and kissed her cheek. "How are you, sugar?"

"Good. You?"

"Feeling a little left out. Who's Mr. Sexy? And what's up with the ass-baring sundress? You look cute as shit, but unless you have a date, you're wasting it on us."

Leanna glanced over her shoulder and looked down. "Can you really see my butt?"

"Just the curve of it," Amy said. "Who cares? It's

just us. Hey, can I have a burger?"

Leanna put one hand on her hip. "How many do you see on my grill?"

"Four," Bella answered as she went inside Leanna's cottage.

"Would I ever leave you girls hanging?"

"Never." Bella came back out with a plate and handed it to Leanna. "I'll get the lettuce and tomato from my place."

"I've got the buns," Amy said as she stepped from the deck and headed toward her cottage.

"I think Leanna has those covered." Jenna smacked Leanna's butt. "Mr. Sexy. Spill it."

"They're overreacting." Just the thought of Kurt sent a little thrill through her, and when she thought of the way his eyes darkened and his arousal pressed against her center as he almost kissed her, her entire body shuddered. God, how she'd wanted that kiss. She could almost taste it. "I met Kurt Remington, and I guess he's a big-time thriller writer."

"No way." Jenna's baby blues widened. "You met him? Like in person?"

"Uh-huh."

"Holy crap. I love his books. What's he like? Is he as cute as his pictures? He seems kind of reclusive from the interviews I've read. The way he answered their questions, it seems like he never leaves his house—except he did mention his family a lot. Oh, and a house on the Cape. Oh my God. He's here writing! That's what he said in the interview, that in the summers he comes to the Cape to write." Jenna tucked her straight dark hair behind her ear and closed her eyes for a second. "I wouldn't mind being reclusive with him."

"Yeah, me either. That's the problem." Leanna sighed.

"What's the problem?" Bella took the spatula from Leanna's hand and flipped the burgers.

"Leanna wants to write a new chapter in Mr. Sexy's book." Jenna took a tomato from Bella's plate, and Bella smacked her hand.

Amy returned with a plate of buns. "A dirty chapter?"

"Oh! I almost forgot to show you!" Jenna reached into the deep cleavage between her enormous bosoms and pulled out a perfect, white oval rock. "Cool, right?"

Leanna, Amy, and Bella exchanged an eye roll.

"What? Look at it." Jenna ran her hands over the smooth stone. She collected rocks like other people collected antiques or figurines. She refused to carry buckets while she trolled the beaches for rocks, and she often came back with her cleavage overflowing and tiny rocks tucked in between her cheek and her teeth. She stuck out her lower lip and stroked the rock. "Well, I like it. At least I'm not hitting the yard sales this summer and bringing home all kinds of stuff that you guys hate." Jenna was an elementary school art teacher, and her direct personality and hearty laugh made her seem much taller than her almost five-foot stature. She summered at the Cape each year in her one-bedroom cottage, and she lived on a shoestring budget, but last year she'd gone to a string of yard sales and brought home some of the gaudiest yard decorations they'd ever seen. The girls had formed an intervention and stolen every one of them one night while she was asleep, and in their place, they'd left little notes that read, *We love you, but...stick to rocks, please!*

Leanna leaned closer to her. "Let's not revisit that little tangent of yours. I like the rock, too, but I thought you were cutting back on your rock collection."

"I am," Jenna said.

Mm-hm. And I'm not thinking about Kurt.

"Oh, crap. I forgot the wine. Be right back." Jenna hurried off the porch.

"Okay, enough rock talk. Tell me about the dirty chapter." Amy handed out the plates and lit citronella candles as they sat around the table. "I want all the dirty details."

Jenna ran back onto the deck with two bottles of wine.

Bella went into Leanna's cottage and came out with plastic wineglasses. She filled them each a glass and passed them out, then sat down with a loud sigh.

"To a dirty chapter." Bella held up her glass and clinked it to the others'.

Leanna shook her head. "You guys are awful. There is no dirty chapter."

"But you want there to be. You have that look in your eyes." Jenna tossed a piece of hamburger to Pepper.

"Maybe. Maybe not. He's all..." *Hot and bothered when I'm near him.* "Neat and meticulous and totally focused on his work. I think those interviews were right. He probably doesn't ever leave his computer."

"Neat and meticulous. I love that." Jenna was so

OCD she wanted to put the letters *OCD* in alphabetic order. Every photograph in her house was lined up perfectly, and her clothing was organized by color, as were her seventeen pairs of cheap, rubber flip-flops.

"Yeah, you'd love him. His whole house is pristine and white with wood trim, just like yours."

"There is nothing wrong with a neat man, unless he doesn't like to get down and dirty." Bella raised her eyebrows.

"Oh yeah, I hear ya." Amy lifted her glass and took a drink.

Leanna's heart warmed. She loved her friends. During the summers when they were growing up, they'd chased boys, shared details, and tested all of their parents' patience. She trusted them explicitly and knew that they'd always have her back, just as she'd have theirs. "I went to see him today."

The women leaned in closer.

"And there isn't much to tell. He said I should stay while he wrote, and I did. I played with Pepper on the beach, and then..." *Almost kissed him.* She got warm just thinking about him.

"Then?" Bella pushed.

"Then he said he had to write." She shrugged. "So I left."

"He kicked you out? You? You're so cute and fun, and sexy, and..." Jenna shook her head. "If he kicked you out, I wouldn't have a chance in hell."

Leanna took a bite of her burger, mulling over *why* he told her to leave.

"Lea, I think we're missing something. No man just kicks out a beautiful woman. Were you giving off a weird vibe?" Amy asked.

"Maybe he's gay." Bella shrugged.

"He's not gay, and I wasn't giving off a weird vibe. I'm just me, you know. I went in the water, and when I came back onto the deck things were...different." *Hotter.*

They finished their wine, and Amy refilled the glasses. "Were you wearing your pink bikini?"

"Yeah, like that would scare off any man." Bella laughed.

"Charcoal gray."

Bella and Amy exchanged another look.

"You did not." Bella smacked the table, threw her head back, and laughed.

"Leanna, really?" Amy shook her head.

She looked between them. "What?"

"Leanna, that bathing suit makes you look like a Victoria's Secret model," Jenna explained.

"Oh, it does not." Leanna shook her head. She wasn't a woman who looked good in a one-piece bathing suit. Her waist wasn't exactly small, but it was small enough to make her hips look quite round, and her full breasts needed the lift and support of a good bra. A bikini definitely suited her curves, but she felt very far from anything remotely similar to a Victoria's Secret model.

"It's so small," Jenna continued. "And let's face it; you're not Amy's size. None of us are."

"Hey!" Amy crossed her arms.

"Sorry, honey, but Leanna has boobs and hips. You have itsy-bitsy anthills, but you're gorgeous and you know it." Jenna winked at her. "You probably stole the breath right from his lungs."

"And shot it right between his legs." Bella did a little shimmy with her shoulders.

"Ha!" Jenna laughed.

"Uh, yeah. Maybe." *Definitely.* "But even so, he's a guy who knows just what he wants in life and he has it. I'm...me."

Amy came around behind Leanna and hugged her. "Aw, Lea. We love you, and any man would be crazy not to feel the same way."

"I need to try to figure out my life before I can jump into anyone else's. I mean, I love the jam business and the flea market, but let's face it; I've gone through more careers than underwear in the last four years."

"You're just finding your niche," Jenna said.

Leanna crinkled her nose. "What if I have no niche?"

"Everyone has a niche," Bella said. "What's happening with your jams?"

She shrugged. "Nothing really. They're selling pretty well. I sent out proposals to a few grocery chains, and I've been talking with a few mail order and online businesses who want to carry my stuff."

"But?" Bella asked.

Leanna shrugged.

"Oh no. Do not tell me you're bored." Bella leaned forward and touched Leanna's hand. "Leanna, listen to me. Once you get rolling and you're in more places, you'll have more orders than you could ever imagine."

Leanna had yet to find a job that held her interest for longer than a few months. "It's not that. I like doing a few shows and not being locked down fulfilling orders. And I really love coming up with new flavors and dealing with the customers. It's all fun for me. I mean, I really love it, and I have the added benefit of knowing I'm following in Al's footsteps."

"Aw. I miss Al." Amy's lips turned down in a frown. By becoming friends with Leanna, Al had also become friends with her Seaside friends. They'd spent time at his flea market booth each summer, listening to stories about his family and the jam-making business, but it was Leanna who'd kept in touch with him over the winters.

"I know. I do, too." Leanna petted Pepper. "I just feel like something is always missing, and I have no idea what it is. Like there should be...more."

"You haven't gotten laid all summer. Maybe that's it." Bella laughed, then finished her wine in one gulp.

"Neither has Amy, and she's not feeling like something's missing."

Amy picked up the empty plates and carried them inside. "She's right. I love my job at Moby Dick's, and I love my cottage and seeing you guys. I just love my summers." Amy had been a waitress at Moby Dick's restaurant for the past six summers. She had a sweet deal worked out with her *real* job in Connecticut, where she worked as a bookkeeper. She worked remotely during the summers, and she worked at Moby Dick's to pick up extra income—and meet men. But Amy was picky when it came to men, and this summer she seemed especially picky, though she claimed nothing had changed.

"I love what I'm doing. I don't have a clue what's

missing." Leanna went inside and brought out a loaf of the bread she'd baked the night before and the apricot-raspberry jam she'd made. Maybe she could fill her emptiness with food.

Chapter Five

IT WAS NO use. Kurt couldn't run on the beach without thinking of Leanna. Yesterday morning he thought about her in his arms as he carried her to the beach, and this morning all he could think about was her delicious curves in that obscenely small bathing suit. She'd forgotten her clothes when she left yesterday evening and he'd washed them last night, then spent two hours debating taking them over to her. Every minute he spent thinking about her was a minute he wasn't thinking about his writing. And that, it turned out, was a major problem. He'd stayed up until two o'clock in the morning writing what he should have written while she'd been there in that itsy-bitsy bikini—and in the hours afterward when he couldn't concentrate.

He jogged up the beach access road and ran the rest of the way home on the hot pavement to try to refocus on *Dark Times* instead of Leanna. By the time he returned home, he was drenched in sweat and only moderately more focused. He showered, ate breakfast, skimmed the newspaper, and checked his email. While refilling his coffee cup, he eyed Leanna's shirt and shorts, folded neatly on the counter. He doubted she'd even miss them. She didn't seem like the type of woman who worried about where she'd left her things, given that she'd left his house without shoes the first night. Neither of them had remembered to put her bike into her van, either.

He fought the urge to drive them over to her now. He couldn't afford any more distractions. He had to focus on his writing. On his way out to the deck, he glanced at the basket she'd given him and smiled.

You really are sweet.

He opened the apricot-lime jam and tore off a hunk of bread. Inside the basket he found a plastic knife, which, given Leanna's propensity for forgetting, struck him as quite thoughtful. He layered the thick jam on the bread and sank his teeth into it.

"Mm." He closed his eyes and savored the sweet, tangy flavor. He finished that helping and made himself another. He'd never tasted anything like it. The bread was fresh and also a little sweet. He took the basket inside before he devoured the whole loaf.

A few hours later, with the afternoon sun high in the sky and his fictional victim safely tucked away in the cellar of the villain's secret hideaway, Kurt closed his laptop and stretched his legs. He'd written a fair amount and chewed on the idea of bringing Leanna her clothes at the flea market. He should write more. Another four or five hours and he would be comfortably ahead of schedule.

A few days ago this would not have been debatable. He'd stretch, freshen his ice water, and return to the keyboard inspired and ready to write for hours.

A few days ago he hadn't known Leanna.

Now he couldn't stop thinking about her.

Kurt took a quick shower, threw on a pair of khaki shorts and a short-sleeved, button-down linen shirt, and headed toward the flea market. His cell phone rang as he pulled onto the main road. He clicked his Bluetooth button and answered his sister's call.

"Hi, Siena. How are you?"

"Hey, Kurt. I'm great. You? How's the Cape?"

"Perfect." *Almost.*

"Are you doing anything other than writing, or do I need to come out there and drag you down to the beach? It would be a hardship to spend time at the Cape and all, but if you need me to…"

Siena was a model in New York City, and he pictured her wide smile and bright blue eyes with a glint of tease in them. Siena and her twin, Dex, were Kurt's youngest siblings. He'd always felt protective of them, but not in the same way as his brothers Jack or Sage had. They had no issue prying into their siblings' lives or forming an intervention of some type—gathering all the siblings together to take a stance—and giving their two cents. Kurt preferred to remain in the background, and when he took issue with something, he'd talk with his siblings privately. Siena, on the other hand, took far too much pleasure in prying into all of her brothers' lives.

"Actually, I'm on my way to the flea market right now."

Siena gasped. "No."

"Yup." He smiled, because he knew she wouldn't believe him. He left his keyboard only under duress. She'd had to bug him for seven weeks before he'd agreed to go on the blind date with her friend, and then he'd accepted only to shut her up. "Listen." He clicked off his Bluetooth and held his phone up in the air, then brought it back to his ear. "I've even got the top down."

"Holy crap, Kurt. Are you sick? Have you lost your mind? What will your poor laptop do without you there pounding away at it?" She laughed.

Kurt smiled. It was just the reaction he'd expected.

"I'm actually calling about Jack's wedding. Do you need me to do anything for you here in New York? Do you have your suit? Are you coming straight from the Cape, or are you going home first?"

Kurt lived just outside of New York City, and when he summered on the Cape, Siena often took care of things for him back home. "Thanks, sis, but I'm going straight from here. I've got my suit, and my flight arrangements are all set. I land in Colorado the night before the wedding."

"Perfect. Are you really going to a flea market? That's so unlike you."

"Yes, I really am. Hey, listen. I'm pulling in, so I have to run. How are you and Cash?"

She sighed. "Also perfect. He's the greatest thing that's ever happened to me."

Siena was bossy, noisy, and gorgeous, and when

she was with Cash—her new boyfriend, a New York City fireman—she was all those things, but as had happened with each of his brothers, when she'd fallen in love, another side of her personality has begun to reveal itself. A softer, more vulnerable side.

"I'm happy for you, Siena. Really happy."

"Me too."

He could hear the smile in her voice.

"Now we just have to find you the right woman. I'm going to start advertising for a woman who can drag a six-foot-something man around by his ear. Once I find her, I'll send her your way."

He thought of Leanna and almost told Siena about her, but he didn't want to deal with the litany of questions that would surely follow. "You do that," he teased. Siena had been saying the same thing for five years. He knew he was safe from her doing any such thing. Despite the blind date a few weeks back, Siena had been all talk. "Love you, sis."

He ended the call and pulled onto the grounds of the Wellfleet Drive-In. There were only about two dozen cars in the parking lot, and when he glanced at the clock, he realized it was already four. Each parking place had a metal pole with a speaker attached, which were used to hear the movie playing at the drive-in theater. Kurt had never watched a movie at the drive-in. He parked by the snack bar, and as he stepped from the car, Leanna came into view. He wondered what it would be like to go to the drive-in theater with her. Hell, he'd like to go anywhere dark with her.

A banner hanging from the front of her table read LUSCIOUS LEANNA'S SWEET TREATS in red letters on a white background. She was talking with a young guy in the next booth as Kurt approached. Pepper began barking and running toward him, but he was tethered to the table by a long white rope. The jars on the table collided.

Leanna flipped her hair over her shoulder with one sharp turn of her head. "Peppe—" Her eyes widened. "Kurt."

Pepper clawed at his legs. Kurt narrowed his eyes at him. "Sit."

Pepper sat on his butt, wagging his tail.

"What are you doing here?" Leanna asked. She glanced back at the young guy in the tank top she'd been talking with.

Kurt sized him up as he loaded crates full of records into his old orange van. *Handsome. Well built. Looking at Leanna like she's the main course.* He nodded in greeting to the guy, then handed Leanna her clothes.

"You left these at my place, so I thought I'd bring them over." Now he had the guy in the next booth's full attention.

"I did? Oh gosh. I'm sorry." She put the clothes in her van and began packing the jars into insulated coolers.

"I'm not." Kurt felt the guy's eyes on him.

She stopped packing and met his gaze. "But you brought them all the way here and you could be writing."

"You look familiar. Are you that thriller writer?" the guy from the other booth asked.

"Oh gosh. Carey, this is Kurt. Kurt, Carey." Leanna

continued packing the jars as she spoke.

Kurt held out a hand. "Nice to meet you."

The guy's eyes lit up. "Cool. I read all your books."

"Great. Hope you enjoy them." *And keep your eyes off of Leanna.*

"Yeah, they're really good." His eyes darted between Leanna and Kurt.

Pepper began whining and pulling against the rope again. Kurt caught two jars as they fell from the table.

"Sit," he said to Pepper.

Pepper obeyed with another whimper.

"Good catch." Leanna came around the table and reached for the jars.

Kurt trapped her finger beneath his, and when she looked up at him, his pulse sped up. She was breathing hard, and he could see the strap of her dark bikini beneath her tank top, and the image of her in the itsy-bitsy teeny-weeny bikini sent heat right through him.

"So, Leanna, are we still on for the beach?" Carey asked.

She looked at Kurt and trapped her lower lip between her teeth.

On for the beach? Holy hell, you're dating this guy? He glanced at Carey's beaten-up old van parked behind Leanna's van. *I'm a fucking idiot.* He released Leanna's fingers.

"Um." She looked up at Kurt again with an *oh-shit* look in her eyes.

"Hey, don't let me interrupt. I just wanted to bring you your clothes." He nodded at Carey, then forced a smile for Leanna. "I'll see you around."

"Yeah. I guess," she said.

He turned to walk away, feeling like a complete ass. Of course a woman like her would go out with a young, free-spirited guy with similar interests. What was he thinking? What would a woman like Luscious Leanna see in a man who spent hours behind a keyboard, found the ocean sticky, and rarely left the house? Pepper barked and barked. He whimpered and whined, and Kurt kept walking.

There he was getting excited just thinking about taking her to a damn drive-in movie when he should have been writing. He shook his head. What the hell was wrong with him?

He tried to block out Pepper's incessant barking. A loud crash—glass shattering against pavement—broke through his thoughts. He turned as Pepper arrived beside him, barking, clawing at his legs. With his eyes, he followed the trail of rope hanging from Pepper's collar to Leanna, standing among several broken bottles of jam, her legs splattered with red goo.

Kurt closed his eyes and took a deep breath. *Walk away. Just get in the car and leave.* Carey had staked claim to Leanna, and she obviously was interested in him. Kurt should climb into his car, drive the hell away from there, and go write. Wasting time was not on his agenda. He had no business walking to the men's room and filling his hands with wet paper towels. He shouldn't have made a beeline for her, or gotten down on one knee to wipe off the jam from her lean, sexy legs. She wasn't his to take care of, and Carey was right there beside her. But Carey was busy taking down his own booth, and other than handing Leanna a towel, he was doing nothing to help her—and that pissed off Kurt. He didn't deserve Leanna. What type of man didn't help a woman in a situation like this? Kurt wasn't working on what he should or shouldn't do. He was driven by something stronger—something he hadn't ever felt before—the desire to be someplace other than in front of his beloved keyboard. He wanted to be right there, helping Leanna.

He picked up Pepper and put him in the van with a sharp, "Stay."

"I'm okay. It's okay. Really. Go write. I'm a total time suck," Leanna said.

She had a sliver of a cut along the top of her right foot, and he knew she could handle a few broken jars—although the thought of Leanna with a broom and broken glass scared the hell out of him. And hearing the word *suck* coming off her lips gave him a few dirty ideas. She'd be fine without him, but damn it, he *wanted* to handle it with her. *For her.*

"I've got this." He borrowed a broom and dustpan from the snack bar manager and arranged to have buckets of water brought out to clear the sticky jam from the area.

Half an hour later, he returned the push broom and other supplies he'd borrowed, and Leanna's booth was clean, her van full.

"So? Off to the beach?" Carey flashed a smile and ran his hand through his hair.

Leanna met Kurt's gaze. The sun was slowly descending, and it cast a soft light along her hair, highlighting nearly blond natural highlights in her brown hair that he had somehow missed yesterday.

Her skin glistened from her efforts, her tank top hung off of one shoulder, wet between her breasts from sweat, and her short, white cotton skirt was speckled with red jam. She looked like the most adorable hot mess he'd ever seen, and Pepper stuck his head out of the van window, panting happily, as if he hadn't just caused the mess.

Kurt touched the edge of her skirt and *tsk*ed. "Make a paste with baking soda; soak those spots and then wash it. That'll come out."

Leanna tilted her head. "How do you know that?"

"I looked it up on the Internet last night before I washed your shorts. I didn't think you wanted red handprints on your ass forever." He nodded at Carey. "Have fun at the beach." *Lucky bastard.*

As he walked away, he felt the heat of Leanna's stare on his back, and while it brought a smile to his lips, it wasn't nearly enough.

Chapter Six

HAVE FUN AT the beach? How could she have fun at the beach after he'd been such a gentleman and stuck around and cleaned up her mess knowing she was going someplace with Carey? She glanced at the passenger seat, where Pepper was fast asleep on top of the clothes he'd brought. *And washed. And looked up how to remove the stain. Ugh.* She'd never understand men. If he was interested in her, he could have asked her out or said something. Maybe he wasn't interested. Maybe she'd misread all of his signals. *And his hard-on? No way. Not a chance.* That much she understood about men. Leanna followed Carey's van in her own on the way to Cahoon Hollow Beach and decided that she couldn't change what had already happened, and she might as well enjoy the beach before the sun went down.

    The sand was still hot from the afternoon sun. Leanna and Carey dropped their towels in the dry sand and ran toward the water with Pepper barking alongside them. Carey dropped his shirt and shorts along the way, and Leanna threw her shirt and shimmied out of her skirt, thinking about what the girls had said about her bathing suit. She'd have to watch Carey and see if they were right. She ran into the icy water with a squeal. Pepper followed her in.

"Cold!" She crossed her arms over her chest.

Carey popped up from under a wave and shook his hair like a puppy shakes its fur. "You'll get used to it. Come on."

She followed him deeper into the ocean, hoping she'd get used to the icy water. They rode the waves until their bodies were numb. Leanna loved the ocean, the bay, the beach, the mountains, snow, rain... There wasn't much Leanna didn't love about life. *Maybe that's my problem. I want to be in the thick of it, and most jobs make me feel like I'm missing something.*

"Your lips are blue. We should get out," Carey said with a wide smile.

He walked beside her as they made their way back to their towels. He was lean and fit and so tan that he looked like he lived on the beach, though Leanna knew he didn't. He, like Leanna, moved around a lot, but unlike Leanna, he often slept in his van.

"That was awesome." He wiped his face with the towel, and Leanna noticed his eyes lingering on her breasts—or more specifically, her cold, erect nipples.

Yup, the girls were right. The bathing suit is a killer.

"So refreshing." She sat down on her towel and slipped her T-shirt over her head.

Pepper plopped down beside her in the sand.

"Hey, so how do you know Kurt?"

Just hearing his name made her feel bad again. She wondered if he was writing, bare chested, sitting on the deck. She wondered if he was thinking of her. She liked the feel of his chest. A map of muscles and smooth skin, with that interesting tattoo. And those bright blue eyes that always seemed so focused and intense. He was...perfect. *Oh my God. What am I thinking?*

"Pepper got caught in the ocean the other night in the rain and he rescued him." She shrugged, as if it were nothing, when in fact it had been the one thing all summer that had stuck like glue in her mind. Or more specifically, he had been the one thing that stuck like glue. She glanced at Carey and felt guilty for wishing he were Kurt.

"Cool." He looked out over the water. "You wanna grab a beer?"

No, I want to go see Kurt. She was torturing herself. Kurt hadn't asked her out, and he'd basically kicked her out the other night. Then she'd kicked him out. *Ugh.* She thought about the moment on the deck when she'd thought he might kiss her, and now she wondered if she'd imagined it. Though she knew she hadn't imagined his erection. It was no use. She sucked at everything having to do with men. She was too outspoken, too uninhibited, too unsettled, which was why she never tried to pick men up, and forget knowing how to show she was interested. She turned into a fumbling, klutzy nimrod when she liked a guy.

A few drinks might be just what she needed to get Kurt out of her head.

"Sure."

After taking Pepper back to the cottage and putting away her flea market supplies, she joined Carey on the deck of the Beachcomber, overlooking the water. The Beachcomber was built at the crest of a bluff with a large covered deck that overlooked the ocean. Loud music, alcohol, and laughs were staples at the Beachcomber. Carey loved to dance as much as Leanna did. They danced, shared a burger and fries, and danced some more. They met a group of women and men who were vacationing from Canada and talked with them for an hour. By the time they headed back to their vans, Leanna was too tipsy to drive.

"Are you pretty sober?" she asked.

"I only had two beers. I'm good. But you were really putting them down. You okay?"

"Do you mind driving me home?" She leaned against his van, wishing she hadn't had the last two drinks. She'd been trying to distract herself from thoughts of Kurt, but nothing seemed to help. She kept picturing him at the flea market, feeling the intimate touch of his finger holding hers when he handed her the jar of jam and how quickly he'd let go when she told Carey she'd go to the beach with him.

"No prob." He opened the door and she climbed in.

They rode in silence down the main drag, and Pepper greeted them with a loud bark as they pulled into her driveway.

"That was fun. Thanks, Carey."

He narrowed his eyes and leaned across the seat. Before she could register what he was doing, his lips were on hers in a hard kiss. When he pulled back, she was still blinking away the surprise, but his hand resting on her thigh definitely registered.

He leaned in close again, and Leanna shook herself out of her stupor and splayed her palm on his chest with a little shove. "Sorry, Carey, but I'm not really..."

"Oh come on. Really? We have a great time together."

They did have a great time together, but she didn't feel that type of attraction to Carey, and if she'd been at all confused before, that absolute-zero-spark-inducing kiss had proved it.

"We do have fun. I love hanging out with you, but I'm not really looking for..." She looked down at his hand on her thigh. "More." *Liar.*

He sat back and put his hands up. "Hey, it's cool. No worries. I just thought we were both on the same page with you asking me to drive you home and all."

"I'm sorry. I really did have too much to drink." Leanna hated making anyone unhappy, and she genuinely liked Carey as a friend, but her mind had already drifted to Kurt, and then she felt even worse. She was leaving a wake of unhappiness everywhere she went, and it was so unlike her that she sobered up quickly and stepped out of the van.

"I'm sorry, Carey. You're great, really. I'm just...Ugh. I'm sorry."

"Hey, no sweat. I had fun tonight."

She watched him drive away and wondered if she should have said something else, but she'd never been good at this type of thing. She headed inside. The flea market wasn't open tomorrow, so at least she could sleep in and work on new recipes. She'd get up early and have one of the girls take her to get her van before they went out for the day. With that settled, she took Pepper for a walk, then took a quick shower and climbed beneath the sheets, wishing it had been Kurt's lips pressed against hers instead of Carey's.

Chapter Seven

IF THERE WAS one thing Kurt was sure of, it was that he was never going to concentrate with Leanna's bike in his garage. Not knowing that he didn't have a chance in hell with her. Dressed for his morning run, he pulled her bike out and looked it over. Pink. *Of course.* With a small basket on the front and a larger basket on the back like Miss Gulch in *The Wizard of Oz.*
Perfect. Just fucking perfect.
He'd found her bike lying on the ground at the end of the beach access road, and he'd ridden back to his house in the dark the night they'd met. He glanced at his sports car, realizing he didn't want to chance marring the leather by manhandling the bike into it, even with the top down. There was no way it would fit in the trunk without some elaborate tying down. With a loud, frustrated sigh, he put the bag of things he'd picked up for Leanna into the basket and felt a pang of longing chased by something akin to anger only not

quite as harsh, directly to his heart. He stared at the bag. He couldn't even get Leanna out of his head enough to forgo buying the things she needed. For the first time in his life—and he'd experienced a lot of firsts since meeting Leanna—he felt like the very definition of the word *fool*. He was sure if he Googled the word, his picture would appear, and he was powerless to do anything short of climbing on the damn bike and riding it the mile and a half to Leanna's cottage.

Thankfully, there wasn't much traffic on the back roads at seven in the morning. He could only imagine what he looked like. He was a foot too tall to be riding the bike in the first place. Add the pink color and the baskets, and he looked like he'd either stolen the damn thing or he was more interested in men than women.

He stepped off the bike when he came to the entrance of Seaside, and instead of heading directly to Leanna's cottage, he walked the bike around the other side of the development, where he found a gray building with LAUNDRY painted over the door and noticed that Leanna's van wasn't parked there. He followed the narrow gravel road around the bend, passing a large house on the left, which seemed out of place among the cozy cottages, and three more cottages on his right, before coming to a pool. He paused for a moment, trying to reconcile the postage-stamp-sized houses with the large swimming pool. There weren't many in-ground pools on the Cape besides the ones at the motels, and it intrigued him. A pool would offer something even the ocean could not. He could jump in to cool off and not have to worry about being sticky with sea salt when he went back to writing. His eyes fell to the bike, and he pushed away the daydream and continued up the road to Leanna's cottage.

Her driveway was empty.

I park it by the laundry room.

His chest tightened with the realization that she'd probably spent the night at Carey's.

None of my business.

Shit.

He opened the gate to the deck, and Pepper barked from behind a window screen, nearly giving him a heart attack.

"Holy hell, Pepper," he said through clenched teeth. "Hush. Please." He leaned the bike against the house.

Pepper stopped barking and panted.

He touched the screen with his finger and Pepper licked it. "Did she forget you last night?"

Leanna's face appeared behind Pepper. She blinked several times and sleepily rubbed her eyes.

"I could never forget Pepper." She hugged Pepper's head, and Pepper licked her cheek.

"Sorry. I didn't mean to wake you." He couldn't take his eyes off of her devastatingly sexy bare shoulders.

"You brought my bike back?"

She smiled, and he felt his anger float away. He stifled the urge to say, *Oh, come on. Not the smile? That's not fair.*

"Come on in," she said through the window.

He watched her walk away and—*holy Christ*—she

was wearing only a pair of lace panties. She disappeared into the bedroom, and when she came back out, her arms were up in the air and a silk camisole was sliding down over her bare breasts. Kurt could. Not. Move.

She came out on the deck, took his hand, and—

A chipmunk ran across the deck inches in front of her feet.

"Did you see him? Wasn't he the cutest little thing?" Her eyes widened, and the joy that she exuded was contagious.

Kurt felt a smile form on his lips. *She* was incredibly cute, but he could not form a sentence to save his life.

Another first.

"Come on. I'll make you some coffee." She led him inside.

The clothes she'd worn the night before were on the kitchen table, her shoes were in the middle of the floor, and there she stood, barefoot, in a pair of lace panties and that seductive silky camisole, setting a teakettle on the stove. He might not be able to speak, but he could feel the rise in his pants and the squeeze of his heart, and his legs had a mind of their own. Two silent steps put him behind her. His hands found her glorious hips—the hips he'd dreamed about more times over the past two days than he cared to admit.

"No coffee," he whispered in her ear. "I...I'm jogging back home." His heart thundered in his chest, and when she turned to him and pressed her hands to his pecs, she stole his breath.

"I'm sorry about yesterday." Her voice was soft

and tender.

Pepper whined at his feet, but he was too focused on Leanna blinking up at him to notice.

"Is...Carey your boyfriend?"

She shook her head. "I don't do boyfriends very well."

He narrowed his eyes but didn't want to—couldn't—take the time to decipher what that might mean. He had to taste her sweet, sexy lips. He had to be closer to her. He lowered his mouth to hers and wrapped his arms around her body. He placed one hand on the graceful curve of her lower back, and the other snuck beneath her hair. Her lips parted as she opened up to him. Her hands slid up his chest to his shoulders, and her tongue—her luscious, hot tongue—stroked his in perfect sync. He had to feel more of her. He slipped his hand beneath her cami, reveling in the soft, tender feel of her back. The back he'd been envisioning since she'd first changed into his sweatshirt. Her breasts pressed against his chest, and he craved more. So much more. He drew back and searched her eyes, and the desire in them mirrored the heat raging through his veins.

"Wow," she whispered.

A half smile was all he could manage, because *wow* was right. That kiss sent a bolt of lightning right through him. "Sorry."

"Sorry?" She wrapped her arms around his waist and snuggled into him. "That's the best kiss I think I've ever had in my life, and I really, really want another."

He lowered his lips to hers again, and she made the cutest, sexiest little sounds of pleasure. He wanted to kiss her forever just to hear more. She reached up and stroked his cheek, and he couldn't help but back her up against the bathroom door and deepen the kiss. She pulled back. They were both breathing hard.

"Teeth. I have to brush them."

He hadn't even noticed. She reached behind her and turned the doorknob. The door opened, and he kept his grip on her, then lifted her up and set her on the sink before he kissed her again—deeply, greedily, hungrily devouring her. She opened her legs, and he stepped between them. She arched into him.

"You taste delicious." He kissed her again just to prove it. His lips slid to the corner of her mouth, where he placed another soft kiss, and he couldn't stop there. He kissed her jaw, her neck, her sweet shoulder before reclaiming her mouth again.

She took his face in her hands and looked into his eyes.

"I'm a train wreck, and you're anything but," she whispered.

He loved her honesty. "You are. I am."

He kissed her again, and she pressed her hands against his back, closing the inch gap between them. He couldn't believe she was in his arms, and relief from what he knew now had been disappointment, not anger, forced his lips from hers, and he gazed into her eyes.

"I thought you went home with Carey."

She shook her head and brought her lips to his chest, pressing soft kisses along the tattoo over his heart and making him want her even more. Kurt buried his hands in her hair and tilted her head back so he could look into her eyes again. What the hell was it about her that enraptured him so? Time was ticking away. He should be back home eating breakfast, reading the paper, and getting ready to write, and all he wanted to do was carry her into the bedroom and make love to her.

He was too torn to move. Another day of not writing would set him back, and his deadline was looming. "Leanna."

She smiled. "I know." She dropped her eyes to his chest and ran her finger over the ink again. "You have to write. I need to get my van."

"Go out with me tonight." He didn't wait for her to respond. He kissed her again and groaned as he forced himself to tear his lips away again before he became too lost in her and wasn't able to.

"Okay," she whispered.

"Okay?"

She nodded. "Tonight."

He'd forgotten what he'd asked. His mind was running down another path—swooping her into his arms and making love to her until he forgot how to write and she forgot...Oh hell. Until she remembered everything. No. He wanted more than that. More of her than an hour of ravaging her heavenly body.

"Tonight." He took a step back to try to cool the heat between them. He ran his hand over his face and his eyes down her captivating curves. Kurt lowered his forehead to hers. "You are the most alluring woman I have ever met. I can't stop thinking about you."

Her finger got busy tracing him again and he lowered his lips to hers, then took another step back and helped her off the sink. Her hand remained a soft pressure on his chest, her hips found his, and he noticed how perfectly they fit together. The thought of making love to her right there against the sink, then in the shower, then in the bedroom, shot another bolt of desire through him. *Christ Almighty.* He needed to put space between them.

He caressed her cheek before stepping out of the bathroom with Pepper on his heel. He looked down at his erection. There was no way in hell he could run with *that*. He glanced back at Leanna. She held up one finger, then closed the bathroom door. He sat down on a chair and buried his head in his hands. He was hard, hot, and his brain couldn't think past Leanna's scent, the feel of her, the look in her eyes—and the way she read his mind, then reacted without throwing him out. She knew he needed to write. *Knew!* He'd been with enough women to know that her reaction was not typical. He had to get a grip. He was becoming more enchanted by her every time he saw her.

Pepper whined at his feet, his tail wagging for attention.

"Good dog," Kurt said.

Pepper barked.

Kurt gave him a stern look, and Pepper lay down beside the chair.

A few minutes later, Leanna came out of the bathroom fresh faced and still clad in her panties and camisole. She straddled his lap and looked him in the eyes. So much for letting his erection fade.

"Thank you for bringing me my bike." Her breath was minty, her smile still a heart slayer.

"You're welcome."

"And thank you for helping me with the mess yesterday." She kissed his cheek.

Jesus, do I really have to go write? "I have no doubt that you could have cleaned it up yourself, but you're welcome."

She crinkled her nose. "You've seen me with a broom."

He kissed her crinkly nose. "That I have."

"Since even I know you can't jog home in your present state, can I make you breakfast?"

There was that honesty again. "Are you as good in the kitchen as you are at kissing?"

She shook her head as she rose to her feet. "But I'm better than I am with a broom."

Chapter Eight

AS KURT JOGGED out of the development, Bella, Jenna, and Amy burst into Leanna's kitchen, each still in their sleepwear and carrying a mug of coffee.

"Details. I want every last detail." Bella sat at the table in her cotton nightie that stopped two inches below her butt.

"He arrived shirtless and with your bike. I saw him." Jenna tugged at her T-shirt, which was hung up on her enormous braless breasts above a pair of men's boxer shorts. She looked down and wiggled her boobs into submission, then gave up with a defeated sigh and leaned against the counter. "And I want to know why he brought these." She tossed a dog's leash and a box of baking soda onto the counter; then she put the empty bag she'd taken from the basket on the bike beside the contents.

Amy popped two pieces of bread into the toaster. She wore a T-shirt and plaid pajama shorts and looked like a teenager rather than a twenty-seven-year-old woman. "Morning booty call. Nice. I like that. You get all the action and still get a good night's sleep. But baking soda?"

Leanna laughed as she fingered the leash. "Yesterday he was at the flea market and I had Pepper tied up with rope because I couldn't find his leash, and the baking soda?" *Because he's thoughtful.* "Pepper went kind of crazy, and a couple jars of jam broke. My skirt got splattered, and I guess he'd Googled how to clean the stain on my shorts that I'd left at his house because when he brought them back, they were perfectly clean."

"Left your clothes at his house?" Bella puckered her lips and made kissing noises.

"You guys are awful. It wasn't a booty call. How often have you seen me have any type of booty call? I swear, I'm at the point of needing a chimney sweep to clean out the cobwebs."

"Oh, that's just sad." Bella shook her blond hair in front of her eyes and then gathered it in her hand and drew it all away from her face.

"Seriously. Sex is hardly a priority. But it was really thoughtful of him to bring this stuff, don't you think?" Although, now that she'd kissed Kurt and felt him, really felt him—all of him—against her, thoughts of climbing between the sheets with him were lingering. *Taunting.*

"Yes. Very thoughtful. So, nothing happened? The guy washes your clothes and brings you stuff to keep stains away, and nothing happened?" Amy pulled her toast from the toaster, grabbed a jar of jam from the fridge, and read the label. "Apricot-lime? Is it okay if I try it?"

Leanna shrugged and set the leash down. "Sure. It's a new flavor. Go ahead."

Amy spread it on the toast and took a bite. She narrowed her eyes, and a second later they widened. "Oh my God," she said with a mouthful of toast. "This is amazing."

"Really? I wasn't sure anyone would like it."

"Mm. It's like a cool summer drink."

"Can we cut to the chase here? I'm glad you like her new flavor, but I want to hear about Kurt's bite." Jenna leaned forward a little. "Oh, and, Amy, make me one? Pretty please?"

"Sure." Amy popped more toast in the toaster.

"Me too," Bella added.

"Already on it," Amy said with a smile.

Leanna thought about kissing Kurt, and she sighed. "All I can say is that the second our lips met, it was like...like, you know that feeling when you're going up on a roller coaster? Not down when your stomach falls, but that ride up when everything in the world seems possible, when the wind is at your face and you feel like you could just close your eyes and be carried right up to the clouds?" She sighed again. "Kissing Kurt was like that, only about a million times better."

Bella shook her head. "Jesus."

"Imagine how good the sex will be," Jenna added.

"I want a kiss like that." Amy set a plate in front of the others with toast and jam on it.

"That's not all." Leanna covered her face. "I can't

even believe I'm telling you all of this two seconds after he left."

Bella kicked Jenna under the table. "Told you. Booty call."

"No, no. Not like that. When he wrapped me in his arms, it was like everything else fell away."

"Wait. What?" Amy took a bite of toast and tossed one to Pepper, who ate it quickly and then whined for more. "Fell away?"

"The chaos in my head. You know how my mind goes a mile a minute? Well, for those few minutes it calmed."

"He really is magical." Bella took a bite of the toast and jam. "This is fucking amazing. It really is like a summer drink, but better. It reminds me of that night last summer when we had the bonfire on the beach. Why didn't you give me a jar of this?"

"I was afraid you guys wouldn't like it."

Bella pointed at her. "There are two things I like to make up my own mind about. Food and men. Don't tell me what I want to eat or who I want to fuck. Got it?"

"I know that about men." Leanna smiled. "You're definitely a taste tester."

Bella ripped off a piece of toast and threw it at her. Pepper caught it midair.

"So, no bing, bang, boom? Why did he leave?" Jenna asked.

"He has to write. He's so focused. I'm not sure I've ever met anyone more focused than him."

"I'm focused," Jenna said.

They all laughed.

"Really? What's on your agenda today?" Leanna

asked.

Jenna tucked her hair behind her ear and looked up at the ceiling.

"Right." Leanna rolled her eyes. "You're organized and efficient, very obsessive, but over the summer, you're focused on finding rocks and drinking and men, like the rest of us. I think he's always focused on writing."

"Always, like too much?" Jenna bit into her toast.

"I don't know that it's too much, because I'm not really an expert on focusing, but I can see it in his eyes. When he's not writing, I can tell he's thinking about it." She ran her eyes over her friends' concerned faces. "And we're going out tonight." She watched the concern lift, replaced with delighted smiles.

"Finally. Hope for some action," Bella cheered.

"But what if he has that look all night? I could tell today. We were making out and he looked at me, and in that split second I knew he was thinking that he had to go write. It was like from his brain to mine, I knew it."

Amy put her arm around Leanna. "Honey, I think you had your signals crossed. He was probably wondering how he could get you into your bed and out of those sexy little panties."

Leanna shook her head. "You could be right, I guess, but I don't think so. When I said he had to write, he agreed. Lord knows I never get my signals right." She shrugged. "Other than with you guys, I'm never in sync with anyone."

"I say just follow your gut. I mean, you'll know pretty quickly if he'd rather be writing. Hell, you'll know if he would rather be doing anything else, and then you can decide what to do." Bella took another piece of toast from the plate. "You look so worried, and there's nothing to worry about."

Leanna sank down to the floor, and Pepper rested his head on her thigh. "Yes, there is. I'm totally awkward when things heat up with guys. I can never get my timing right, and I mess everything up."

Amy sank to the floor beside her and petted Pepper. "You don't mess up everything. You're doing great with your Sweet Treats business, and your timing must be okay or he wouldn't have asked you out."

"Yeah, but..." He brought Pepper a leash. He didn't even really like Pepper. Although she had heard him say, *Good dog*, when she was in the bathroom. *Hmm.*

Jenna slid off her chair and sat by Leanna's feet. "You can't mess up sex, honey. You know that. You've had sex."

Leanna sighed.

Bella threw her hands up in the air. "Are you freaking kidding me? This is what worries you? Leanna, honey." She sat down with the others. "You could just lie there and the guy will be happy. Seriously, how *off* can you be in the bedroom? You would have told us by now. We've known you for years."

Leanna swallowed hard.

"No way." Bella smiled. "This, I have to hear."

"I can't." Leanna covered her face and took a deep, mortified breath before dropping her hands. "Ugh. I'm fine. Really. I'm just not one of those delicate girls who knows how to be all sexy and feminine and…I don't know. I'm just always a little off with my moves."

Jenna swatted the air again. "With a body like yours, it wouldn't matter if you were off, on, or ten paces behind. Girlfriend, you've got this. Just relax. Drink some wine beforehand, and you'll be fine."

"I guess. It's not like I'm having sex tonight anyway. He asked me out, not to bed."

The others exchanged a glance.

"You said you made out with him?" Amy asked.

"Yeah."

"What are you thinking about right now?" Amy narrowed her eyes.

"Sleeping with him."

"And what do you think that handsome hunk is thinking about after making out with you dressed in your take-me-now outfit?" Amy touched her shoulder. "You're doin' the dirty tonight unless you don't want to."

Leanna traced circles on her thigh. Oh yeah, she wanted to. She wanted to so badly that her stomach was tied in knots and she worried that her heart wasn't far behind.

Chapter Nine

KURT WROTE UNTIL four in the afternoon, when it dawned on him that he didn't have Leanna's phone number and they hadn't made any firm plans. She really did steal his cognitive abilities. Although, for the first time in the last forty-eight hours, he'd been able to really focus on his writing, and he'd knocked out four chapters that resonated so strongly with him he half expected to find his villain standing next to him when he finally pried himself away from the computer. He wondered if in some convoluted way it had anything to do with their impending date. He took stock of his emotions. He was definitely feeling more enthusiastic about...hell, everything...and more driven since she'd agreed to go out with him.

Kurt saved his work and brought his notebook inside, thinking about where to take Leanna that evening. They could go to the drive-in theater, but he really wanted time to talk with her and get to know her a little better. If they went to the drive-in, there was no way he'd be able to keep his hands off of her long enough to do any talking. He smiled to himself, because he also knew that once he got her talking, he might be in for an entire night of listening to her sweet voice.

Kurt showered and changed into a pair of linen slacks and a button-down shirt. On the way to Leanna's, he drove into the town of Wellfleet to pick up a few things at the Wellfleet Market and noticed a poster announcing a movie that was showing on the back of Town Hall later that evening. Kurt rarely ventured out in the evenings, and he was excited to do so. He realized that he wasn't thinking about writing. His mind was completely consumed with Leanna and their impending date.

He drove down the main drag toward Seaside and glanced at the bouquet of wildflowers on the passenger seat. It had been years since he'd bought flowers for a woman. He hadn't been planning on buying them, but when he saw the bouquet of colorful wildflowers, their haphazardness reminded him of Leanna. This was the first date he'd looked forward to going on in years.

He parked in her driveway and took a deep breath to calm his nerves. She rattled him. She sent his heart off kilter with everything she did, and while she wasn't a train wreck, as she thought she was, she was definitely not the most organized person, and she didn't seem to live with any method to her days. Leanna breathed new life into everything around her. Including Kurt. When he was with her, things didn't just *look* different; they *were* different. Days seemed brighter. Scents were more aromatic. Even the feel of her hand on his skin brought a heightened sensation. It was as if he'd been living life through a cloud, and Leanna breezed in, bringing clarity and lighter, happier feelings. She even seemed to have improved his creativity and writing. She lit up the darkest corners of his world. And although Kurt was a creature of habit and didn't like surprises, or change, very much, he was drawn to Leanna like pen to paper.

He climbed from the car with his purchases in hand and was greeted by Pepper's bark through the window.

"Hi, Kurt."

He turned and waved to Bella and two other women sitting on the deck of one of the cottages before heading up to Leanna's door. Pepper clawed at the screen, and Kurt crouched so he was eye to eye with the white fluffy pooch.

"Sit."

Pepper did.

"Good boy."

"Did I hear you call Pepper a good boy?" Leanna came out of the bedroom wearing a white gauzy dress, cut midthigh in the front and below her knees in the back and belted at the waist with what looked like a brown scarf of some sort. Her hair cascaded in loose waves over her shoulders. She pulled open the screen door with a sweet smile.

"Wow, Leanna. You look incredible."

That earned him a smile and a tippy-toed kiss. Her sweet, summer scent enveloped him.

"You smell amazing, too. What is that?"

She shrugged. "I have no idea. Whatever lotion I grabbed from my dresser, but thank you. Now I wish I knew which one it was."

He was slowly coming to understand and appreciate that this was how she lived her life, easy, free from worry, natural, and that those moments he'd witnessed—forgetting her bike, leaving her clothing in his car and at his cottage, and even the disarray of her kitchen—hadn't been moments at all, but peeks into the remarkable woman that she was.

And he liked it. A lot.

"These are for you." He handed her the bouquet.

"Wildflowers? How did you know they're my favorite?" She wrapped her arm around his hip and snuggled against him in a one-handed hug. "Thank you."

While Leanna put the flowers in a vase, Kurt opened the bag he'd been carrying and crouched beside Pepper, who was wagging his tail and panting for all he was worth.

"Yes, I brought you something, too." He held a doggy treat in his hand, and Pepper climbed right up onto his white pants and licked his cheek. Kurt laughed as he pulled back from him. "Sit," he said a little less sternly than he had before.

Pepper obeyed.

"Good boy." He handed Pepper a treat, and Pepper carried it beneath the table and scarfed it down.

"I can't believe you brought Pepper a treat." Leanna crouched to watch Pepper eating.

"I figured he deserved it. He might be lonely if I

steal you for the evening."

She slid her arms around his waist again, as if she'd done it a million times before, and she gazed up at him.

"Thank you for the leash. I can't believe you bought that and the baking powder even though you thought I was going out with Carey."

"I didn't want to come between you two, but the thought of you trying to walk Pepper with a rope long enough to trip a thousand kids worried me."

"It was very thoughtful of you." She moved away to slip her feet into a pair of flat, strappy sandals. "Where are we going?"

"That depends on what you feel like doing. There's a movie playing on the back of Town Hall, and I brought a bottle of wine. We could grab a quick dinner and head there, or have dinner on the beach, or go to a restaurant in town. Or maybe head up to Provincetown and walk around, grab a bite to eat?"

"You gave me so many options. It's hard to decide."

Pepper whined up at them.

"Oh, hush. You'll be fine." Leanna reached down to pet Pepper, and he pawed at Kurt's pants leg. "Are you starved?" she asked Kurt.

"Never."

"Really? Sometimes I'm so hungry I can't see straight." She tucked her hair behind her ear as she rose to her feet.

Why doesn't that surprise me?

"I love the beach at night, and I haven't gone much this summer. Why don't we grab something quick to eat at PJ's or Mac's and take it to the beach with the wine? If we get bored, we can go see the movie."

Bored? Between his writing endeavors and his love of exercise, Kurt had never experienced being bored a day in his life.

She took his hand and they went outside.

Pepper whined and barked behind the screen door.

"Let me just go ask Bella to take care of Pepper. She won't mind, and I'll only be a minute."

Kurt looked down at Pepper's big, sad eyes.

"If we're not going to a restaurant, we can bring him with us. Unless you don't want to."

She stopped cold. "You...*want* to take him?"

Kurt looked at Pepper again. "He's kind of like your kid, isn't he? Doesn't he go everywhere with you?"

"Pretty much, but I never date, so he doesn't really know dating etiquette."

"As opposed to...flea market etiquette?" He reached for her hand.

She stared at their linked fingers. "Point taken, but won't he be a total mood killer?"

He brought her hand to his lips and pressed a soft kiss to it. "I'm not sure there's any such thing when I'm around you."

She stepped in close and ran her finger down the center of his chest. "Well, Mr. Remington, you know how to cut right to a girl's heart. Are you sure you don't mind?"

He eyed Pepper again. "You're a package deal, and I have a feeling that I might as well get used to it." He leaned down and kissed her long and slow, and when their lips finally parted, he wasn't so sure he even wanted to leave the cottage.

Chapter Ten

THEY DROVE TO Duck Harbor and left their shoes, a blanket, and a bag with the wine and sandwiches that they'd brought on the side of the dune and walked hand in hand by the water's edge. Pepper trotted happily beside them, tethered by his new leash. The wet sand was cold between Leanna's toes, and a light breeze came in with the crashing waves. It had been a long time since she'd walked hand in hand with a man. Kurt's hands were big and strong, and as strange as it seemed, the word *safe* came to mind when she thought about their interlocked fingers.

"Tell me about your life, Leanna. You said you're here for the summer, but where do you live when you're not at the Cape?"

She'd been trying to figure out how to explain her crazy life all day, and now, walking beside Kurt, she threw out the preconceived ideas she'd come up with and decided to go with complete honesty. What did she have to lose besides maybe the most thoughtful guy on earth?

"I lived in Pullman, Washington, for a few months, where I was helping a friend with her floral business. I gave up my apartment when I came here to start my business. I'm kind of a wanderer, I guess. Growing up as a military brat sort of set me up to move around a lot."

"Your family is military? My dad's retired army, four-star-general through and through."

"Yeah? Did you move around a lot?"

Kurt shook his head. "No. I guess we were lucky in that regard. I like knowing I'm coming home to the same comfortable and familiar house. But my dad is the epitome of a military father. Strict and maybe a little cold at times. How about you?"

"Cold? Really? My father's one of the warmest men I know. He's not at all a typical military guy, I don't think. In fact, I'm sure of it. He's very forgiving of his children. Probably too much so." She noticed tension lines around Kurt's mouth that hadn't been there a moment ago. "Do you and your dad get along?"

He shifted his eyes to her. "Yeah, sure. He's a good guy, and I respect the hell out of him for all he's done. He's just...He pushed us all pretty hard when we were growing up. You know the type. *Do better. Do more. Be the best at whatever you do.*" He stopped to pick up a stone and tossed it into the water. "I think it's what's driven me to be so focused on my career, so it was a good thing. At least for me."

"If my dad had a little of that in him, then it might have helped me," she admitted.

He pulled her close and gazed into her eyes. She loved his face, the soft crease beside his nose, the sweet fullness of his lips, and she could look at his eyes all night. Kurt had kind, emotional eyes. She read a thousand things in them in the space of a breath. Happiness, hope, generosity, desire. What she didn't see was what she'd seen earlier—the restrained yearning to be writing. And she was relieved.

"Helped you with what?"

She shifted her eyes away. This was the hard part. A little fear weaseled its way into her heart and kicked up her pulse.

When she didn't answer, he took her hand and turned back in the direction they'd come. He didn't push her for an answer or act as though he was annoyed by her silence. She added that to the growing list of things she really liked about Kurt.

"Do you have a big family?" she asked.

"Yeah. Four brothers and a sister. We're all pretty close. I meet them for drinks about once a month, and we all have dinner with our parents every few weeks. You?" he asked.

"Mm-hm. Three brothers and a sister." She stole a glance at him, and he draped his arm around her shoulder.

"I'm not going to judge you, you know. Not that you have to tell me anything, but I can see you're worrying about something." He kissed the side of her head. "I like who you are."

"You might not after you get to know me better." She held her breath, and when he squeezed her shoulder, she relaxed a little. They made their way back to the blanket, and Kurt tied Pepper's leash around his ankle.

"Sit," he told Pepper. Pepper lay down with his head on his front paws.

"I still can't believe you can get him to do that." She held the plastic wineglasses as he filled them.

"I think it's all in the voice. My father used that trick with us. You know, the one tone that had you shaking in your shoes."

"I guess, but my dad never used that with us." She watched him closely, looking for signs of his wishing he were elsewhere.

He leaned his elbows on his knees, and for a few minutes there was only the sound of the waves.

"I'm not thinking about writing, if that's what you're wondering."

"What makes you think I'm wondering anything at all?"

He turned to look at her and smiled. "You've got an assessing look in your eyes. When you look at me, you're kind of sizing me up, or weighing what you should or shouldn't say. I can feel it." He took a sip of wine. "Am I wrong?"

She traced the line of a muscle up his arm. "No. You're right. Here's the thing. I'm twenty-eight, well educated, well traveled, and besides being with Pepper, I've never found a single thing that I knew without a doubt was right for me. I've gone through eight jobs in the last two years. I've moved to three states in four years, and my Sweet Treat business is my latest effort in finding a fulfilling career. And I know that's totally not the type of person you are, so I was a little afraid to tell you."

He nodded and took a sip of wine. Then he wrapped his arm around her. She snuggled in against his warm, muscular body, one arm draped across his stomach, her head against his chest and arm, and she waited for him to say something. Anything. For the longest time, he was quiet. He was careful, she realized. Words were his life, and he seemed to choose the most meaningful words, or the ones that most accurately reflected his thoughts. Another thing to add to her Like List.

When he finally spoke, his tone was thoughtful and tender.

"Sometimes it's the interest we take or don't take in things that makes them fulfilling—or not."

"I'm not sure I follow."

"Well, like with writing. If I wrote about characters or topics I didn't enjoy, writing wouldn't hold my interest. But writing is such a personal endeavor that I make a conscious effort to write about the things that do hold my interest. I break the rules. My work isn't formulaic, and if people don't like what I write..." He shrugged. "They don't have to read it, but at least I'm happy while I'm writing."

"But not every job is like that."

He set down his wine and turned to look at her. "Tell me about your business. Why did you choose it? Do you enjoy what you're doing?"

"I love what I'm doing. It's creative and fun, and I get to meet a lot of interesting people. I have flexible hours. I mean, I really love it, and I know that's weird, because I'm just making jam."

"Just? I couldn't make jam. And you're not just making jam; your jam is incredibly sweet." He leaned over and kissed her. "I'm dying to know how you chose that path."

"It's kind of weird, I think. There was this really sweet old man, Al Black, and he used to sell jam at the flea market. We were friends for years. I was just a kid when we met, but every summer I'd spend a few hours a week with him at the flea market, and I really came to love him. Like a grandfather, you know? He told me stories about his family, and when he spoke of making jam..." She shook her head, remembering the look in Al's eyes. "The way he looked, his eyes. It was like making jam was the most romantic thing in the world." She ran her finger along his forearm, tracing a vein. "He died last winter, but before he passed, he called me and shared his recipes, and I don't know. Everything came together in my heart. I knew I wanted to do the same thing. It only made sense to do it here, you know, to honor him?"

He cupped her cheek, his eyes laden with compassion. "Leanna, that's the most beautiful thing I've ever heard. Do you miss your friend?"

No one had thought to ask her that, and she had to swallow past a growing lump in her throat. "Yeah. I do. This summer is the first summer he hasn't been here, and I find myself looking for him sometimes. You must think I'm weird." She looked down at the blanket, and he lifted her chin with his finger and drew her eyes back to his.

"Not even close. I think you're smart, and kind, and funny, and...special in the very best way."

She felt her cheeks flush. "I'm not. I'm just trying to find something..."

"Are you fulfilled?" He searched her eyes.

She inhaled deeply before answering, letting the salty sea air fill her lungs. "I guess I don't know. I always feel like I want to do more."

"Me too. I always want to do more. I want to write more, write differently, take my readers to new places. Do you want to take your business to another level? Try new things with it? New flavors? Travel more? Or do something else altogether?"

She shrugged, which she knew wasn't an answer at all. "I never really overthink things. I want to enjoy my job. I want to love it, actually, but I also love life so much. All of it, from the yucky parts to the good parts. I hope to one day find something that fits that part of my personality. I'm enjoying the jam business so much, and the flea markets, that I'm kind of hoping this feeling remains. I just wish I could know for sure now." Pepper inched up beside them and put his head on Kurt's leg. Kurt's eyes never wavered from her.

"Is there some reason you are putting so much pressure on yourself? I can see you're a little stressed over this. Do you have a career deadline?"

She laughed. "A career deadline? No, but I'm almost thirty. Shouldn't I know what I want to do?"

He kissed her softly, and she nearly melted into him.

"My mother would say that no two people are the same and not to compare yourself to what others think you *should* be like."

Kurt's voice—and his words—soothed the rough

edges of the pressure she had been putting on herself. He made her feel better about her inability to commit to a career.

"So you don't think I'm a hopeless, reckless, nightmare?"

He smiled. "Wow. All those things and a train wreck? No. You seem like you're very passionate, and you just haven't figured out where to direct your energies yet. You'll figure it out." He shrugged. "Or you won't, and if you don't, you'll have spent your life doing all sorts of things along the way that you, hopefully, enjoyed, so will it really matter?"

He leaned in closer, and she could barely breathe. He wasn't judging her. He wasn't telling her all the reasons she needed to make a career choice. Him of all people. Kurt Remington. The man who knew exactly what he wanted—the man who was slowly stealing little pieces of her heart.

"The truth is, most people spend more time with their jobs than they do with their spouses, so if you don't enjoy it, you'll...divorce it." His voice grew serious. "Life's too short to stay married to a career you hate. You're probably smarter than half the people out there who are begrudgingly going to their jobs every day."

His lips were a breath away from hers. She could smell the sweet wine on them, and she could feel the heat coming off of him in waves. She didn't think before she spoke. She looked into his eyes, and the words came from her heart.

"Kiss me."

His eyes narrowed, and in one gentle move, he

took her in his arms and kissed her until she couldn't think, could barely breathe. He lowered her to the blanket, still in his arms, their lips joined, their tongues colliding in an erotic, sensuous, lavish kiss. He lay beside her, one leg draped over her hips, his chest pressed to hers, breathing air into her lungs. He brushed her hair from her forehead and slid his hand to the back of her head, tilting it just enough that they both deepened the kiss. He wasn't groping her body or pushing himself on her—and as much as she craved his big, strong hands on her body, she loved this. The closeness, the way he was kissing her, as if kissing her was all he ever needed. She'd never felt so treasured in all her life.

Pepper whined, and they drew apart, both breathing heavily.

Kurt held her face in his hands and pressed another kiss to her lips. "I like you way more than I should after just a few crazy days." He breathed heavily.

Oh God. Me too. She opened her mouth to say just that, but all she could manage was, "Uh-huh." She felt her cheeks flush again.

He smiled and kissed her again.

He stroked her hair. "This is the first time I've really taken time off in weeks."

"And." *Kiss me. Touch me.*

"And there's no place I'd rather be."

She reached her hand around the back of his neck and brought his mouth to hers again. God, she loved kissing him. She couldn't mess up kissing. It was the mechanics of taking clothes off and maneuvering bodies that she was worried about. But kissing? She could kiss him forever.

He ran his hand up her thigh, and her whole body shuddered. His lips slid to the corner of her mouth and he pressed a soft kiss to it; then he kissed a trail along her jaw to her neck. His strong hand gripped the outside of her upper thigh and held tight. Leanna closed her eyes and arched into him as his lips worked their way up her neck to the sensitive area below her earlobe, where he licked and kissed, then grazed his teeth along her earlobe until her heart thundered against his. She needed more of him, more of his touch, his tongue, his kisses.

He took her earlobe in his mouth and laved it with his tongue, then whispered, "I want to make love to you."

"Yes," she said in one long breath.

He brought his forehead to hers. "The sand?"

"Too messy?"

He looked down at the sand. "The sand will be messy, gritty, and uncomfortable as hell, but I don't care about any of that." He glanced at Pepper. "But if he takes off while he's attached to my ankle, it could get a bit awkward."

She bit her lower lip and glanced at Pepper. "Trust me on this. You're having sex with me; it's *going* to be awkward."

He nuzzled against her neck. "Why does that totally turn me on?" Kurt kissed her again. "This might sound lame, but I've never been a very adventurous guy. I've never had sex on a beach."

"You? Not adventurous? You waded out into a

storm and saved me. That's pretty damn adventurous. But I've never had sex on a beach either."

He cocked his head to the side. "My free spirit"—he kissed her neck—"beautiful Leanna"—he kissed her lips—"has never had sex on a beach? But you'll whip off your clothes in my living room and put on my sweatshirt when you've known me five minutes?"

She was still relishing in his use of the word *my*. "I knew you about thirty minutes, and there's a big difference. I'm not shy about being seen naked, but being seen having sex? Not such a pretty sight." She looked up and down the beach. They were alone, tucked against the side of a dune. The moon reflected off of the ocean, the waves lapped at the shore, and Leanna's heart thundered inside her chest. At the moment Pepper was being very well behaved, lying in the sand beside them, and the idea of getting out from under tender and sexy Kurt did not seem appealing at all.

Nervousness and desire vibrated through her body. "I'm game if you're game."

"Oh, baby, with you? I don't know what you've done to me, but I'm game for just about anything as long as it doesn't involve a broom or broken glass."

He covered her mouth with his and kissed her until the last bit of worry about being seen and out of sync slipped away, and all that remained was the feel of his full lips, his hard body against her, and the sound of the breaking waves. Kurt's hand moved along her thigh, and when it slid beneath her dress, her whole body went hot. She arched into him, and he pressed his cheek to hers as he worked her belt free.

"I've thought about you in your lacy panties all day."

His seductive whisper sent a shiver through her, and when his fingertips touched the edge of her panties, she sucked in a breath. He gazed at her with serious eyes.

"Want me to stop?" he whispered.

God, no. She shook her head, reached her hand around the back of his neck, and pulled his mouth to hers again. His big hand moved up her body, his palm covered her ribs, and his thumb grazed the underside of her breast. She moaned against his lips, and he deepened the kiss. When they came apart, she could barely breathe for the need to kiss him again. But his mouth was moving slowly down her body, kissing a hot path between her breasts. He lifted his eyes and met her gaze and she held her breath; then he moved farther down and lifted her dress above her hips. Leanna gripped the blanket in her fists and closed her eyes, stifling the urge to beg for more as he ran his finger along the edge of her lacy panties, teasing her with his touch. Her body tingled, aching for more of him. Then his lips were on her stomach again, burning a path from her belly button to her hip. She exhaled in pleasure and he gripped her hips, causing her breath to hitch in anticipation. He used his teeth to drag her panties down her thighs. *Good Lord.* It was the sexiest thing she'd ever seen a man do. Kurt ran his tongue along the crease between her leg and her sex, first on one side, then the other. A cool bay breeze swept across her damp skin, and Kurt worked his way up her body, kissing, tasting, touching every inch of her skin and taking her dress with him. When he reached her breasts, he stopped, and she felt him rise up onto his elbows.

"Leanna," he whispered.

She opened her eyes.

"You're sure you want this?"

"Yes." *God, yes. Now, please.*

He kissed her softly. "You're exquisite. Everything about you, Leanna. You're not at all awkward."

"Take your shirt off." She tried to work the buttons on his shirt, but her hands were trembling.

He pressed his hand to hers and held it against his chest. "You're shaking."

"A little."

He kissed her hands. "Are you nervous?"

"A little." *A lot.*

"We don't have to." His gaze turned serious.

"I want to." She reached for his buttons again. "I've never wanted anything so badly in my life." *Oh, shit. Did I just say that out loud?* She shot her eyes to his. *Oh God!* He was looking at her with an amused little smile.

"Me either." He removed his shirt and rolled it up, then placed it beneath her head. He shifted his eyes to Pepper, fast asleep in the sand. "Think I can untether him?"

"Yes. Quick. Yes."

He removed the leash from his leg, and Pepper opened one eye, then closed it and went right back to sleep. Kurt stepped from his pants, and Leanna drew in another sharp breath at the sight of him, naked, before her. She felt as if she were under a spell, her eyes locked on the gorgeous broad-shouldered creature before her. Planes of lean muscles and warm skin there for the taking, and boy did she want to take. She dragged her eyes down the center of his body to his eager desire between his legs, and anticipation thrummed through her. He came to her then, and she wanted to reach for him, to stroke him and love him, but she couldn't move.

"You're beautiful," he whispered against her neck as he unhooked the front clasp of her bra and carefully removed her clothing, leaving her naked, save for her panties around her thighs. In the next breath, he drew them off. Leanna closed her eyes, breathing harder and shivering against the bay breeze as he came down beside her. He reached into the pocket of his pants and took a condom from his wallet, then tore it open with his teeth. She tried to help him roll it on, but her hands were still trembling. He took her in a sensuous kiss, never missing a beat as he put on the latex sheath.

"Told you I was awkward," she whispered as he gently laid her back down.

Positioned above her, he kissed her again. "You're not at all awkward."

She shifted her eyes away, and he drew her chin back, bringing them eye to eye again. "We can stop."

"No," she said sharply.

"Look at me. Be here with me, Leanna. Share this moment with me."

She held his gaze as he slid inside her, and a streak of heat raced through her body to her heart. She sucked in a breath as he pushed deeper, until their bodies were as close as they could possibly be, and he stilled. She closed her eyes, and he kissed her eyelids.

"Be with me."

His heated whisper drew her eyes open as he withdrew, then pushed in until he was buried deep, again and again, sensuously stroking the coiled heat in her belly free. He lowered his mouth to hers, and in that moment she became his. The rest of the world fell away, and it was only the two of them. His efforts carried her from one breath to the next, breathing, taking, loving her body. She tried not to move, afraid of throwing them off. He buried his hands in her hair and rested his forehead on hers.

"Leanna." Her name was filled with desire. He kissed her again as he pulled out, then thrust in until he was buried deep, and stilled again.

He slid his lips to her cheek and whispered, "Move with me."

She loved his voice, his words, the way he expressed himself. Every word was intense, passionate, and thankfully, he began moving inside her again. *Yes, oh yes.*

"No," she whispered back.

He stilled again.

"No? Why?"

"I'll throw you off, and this feels so good." She looked away, and he drew her eyes back again, searching for understanding. "Really," she pleaded. "Trust me. You don't want me to move."

"Let me be the judge, okay? I want to feel you, all of you, and if that means you move at a different rhythm than me, I'll figure it out."

She bit her lower lip, completely, utterly embarrassed and wanting so badly to let herself go and just be herself with him at the same time. She shook her head.

"Leanna." He caressed her cheek. "I don't care if you buck like a bronco. I'm with you. I want you. The real you."

She smiled. "A bronco?"

He shrugged; then he lowered his mouth to hers, and his tongue moved swift and deep, in perfect tune to every thrust of his hips, and Leanna began to forget her worry and forget her awkwardness. As his hands moved down her body to her breasts and he brushed her nipples, her hips began to move on their own. She knew she was completely off, and when he stilled, so did she.

"No. Keep moving," he urged.

She did, and she prayed he wasn't going to get up and say, *That's some crazy shit you have going on there. I can't do this.* Her last boyfriend had said something similar one too many times.

In the next breath, his cheek was pressed against hers again and he was whispering in that sweet, seductive voice of his. "You feel so good. I love the way you move. Oh yeah, that's it."

His encouragement wrapped around her heart; then his lips met hers and his heart thundered against hers. She felt so safe with him that she didn't object when he rolled over and positioned her on top, even though she hated being on top. Their pleasure was all up to her now, and she sucked at this part of sex. She moved, and she knew her rhythm was off. Then his hands found her hips, and he helped her find a rhythm that he could match. Their rhythm. Once they found their cadence and their bodies were in sync, one of his hands found her breast, while the other found her center, and he teased her most sensitive area. She couldn't help but suck in a breath and arch against his hand.

"That's it, baby. Come for me."

His voice sent another thrill through her. No man had ever talked to her during sex, and Kurt made her feel special and sexy. He sat up and took her nipple in his mouth, still teasing her with his hand, and her eyes slammed shut against the sensation of a million pinpricks along her limbs as she came apart, sending her body into a frenzy of crazy movements and hot pulses. He gripped her hips again, moving with her as she rode out the wave of the best orgasm she'd ever experienced. When she finally let out the breath she'd been holding, he expertly rolled her onto her back and took her in another hard kiss. She couldn't think. The new position brought her quickly to the peak again, and she lifted her hips to meet his thrusts. He smiled down at her, never missing a beat, driving his hard length into her, burying to the hilt and then pushing deeper.

"That's it," he urged. "Come on, baby. Take it right over the edge again."

Pepper whined, and Kurt shot him a heated look. Pepper put his head back down and sighed.

Kurt drew his eyes back to Leanna, totally focused on her pleasure, his muscles hard beneath her palms, his movements efficient and strong. He shifted his hips, and she sucked in another breath.

"Kurt," she panted. "Oh God."

He gripped her hips and held her tightly, thrusting harder, deeper, stroking the spot that tightened every nerve in her body and sent her insides into a pulsating fever of need. He sped up his pace, and she gripped his powerful biceps tightly as he took her to the brink again. She cried out—a loud, indiscernible shriek of pleasure that sent Pepper to his feet, barking and running up and down beside them. Kurt held her tight as his muscles flexed, and his body shuddered against her as he found his own release.

Pepper circled them, barking and whining.

Kurt leisurely reached for his leash and drew him close—carefully, Leanna noticed.

"Sit." He said just above a whisper, still breathing hard. Leanna felt the word vibrate through his chest.

Pepper obeyed.

"Good boy," Kurt managed. He let out a breath and pushed himself up from Leanna's chest.

She pulled him down on top of her again. She needed to feel his heart beating against hers. Being in Kurt's arms stole the emptiness from her heart and filled it with an unfamiliar contentment that she never wanted to lose.

"Told you I was awkward." She bit her lower lip.

He kissed her trapped lip, then kissed her cheeks and her forehead and looked at her with his sea-blue eyes. "I didn't notice a bit of awkwardness. You're perfect."

Chapter Eleven

A COOL BREEZE came off the bay like a sigh and rolled over Kurt and Leanna, now fully dressed and lying on the blanket gazing up at the stars. Pepper's leash was tied to Kurt's belt loop, and the dog lay quietly beside them. Leanna's leg was draped over Kurt's, her head rested against his chest, and her index finger traced the ripples of his abs.

Kurt covered her hand with his. "You're nervous."

She didn't respond.

"Was this too public? It was new for me, too. I'm sorry. Maybe we shouldn't have—"

"No. It wasn't that. I mean, it was public, but I wanted to be with you as much as you wanted to be with me, and this was fun. I'm glad we have a first for both of us."

A first. Our first. He loved that. Kurt brushed her hair over her shoulder, thinking about firsts. Women thought about their first time, their first kiss. He knew that many of the things that were momentous in women's lives revolved around men. His firsts, however, were tied to his writing. The first manuscript he completed, *Beneath the Stillness*. His first rejection letter. His first agent request for a full manuscript. The first offer of representation. His first publishing deal. His first live television interview. His first book award. If he really drew on his memory, he could pull the name of the first girl he'd kissed, Madeline Bern, but it was last in a long line of firsts. Firsts with women had never felt very momentous. This first went to the head of the line.

A first for both of us.

Kurt wasn't a talker. His family and friends knew this about him, and they accepted it. He enjoyed observing more than being in the midst of the goings-on, but Leanna had flipped a switch inside him. He felt himself changing, wanting more, and it surprised him. Rather than fight these new feelings and climb back into his writer's mind—the safety of his writer's cave—he wanted to remain in her world.

"I feel like I've had a few firsts tonight," he admitted.

"A few?"

She touched his cheek, and he closed his eyes for a breath, relishing in her touch. Her palm was warm and soft, loving.

"For the first time in years, I'm not thinking about writing." He leaned up on one elbow and gazed into her eyes. "For the first time in as long as I can remember, I really and truly enjoyed making love." He leaned in and kissed her. "I enjoyed making love to you, Leanna, being close to you. I like you. A lot." His pulse sped up again. "And you're wearing off on me. I never talk this much."

She smiled, but she didn't respond, and Kurt's stomach tightened. He was moving too fast, baring his heart when he shouldn't. He'd watched his siblings fall in love, and he'd caught glimpses of what it was like for them to really let someone into their lives. Something inside him that he didn't even know existed felt drawn to Leanna in that way. He wanted to let her in.

But was she pulling back? He wasn't practiced enough at reading women to be sure. Worry snaked its way into the back of his mind.

"I didn't exactly take you on a date, did I?" He sat up and leaned his arms over his knees. "I'm sorry. I'm not very good at this."

She laughed softly as she pulled herself up beside him. "What are you talking about?"

"We had sex on the beach when I should have taken you to dinner, a movie, something more date-like. There's probably some dating rule I know nothing about. No sex until the third date or something?" He shifted his eyes to her with a smile.

"You're so funny. I don't know many people who go out on three dates before they have sex."

"Really?" He had always thought timelines for intimacy were odd. He either felt something or he didn't, but he also wanted Leanna to know he really liked her in a way that was much deeper than just sex. "That's kind of weird, too, isn't it?"

She shrugged. "I don't know. I probably would

have slept with you at my cottage this morning, and we hadn't even gone out on one date."

He pulled her close. "Then why do I feel like something's wrong right now?"

"Nothing's wrong. I'm just embarrassed. Now you know about my weird inability to be in sync while we're..." She glanced at the blanket.

"Oh, thank God." He breathed a sigh of relief.

"Thank God?"

"Yeah. Here I was thinking I'd done everything wrong." He pulled her onto his lap and gathered her thick hair in one hand and lowered his lips to her bared skin. "You're perfect, sensual. Not awkward. Not weird. Perfect."

"Come on, Kurt." She rolled her eyes.

"Maybe we should do it again so I can prove it." He smiled and she laughed. "Seriously. I'm not sure why you are so worried. We were perfectly in sync."

She lowered her forehead to his. "I love when you lie to me."

"I never lie, babe. It's one of my faults. I'm not even sure how to lie."

"Everyone lies."

He pulled back and searched her eyes. "I don't. I've never been able to fake feelings either. They're either there or they're not. It's who I am."

She rested her head on his shoulder and whispered, "Then we're a perfect pair, because I'm who I am, too."

THERE WERE NOT many things in life that scared Leanna. Starting over in a new city was exciting;

quitting jobs was as easy as changing her clothes. She knew she could pick up the pieces of her life and find a way to carry on no matter what was going on around her. She might not be the neatest girl on the planet, or the most organized, and she might not remember everything—like where she left her bike or Pepper's leash—but she knew the moment she set her head on Kurt's shoulder that her heart had opened to him in a way it never had before. And that scared the crap out of her. One of her biggest skills was being discontent—and although this felt a world away from anything remotely similar to discontent, she hoped her mind didn't steal this happiness from her.

As Kurt drove toward her cottage, her heart told her to invite him in and ask him to stay for the night, but her head told her that was stupid. They'd gone out once. She didn't know him well enough. Yet her gut reaction was that he was not only trustworthy, but different from—maybe even opposite of—any man she'd ever met. It was after midnight when they pulled into Seaside. The lights in Bella's and Jenna's cottages were still on. *Of course.* Directly across from Leanna's, Amy's cottage was dark.

Kurt opened the car door for Leanna, something no man had done for her in the past. And there he was, standing tall and handsome in his linen pants, with those piercing blue eyes. A perfect gentleman. And what was she thinking? She wanted to rip his clothes off and climb on top of him again.

She stepped from the car, and he folded her in his arms.

"I wish I had thought to take you to my place for

the night," he whispered.

Could they possibly be in sync?

"I...um..." She turned at the sound of whispering behind her and noticed Amy, Bella, and Jenna walking up the street from the pool. Pepper took off in their direction, dragging the leash behind him.

Kurt followed her gaze. "Were they swimming?"

"Chunky-dunking."

"Chunky-dunking?" He laughed. Their hair was piled up messily on their heads. Each woman was draped in a towel that barely covered her private parts, and they were grinning like fools.

"It's what we call skinny-dipping," she whispered. "The pool closes at eight, but we sneak in sometimes."

"I'll have to set my alarm so I don't miss the next episode of Seaside Skinny-Dipping. May I see you tomorrow?"

May I? She reminded herself that words were his life. "I'm making another batch of jam tomorrow, so I'll be here all day. Aren't you writing tomorrow?"

"I write every day, but I'd like to fit some time in to see you. Unless you have plans or would rather not."

Leanna sensed her friends behind her, turned, and nearly bumped into Bella.

"Bella," she chided her. Pepper was legs to the sky with his tongue hanging out of his mouth as Amy scratched his belly.

"Sorry. I wanted to say hi to Kurt. Hi, Kurt." Bella smiled and tilted her head.

"Hello, Bella."

"This is Jenna." Bella pointed to Jenna, who waved.

"And Amy's loving up Pep."

"Hello, ladies. Nice to meet you." He glanced at Leanna. "Tomorrow?"

"Sure. I don't know what time I'll be done. What do you have in mind?"

He leaned in close. "It doesn't matter. I just like being around you. Although, I kind of owe you a real date."

"A real date," Bella whispered.

Leanna shot her a look.

"Sorry. We were talking about having a bonfire here in the quad tomorrow, if you guys want to join us." Bella turned away and tightened her towel.

"That's not exactly a real date, and I'm sure the last thing Kurt wants to do is hang out with a bunch of women." Leanna touched his hand. "I'd love to see you."

"I don't mind hanging out with your friends if that's what you'd like to do."

"Great. Then it's a date," Bella said.

"Oh my God, Bella." Leanna glared at her. "Jenna, please take her home."

Jenna looped her arm into Bella's. "Come on, Bell. Let's give Leanna a little privacy."

"I'm going, too." Amy picked up Pepper's leash and handed it to Leanna. "Nice to meet you, Kurt."

"You, too, Amy." Kurt settled his hands on Leanna's hips, and she lowered her forehead to his chest.

"I'm sorry. Bella's a little pushy."

He lifted her chin with his index finger. "They seem nice. I don't care what we do, as long as I'm with you. Why don't you decide, and I'll come by around six or so?"

"Perfect."

He kissed her good night, and Pepper whined at his feet. Kurt shook his head. "Good night, Pepper."

As he drove away, Leanna wondered if her luck had changed—or if she was on the way to a crash-landing but too high up in the clouds to notice.

Chapter Twelve

COLD. WET. STINKY. Leanna opened one eye and found Pepper's nose pressed against her cheek. She groaned and rolled over.

"Five more minutes?" she pleaded.

Pepper yelped in her ear. She pulled the covers over her head and felt Pepper pawing at her. Leanna drew the covers back down and sighed at Pepper's tongue hanging from his mouth, his tail wagging. She dragged herself from bed, peeked out the window, and spotted Pete the pool guy's truck. *Nine o'clock.* Another late start to her morning.

Totally worth it.

She'd stayed up for hours thinking about her evening with Kurt, reliving his touch, his mouth on her skin, his teeth on her panties. She shivered in her T-shirt and panties as she opened the door for Pepper to go out. He ran straight down to the pool to greet Pete. Leanna grabbed her laptop from the bedside table and checked email. She skimmed the junk messages announcing sales and ways to make her love life *sizzle*. *My love life is already sizzling.* The thought surprised her, because for once in her life it was true.

The mouse bounced between two unopened emails. One was from Mama's Market, a local farmers' market, and the other was from Daisy's Chain, the largest grocery chain in New England. She'd sent a proposal to each three weeks ago. She was two clicks away from either the end of her dream or the beginning.

Too nervous to read either yet, she closed her laptop. Pepper scratched at the door as Bella barreled in behind him, wearing her bathing suit beneath a sarong, her thick hair tamed in a high ponytail.

"Hey there, girlfriend. You're finally up. Were you up having phone sex all night?"

"No. Mental sex. Oh gosh, you know what? Kurt doesn't even have my phone number. Come to think of it, I'm not even sure where my cell phone is." She looked around the cottage, trying to remember the last time she'd used it.

"That's the thing about the Cape. No one uses their cells." Bella turned on the teakettle.

Leanna ran her hand through her hair. "Weird, isn't it? It's like when we're here, watches and cell phones don't exist. I swear I only use my email for checking on those proposals, too. But I really like living less electronically."

"Do batteries count? Because I'm not giving up *that* little electronic toy anytime soon."

Leanna shook her head as she filled Pepper's

bowls with clean water and fresh food. "I got emails from the two grocery places."

Pepper shoved his nose in his bowl until half of the food fell over the rim and onto the floor. Then he lay down and ate the pieces off the floor.

Bella's eyes widened. "And?"

"I don't know yet. I haven't opened them."

"Well, why the hell not?" Bella reached for the computer, and Leanna gripped it tight.

"Because. What if they both aren't interested? Then I'm screwed."

"Screwed? You're kidding, right? You know that those are just two tiny places in this big wide world. You could submit proposals to hundreds of places anywhere in the United States."

"I know. I'm just nervous. I really love making jam. Isn't that completely crazy? I mean, it's messy, sticky, not anywhere near a *real* career, and something about it makes me happy." She shrugged.

"Most things in life that are fun are messy and sticky." Bella winked and handed Leanna a cup of coffee. "Speaking of which…"

Leanna turned back to her computer to avoid answering Bella's need for details about sex with Kurt. "Let's see what the markets said."

"That bad, huh?"

"No." Leanna looked up at her with a smile. "That good."

"Thank God. After what you said about being off with your timing, I had awful images in my head of things a friend should never think of."

"You're so weird." Leanna laughed.

"So? It wasn't awkward? I told you, guys don't care about all that."

Leanna sat back and sipped her coffee. "I think they do care. At least the ones I've been with. Most guys get all irritated, like you just ruined all their fun. But Kurt didn't."

"Maybe you're not as awkward as you think and the other guys were jerks."

"No." Leanna shook her head. "I'm definitely out of sync with most men, but Kurt...Oh God, this is kind of embarrassing. Can we just look at the emails?"

"Nope." Bella reached over and closed the laptop. "I haven't had a date in weeks. Let me live vicariously through you."

Leanna sighed. "He *helped* me. He was tender, and attentive, and sexy, and..." She felt herself smile. "I don't know. It was just different with him. I've never felt so close to anyone in my life."

"Wow. That good, huh? I want one of those. Does he have a brother? A father? A cousin?" Bella crossed her legs. "You wouldn't want to share, would you?"

"No way. Not a chance in hell. But you know me. He probably won't be around for long. He's got his whole life in order, and I..."

"Oh, stop it. Open your computer and let's see what's going on with your life."

Leanna checked the email from Mama's Market first. "Oh. My. God. They want to meet with me this week." She looked up at Bella. "Oh God. Bella!" She jumped to her feet and paced. "Now what? I never thought they'd want to actually meet with me."

"What did you think? That you'd just give up? That

you were wasting your time? Then why'd you send the proposals?" Bella turned the laptop toward her. "Let's see what the other one said." She clicked on the email from Daisy Chain.

Leanna held her breath.

"Check it out, Lea. They want to meet with you next week!"

"Next week? This week? Oh my God. I have the flea market Friday, so that leaves tomorrow or Thursday. I have so much to do. What should I do?" She sat down, then popped right back up again. "I need to answer them. I can meet with them Thursday, and that gives me today to go pick fresh berries and gather supplies and tomorrow to make fresh batches of jam. Good." She paced again with Pepper on her heels. "I can do this. I can definitely do this." She stopped pacing and looked at Bella.

"You can do this, Leanna. You can definitely do this."

KURT HAD BEEN riding the dark torrent of his villain all afternoon, and by the time his alarm chimed at four, his muscles were so tense that his fingers ached. Thrillers were emotionally intense, and after spending all day writing, he was often in too dark of a mood to climb out of easily. That was the danger of writing thrillers and, Kurt admitted to himself, one of the reasons he never sought out relationships. He was also a smart man, a man who did his research and thought things through before jumping into them. He liked to know where he was heading in his life, and his belief in always having the best-laid plans rarely led him astray, which is why his attraction to Leanna totally threw his equilibrium off.

He stood on the deck and looked out over the water. The tide was on its way out, leaving trails of shells and seaweed behind. He thought about making love to Leanna on the beach, and a thrum of excitement ran through him. She *was* a little awkward, and her timing was a little off, but with his help and the right encouragement, they'd found their rhythm and fell into wonderful, blissful sync. The truth was, he loved that she was a little off. That's what made Leanna, *Leanna*. Real. Unique. More special than any other woman he knew. Anyone could study the art of lovemaking and learn sensual tricks to heighten the experience, but not many women were brave enough to allow themselves to be who they were without extra layers of fabricated sensuality.

He made a mental check of his current emotional state as he stretched the tension from his limbs. Thinking of Leanna helped put him in a lighter frame of mind, but the villain was still tugging at the fringes of his nerves. He went inside and up to the small weight room, where he ran through a quick workout of his biceps, triceps, and chest, and for good measure, he worked in a few sets of abs exercises. Forty minutes later, his head was much clearer and his body craved Leanna.

He took a cold shower, threw on a pair of khaki shorts and a white T-shirt, and headed over to Seaside. He heard the music as he pulled into the community, and as he neared Leanna's, he realized it was coming from her cottage. He followed the sound onto her deck and to her screen door. The music was so loud he could barely hear her and her girlfriends talking. Every square inch of counter was covered with cooling jars of jam, and on the stove was a giant pot. Leanna wore a bikini top and a miniskirt—and about a pound of jam.

Pepper barked, and Leanna turned with a spoon in one hand and a streak of dark red jam across her cheek that Kurt wanted to lick right off.

She gasped. "Is it five or six already?" She turned down the radio and let him in, then lifted up on her tiptoes to kiss him.

"You taste sweeter than sweet." Kurt licked his lips and then went in for another kiss.

"I taste good, too. Wanna taste?" Bella hollered above the music with a wiggly wave of her fingers.

"No," Leanna answered for him. She took his hand and led him farther inside the crowded cottage. "I'm so sorry. I lost track of time, but I came up with a new flavor."

"She's meeting with Mama's Market on Thursday," Jenna explained while struggling to confine her breasts in a bikini top that looked like two thongs trying to trap Beyoncé's butt against her chest.

With the smell of sugar in the air, her hair pulled back in a messy ponytail, and wearing streaks of jam like camouflage, he couldn't help but wrap his arms around Leanna from behind and kiss her cheek.

"Mama's Market? That's impressive. Congratulations."

Feeling proud, she turned to him. "Guess what else?"

"You came up with a new flavor?" Then he leaned down and kissed the jam from her cheek. "Strawberry and something?"

She blushed and stumbled backward, knocking the spoon from her hand onto his white shirt. "Oh gosh." She reached for a towel.

Kurt gently grabbed her wrist. "Slow down and tell me."

"Strawberry-apricot, but that's not what I was going to tell you. Daisy Chain wants to meet with me next week about carrying my jams." Her smile reached her eyes, and Kurt pulled her close.

"Ah, babe. That's fantastic. I'm so happy for you." When he pulled back, the streak of red jam that was on his shirt left a trail between her breasts. He couldn't take his eyes off of it as all sorts of dirty, sticky ideas came to mind. Dirty and sticky had never been words that he'd found alluring, but when he was with Leanna, everything he thought he knew about himself was beginning to look different, and after last night, he doubted there was much he wouldn't consider trying with her.

"So, what's your plan?" he asked.

"Plan?" She washed the spoon that had fallen and was dabbing at his shirt with a wet sponge, deepening the stain in the process. "I'm going to bring the new stock of jam with me and talk to them."

"Do you have brochures? A marketing plan to show them?"

She looked at him like he was speaking a foreign language and went back to work on the jam on his shirt, which was now ground into it.

He pulled the shirt over his head and was rewarded with gasps from the other women as he rinsed it under cold water.

"Now we're talkin'," Bella teased.

"Where have you been all my life?" Jenna added.

"You guys, that's Leanna's boyfriend. Give him a break." Amy placed her hand over the tattoo on his arm. "Sorry, just had to touch him once. Now he's all yours."

"Oh my God. Sorry, Kurt. And he's not my boyfriend," Leanna said.

Kurt's hands froze beneath the water. He looked up at her and saw the worry in her eyes. "I'm not?"

"Well, I mean, we didn't talk about it."

"Hey, girls. Let's go walk Pepper." Amy dragged the others out of the cottage. Pepper followed on their heels.

"You're right. We didn't talk about it. I'm sorry." Kurt rinsed his shirt, trying to ignore the tightening of his gut. Maybe he had jumped the gun. He grabbed the baking soda he'd given her and worked his shirt clean. "I didn't mean to assume…"

Leanna leaned her back against the counter, her eyes trained on the towel clenched between her hands. "I know. Do you want that?"

"To be your boyfriend?" *God, yes.*

Her eyes remained trained on the towel. "I haven't had a real boyfriend in forever."

"I haven't had a real girlfriend in years, and I didn't realize I was even thinking in terms of boyfriend and girlfriend until just now." He leaned his hip against the sink and placed his hand on top of hers.

He felt them relax beneath his touch.

"Yes. I want to be your boyfriend, Leanna. I know we haven't known each other long, but I feel something for you that I've never experienced before."

Her lips curved up. She lifted her worried hazel eyes.

"Even after I ruined your shirt?"

"Even after you ruined my shirt."

He lowered his mouth to hers and kissed her like he'd been wanting to since he left last night. He felt himself getting hard, and Leanna dropped the towel to the floor and cupped the back of his neck, deepening the kiss. Her touch sent heat right through him. He buried his hands in her hair, kissing her hungrily, pressing his chest to her beautiful, soft, full breasts. Without thinking, he lifted her into his arms, and she wrapped her legs around his waist.

"Bedroom," she said against his lips.

He carried her into the bedroom and kicked the door shut. Kurt couldn't remember ever wanting a woman the way he wanted Leanna. He longed to be close to her. Her friends' voices filtered through the window screen, and he pulled back, breathing heavily.

"We can't. Your friends. Your jam."

She nodded. "Right. Bad idea, unless we want three sets of eyes watching us while they eat popcorn outside the bedroom window."

"Popcorn?"

"My friends, they'll...Never mind." She leaned her forehead on his. "The bathroom."

"What?" *Oh yes. Holy hell, yes. Anywhere.*

"Bathroom. There's no window in there."

"Your jams?"

"They're cooling. The stove is off." She kissed him and said, "Bathroom," in a breathy voice.

He carried her into the bathroom, and with the door closed and locked—*because Bella knows no boundaries*—Kurt hooked his thumb into Leanna's skirt and drew it down, then stepped from his shorts. Leanna reached her arms around his neck, and he lifted her up again. She slid down upon him, taking in every inch of his desire, and they both sucked in a breath at their bodies coming together. Her hair fell over their faces like a curtain as he moved inside of her.

"Jesus, Leanna. You're so hot and so wet." Sex hadn't ever felt that—*fuck!* He stilled. "Holy shit. Don't move."

"What? Why?"

"I forgot a condom. I'm not used to carrying them."

She began moving up and down, and he stilled her hips.

"Leanna. Don't. I'll come."

She leaned back and looked him in the eye. "I'm almost thirty, not fifteen. I'm on the pill. And before you, it had been almost a year since I'd had sex, so unless you've had some worrisome sex partners, I think we're okay."

He shook his head. "Same three women for the last few years and always with protection."

"Then shut up and kiss me."

Their lips met, and Kurt backed her up against the wall for support, thrusting deeper, harder, relishing in the feel of her body embracing him like moist velvet.

He wanted to be in a bed with her, on top of her, with hours ahead of them to love and touch each other, to taste every inch of flesh and tease her until she couldn't remember her name. He didn't have a chance in hell in lasting here. Now. With no condom and Leanna moaning his name into his ear in a husky, lust-filled voice. He slowed his pace, hoping to draw out the sensation, and pulled back from their most delicious kiss to take her breast into his mouth and tease her taut nipple.

"Oh God. Oh God." She closed her eyes, breathing heavily.

He ran his tongue around her nipple, then moved to the other breast as she clawed at his shoulders and writhed against him in one frenetic thrust after another. Her insides tightened around him, and she cried out as she'd done last night—a loud, sensual cry—which drew the come right out of his loins.

Kurt held her close, their bodies shuddering against each other with little aftershocks from their lovemaking.

With a sated look in her eyes, Leanna whispered, "I want to be your girlfriend."

It was another first for him. He wanted Leanna in his life, even if it meant giving up a few hours of writing each day.

Chapter Thirteen

BY THE TIME they took a quick shower and dressed, the sun had nearly set. Thankfully, Leanna knew her friends would allow them whatever privacy they needed and care for Pepper without complaint. She had enjoyed showering with Kurt and dressing together. He was so much more relaxed than when they'd first met. She began noticing all sorts of things she had missed, like the way he watched her when he thought she wasn't looking and the quirky smile when she caught him looking. She loved the way his eyes went dark and intense before they kissed and how his hands were always finding their way to her in some way—reaching for her hand, her hips, her shoulder. Now he was reaching for a jar. She knew it had to be killing him to have the kitchen in such disarray. She touched his hand.

"We can't move them. They have to cool overnight."

"Really? You'll just leave them out here? What if you need your counter? Or your table?"

He furrowed his brow in the serious way that Leanna was quickly coming to love, because what seemed serious in his eyes was never serious in hers.

She shrugged. "I have the table on the deck." She moved to the sink to scrub the big tub, and Kurt embraced her.

"Let me do that."

"I can do it."

"I know you can. I want to. You can do whatever else needs to be done."

She felt his eyes on her as she moved through the cottage gathering the utensils she needed to run through the dishwasher and the dish towels she needed to wash.

"I like having you here," she admitted.

"Yeah? I like being here." He smiled over his shoulder at her.

She was drawn to his thoughtfulness, this man who had a whole life without her and was finding ways to fit her in. She ran her hands up his flanks and over his shoulders; then she pressed her cheek to his back. His skin was warm, his muscles firm, and though he'd used her body wash, his masculine scent came through.

"Do you need any help preparing for the meeting with the market?" he asked.

Preparing? Even the thought of preparing made her stomach queasy. She sucked at preparing, and besides, this was a jam and jelly business, not a million-dollar corporation. "No, I'm ready. Just nervous."

"They'll love you."

"It's my products I hope they love." She leaned on the counter beside him as he handed her a tub to dry and began washing another. She hoped the market did love her. It would be that much easier to sell them on carrying her product if they liked her as a person.

"How was your writing today?"

He turned off the water and began drying the tub he'd just washed. "Great. I was really inspired and wrote a few suspenseful chapters. Dark and scary."

"How can you write dark and scary? Doesn't it creep you out?"

He set down the tub and picked up his T-shirt from the counter. "Nope. I mean, it puts me in a dark frame of mind for a while, but it doesn't scare me."

Leanna placed her hands on his gloriously sexy chest. "I should tell you that while it's totally cool that you write thrillers, I am *so not* a thriller reader. I don't like scary stuff, but I respect what you do."

"Somehow that does not come as a surprise." He leaned down and kissed her. "Where's your laundry?"

She knew he was expecting her to have a central laundry basket with a tidy little pile of laundry. She trapped her lip in her teeth instead of answering.

"This, I have to see."

She took his hand and brought him into the bedroom; then she led him to the far side of the bed, where there were two piles of clothes. She pointed to them as she spoke. "Clean. Dirty." She wondered if he might turn and leave. Just like that. *See ya. It's been fun, but you're a mess.*

"You're kidding, right?" He had an amused look on his face—eyes wide, lips curled slightly up in disbelief.

"Nope."

In one swift move, he picked her up and laid her on the bed, then settled in on top of her. "You need me in your life."

Oh, hell yeah, I do. "I don't *need* any man in my life. But I *want* you in it."

"Fair enough." He eyed the laundry. "Does your laundry room take quarters or dollars?"

"Quarters." She pointed to a plastic container full of quarters on the dresser.

"Mind if I throw in your whites?"

"That's like me asking if you mind if I sweep your deck." *Only better, because you'll do a good job and I can't sweep worth shit.*

He kissed her again and pulled her up by her hand. "I know better than to ask you to sweep anything. Come on. We'll do it together, so your girlfriends don't think you've hired me as your houseboy."

"They're more likely to think I've hired you as a sex slave." She swatted his butt as he bent over to pick up her laundry.

"You're pretty cute."

"You won't think I'm so cute when you're picking up the pile of laundry for the seventeenth time, or when I turn all your clothes into jam rags, or—"

He captured her words in his mouth with a passionate kiss.

"Let me determine how long I'll think you're cute."

"Okay," she said dizzily.

BELLA COOKED CHICKEN on the grill, and Jenna and Amy made a salad. Leanna brought out homemade bread and jam, and Kurt shared the wine he'd brought with him for the evening. They ate dinner by the fire in the grass behind Leanna's cottage and talked. The air smelled sweet and ashy, and Leanna's cheeks were pink from the warmth of the fire. Her friends were friendly and in good spirits, and Kurt noticed how comfortable they were with one another. They passed knowing looks like inside secrets, and they welcomed him into their tight-knit fold seamlessly. He couldn't remember the last time he'd spent time relaxing with friends. In fact, he wasn't sure he really had friends who were as close as these friends were to Leanna, and he wondered if he was missing out on something. But friendships like theirs took nurturing and time, and time was something Kurt hadn't been able to spare—until he met Leanna. He thought about the time he spent with his siblings and the family dinners with his parents. Those were events he enjoyed, but they were different from this. Sitting by a bonfire under the moonlight, enjoying the company of people other than his family, with his arm around his girlfriend? Another first.

He was surprised that Bella hadn't razzed them for disappearing earlier in the evening, but he assumed that although she was brazen, she also knew when not to embarrass Leanna.

"So, Kurt, can you tell us about the book you're working on?" Jenna asked.

"It's darker than my others, set in an old mining

town in West Virginia." *And I don't really want to talk about it because then I'll start thinking about the next chapter, and then I'll want to write it.* He pulled Leanna closer to him. She wore a sweatshirt and shorts, and when her leg pressed against his, her skin was hot from the bonfire.

"Do you base your characters on real life?" Amy had on sweatpants and a sweatshirt, and her feet were tucked beneath her on the bench where she sat.

"Only the ones I don't like. Then I kill them off." That brought a round of laughs, as was to be expected. He needed to change the subject. "So, how long have you known one another?"

The women exchanged smiles and glances.

"Years," Bella said. "There are other people who own here in the community, but this summer has been weird. It's been so empty here. Jamie Reed's grandmother owns that cottage." She pointed to the cottage on the corner. "She's eighty, and Jamie's our age, but he usually comes down to take care of his grandmother, and Vera hasn't been well this summer. Then there's Tony, who owns the blue cottage that faces the pool."

"Tony," Jenna and Amy said with dreamy smiles.

Bella continued. "He's the community hottie, and he'll be down in a few days, I think."

Kurt made a mental note about Tony being the community *hottie*.

"Yeah, that's right. He had that thing in Maui this week, remember?" Leanna said.

"Maui?" Kurt asked.

"Yeah, he's a motivational speaker and a pro

surfer." Leanna ran her finger in circles over Kurt's thigh, and he silently noted her nervousness.

"And, of course, Clark and Vanessa. They own that three-bedroom over there." Bella pointed to the cottage next to Amy's. "And Grumpy Gus, but he's almost never here."

"And Pete," Jenna added. "Our maintenance and pool guy."

"Yeah, we can't forget Pete, can we, Jenna?" Leanna poked Jenna with her toe. "She's sweet on Pete."

"Oh, please." Jenna swatted the air.

"Anyway, we've known each other forever. Where do you live, Kurt?" Bella asked.

"New York," Jenna answered.

Kurt laughed. "Yes. I do live in New York, just outside the city."

"Sorry. I Googled you," Jenna admitted. "You have four brothers and a sister who's a famous model. One brother owns a gaming company, another's an Olympic skier, and then there's a survivalist, and..." She snapped her fingers.

"You're good at the PI stuff. My other brother, Sage, is an artist, and he owns Creation for Hydration, a nonprofit that builds wells in developing nations. He and his girlfriend, Kate, run the company together."

"When do you go back to New York?" Amy asked.

"In about two weeks." Kurt kissed the top of Leanna's head.

"Gosh, if I had a house on the beach, I'd live in it year-round," Amy said.

"That might be nice, but my life is in New York. My

family, agent, all of my publishing contacts. It would be inconvenient to live here year-round."

"That makes sense." Amy moved closer to the fire to warm her hands. "Leanna? If you get these contracts, are you staying at the Cape or...? Where will you live?"

"I haven't thought about it." She sat up and yawned.

Kurt felt a pang of curiosity. Where would she live? How would he see her? He tucked the worry away. He'd make damn sure he saw her.

"I don't know how you can not know where you'll be living in a few weeks. I'd go crazy. I need to know where I'll be and when I'll be there." Jenna joined Amy standing by the fire.

Leanna shrugged. "It doesn't bother me."

"That's because you have a trust fund and we don't." Bella stood in her jeans and sweatshirt and stretched with a loud yawn.

Not that Kurt cared about her money, but this surprised him. "You don't strike me as a trust fund kid."

"That's because I'm not. My great-grandfather left money to my dad, and he put it all in trust funds for me and my brothers and sister. I used it for college, and I've never touched it since. I figure I'll leave it to my kids someday, and eventually, someone who really needs it will have it." Leanna shrugged as if she'd just said what anyone might.

Kurt and each of his siblings were comfortably wealthy, though they'd each earned their way through hard work and dedication in their chosen fields.

Knowing that Leanna relied on her own efforts endeared him to her even more.

"You're remarkable." He pulled her a little closer.

"Hardly." Her cheeks flushed.

"Most people would use that money to kick-start their business, or to travel, or something else. People can always find reasons to spend money." Kurt thought of his own finances. He didn't spend foolishly, and he traveled only when it was thrust upon him. He owned his house in New York and the one on the Cape and kept one car at each. He gave generously to Sage's company and to other charitable organizations, and beyond that, his money was well invested. He felt like another layer of Leanna was stripped away, revealing the empowered, determined woman beneath.

"I don't think my great-grandfather worked hard so I didn't have to."

Leanna smiled up at him, and in that moment, he knew everything he needed to about who she was. It didn't matter where she lived or what she did for a living. A person didn't become as lovely as her by being pretty or owning the right things. Leanna might be beautiful on the outside, but she was stunning on the inside.

She stifled another yawn.

"What are your plans for tomorrow?" Kurt brushed her hair from in front of her sleepy eyes.

"I was going to make the batch of jam I made today, so I don't have much on my agenda at this point."

"Come home with me. Stay with me tonight."

She sat up and searched his eyes. "You're

serious?"

"More than."

"What about your writing?"

He loved that she thought of his schedule. "I'm going to do what I always do. I'll get up and go for a run, and I'll write, but I thought it might be nice to have you there with me. You can work on your presentation for Thursday, or hit the beach, or read, or do nothing but lounge around. I just want to wake up with you in my arms."

He realized Amy, Jenna, and Bella were watching them, and he cleared his throat. "Sorry. I don't mean to take her away from you guys."

"No, no. Take her, please," Amy said, motioning with her hands for him to take her away.

"We're just drooling." Bella wiped her mouth.

"Jeez, Bella." Leanna looked down at Pepper, asleep by Kurt's feet. "What about Pepper?"

"Package deal. Pep comes, too."

"Okay, but are you sure I won't interrupt your writing?" She traced the outline of his pocket on his shorts.

He lifted her hand to his lips and pressed a kiss to it. "No. I'm about eighty percent certain that you will interrupt my schedule, but I want you with me."

Chapter Fourteen

LEANNA AWOKE TO the sound of dishes clanking together downstairs. The pillow smelled like Kurt, masculine and earthy with a hint of something sweet, floral. She turned toward the window and saw a vase full of fresh wildflowers beside the bed. How did she get lucky enough to meet the kindest guy on the planet? By the time they arrived at his cottage last night, she was so tired she could barely stay awake, and he'd tucked her in beside him and held her while he read—and she slept. *Like a log.*

His bedroom, like most of the house, was outfitted in white—white walls with stained wood trim, white fluffy comforter. A breeze whisked the sheer white curtains from the open bay window. There was a thick and inviting tan seat cushion built into the bay window, with brown, tan, and red accent pillows. A thick, white throw rug covered the wide-planked oak hardwood floors between the bed and the window. A house that was primarily white might feel sterile to some, but it felt just right for Kurt. He was clean and neat, with a dash of pizazz in all the right places.

She buried her nose in his pillow and inhaled his intoxicating scent.

Pepper barked, and she pulled her nose from his pillow and found Kurt smiling down at her with a cup of coffee in his hands.

"I'm not sure if that was creepy or sweet," he said with a warm smile.

She cringed. "Let's go with sweet. You should bottle your scent. You'd make a fortune." She'd slept in one of Kurt's T-shirts, and when she sat up and crossed her legs, it billowed around her.

Pepper jumped on the fluffy white comforter and Kurt slid him a dark stare.

"Down."

Pepper obeyed and lay down beside the bed.

"I'm not sure I want a bunch of guys smelling exactly like me." He sat beside her and kissed her cheek, then handed her a cup of coffee. "I wasn't sure how you liked it, so if it's wrong, I'll bring you a fresh cup."

"Thank you, but I can come downstairs for coffee." She took a sip of the hot coffee. "This is perfect." She touched his wet hair.

"I went for a jog; then I took a shower, made breakfast, read the newspaper."

"I slept through all of that? I'm not that lazy, really. I swear."

He laughed. "No one said you were lazy. I loved waking up with you beside me, and if I didn't have a word count to chase, I'd have stayed in bed with you." He leaned over and kissed her. "Or inside you."

She stuck her lower lip out. "Dang word count."

He glanced at the clock. "I promise we'll make up for it later. There are fresh towels in the bathroom. Make yourself at home. I'll be out on the deck writing if you need me." He kissed her again. "I've never had trouble getting out of bed and writing until today. For the first time in my writing career, I really want to climb back in bed and let the writing wait."

She pushed playfully at his chest. "Go. Write. I can't be responsible for the world not getting their next Kurt Remington thriller."

After she showered and put on her bathing suit and shorts, Leanna looked out the bedroom window at Kurt on the deck below. It was a hazy morning, and there was a pretty yellow-gray haze over the water. Kurt's hands flew over the keyboard, and she wondered what went on in his mind. He was careful when he spoke, and sometimes he looked like he was mulling over a complex equation in his mind. Other times, like this morning when he told her he wanted to climb back into bed with her, tenderness softened his eyes and mouth. She thought of the first night they met and the way he'd seemed annoyed by the disturbance. She knew now that he'd been writing, and she *had* interrupted him. She hadn't pictured him as having a tender or romantic side. He was a wonderful surprise.

Leanna didn't hesitate to open a drawer and see if he was as neat in the hidden parts of his life as he was on the surface.

"Yup." She ran her fingers over the stack of perfectly folded shirts. Wanting to feel closer to him, she withdrew a navy blue tank from the top of the pile, slipped it over her bathing suit, and tied it at the waist. Then she set out to explore. She wandered down the hall and peeked into a nicely appointed guest bedroom. She peered into the next room and was surprised to find a full gym, complete with free weights and Nautilus machines. She tried to picture Kurt working out as he took breaks from writing. Then she modified the thought. Working out *before* or *after* he was *done* writing. She peered out the window and was surprised to see another cottage a short distance away. It was the size of her cottage, with weathered shingles, an arched front door, and shaded by the only trees on the property.

She heard Pepper bark and made her way down the wooden staircase, where she found Pepper panting up at Kurt outside on the deck. Kurt sat before his laptop, typing away. He shifted his head in Pepper's direction, then turned back to his computer. Pepper barked again, and that's when she noticed Pepper's food and water bowls beside Kurt, and attached to Kurt's chair was Pepper's leash.

She watched as Kurt untied the leash from his chair and walked Pepper down to the beach. Leanna stepped outside and watched them walk along the water's edge. Kurt's feet were bare as the water lapped at his toes. His broad shoulders were relaxed, his stride comfortably slow. He seemed perfectly content, though she knew he had to be wishing she'd take over so he could write. She took another minute to drink in the sight of him. He was so handsome that he took her breath away, and walking beside Pepper, he warmed her heart. She realized that he looked like the type of guy she and her girlfriends would point out on the beach and stare at until he disappeared into the distance. Only Kurt was *her* boyfriend. She'd never managed her life very well, so it was no surprise that she'd never managed having a relationship well, either. This felt different. She felt different. She wanted this to work.

Leanna took the stairs down to the beach and caught up to Kurt. "Hey, want me to take over?" She reached for the leash.

He switched the leash to the other hand and draped his arm over her shoulder. "Nope. But I want you to walk with us."

"But what about your word count?"

"I might have to work a little later into the evening, but I think you're rubbing off on me. I don't want to miss this. You. Us." He kissed her cheek and glanced at his shirt, tied to fit her figure. "You look cute in my shirt."

"I hope you don't mind. I wasn't snooping." She put her hand on his stomach and leaned her head against his arm. "Well, that's not true, exactly. I wanted to see how neat your drawers were. Weird, I know, but I wondered if you were a closet messy guy and the whole clean house and nothing-out-of-place thing was just for show."

"Uh-huh. I have nothing to hide. I am who I am."

"I like who you are. And now I know how you got those insanely big and sexy muscles. Arnold

Schwarzenegger could work out in your gym."

"I'm a private guy. I've never really liked public gyms." They walked a little farther with their feet in the water. "Do you have to prepare anything for tomorrow? A presentation?"

"I told you, I don't stress over this stuff." But the more he talked about a preparation, the more she wondered if she should be preparing. She'd never really *prepared* for anything in life. She moved on a hope or a whim, and she assumed things would work out for her. Or they wouldn't. Now she wondered if that was part of her issue. Was she unfulfilled because she hadn't taken the interest or put in the dedication that it might have taken to dig a little deeper in everything she'd ever done? She pushed the thought away. She couldn't stress about the meeting now, and the last thing she wanted to do was worry when it was such a beautiful day and she was with Kurt.

"Yeah, but—"

"I've got it covered." *I hope.*

"Okay, duly noted. But I'm pretty good at putting those things together, so if you ever want to put together marketing plans or presentations, I'm right here."

"Thanks."

"Maybe the jam business is just very different from other businesses. When my brother Dex takes a new PC game to distributors, they want to see everything—business and marketing plans, product specs. Even in publishing, forward planning is critical. We develop business and marketing plans for each new release. It's different, but kind of the same thing."

"I know that's how things are usually done, but I guess I think I want to try it my way first. In case you haven't noticed, I'm not really the presentation and business plan type."

He kissed her temple. "I think you sell yourself short. You're the anything you need to be type, but you know your business best."

"I don't know best, but I know so little about marketing plans and all of that, that I think I'm better off going in as me. If I'm wrong, I'll figure it out later."

"That sounds reasonable. I have faith in you, but if you do need more, I'm here."

Kindest man on the planet for sure.

Pepper ran toward a mother walking with a young boy. Kurt reined in the leash. "Come here, Pepper."

"He won't bite." Leanna stopped beside Kurt as he crouched next to Pepper.

"I know, but kids get scared. This way we're near Pepper in case he tries to jump up on them."

The woman and child were walking toward them. She had kind, dark eyes and a friendly smile. Holding her son's shoulder, they stopped a few feet from Pepper. "He loves dogs. Is it okay for him to pet yours?" She wore a floppy green hat and a black one-piece bathing suit.

"Sure. He doesn't bite," Leanna assured her.

Kurt held Pepper's collar while the little boy pet him and giggled.

"His name is Pepper." Kurt smiled at the boy.

"Pepper," the little boy said as he held his hand out for Pepper to lick.

"How old are you?" Kurt's eyes bounced between

the little boy and Pepper.

"Free," the boy answered.

"Wow. You're a big guy. Is this your first time at the beach?"

The boy shook his head.

Leanna felt her heart squeeze at Kurt's tender tone. *He'd be a great father someday. Oh my God. What am I thinking?*

"Me either." Kurt glanced up at the boy's mother. "He's really sweet."

"Thank you." She touched her son's blond hair.

"Thank you." The little boy reached for his mother's hand as they walked away.

"He was sweet, wasn't he?" They headed back toward the cottage.

You sure were. "Adorable."

Back at the cottage, Kurt settled into writing and Leanna sat on a lounge chair a few feet away.

Kurt's cell phone rang, and when he answered it, he spoke quietly. "Hey there." He listened to the person on the line and then said, "I know. Okay. Yeah, I'll get them something nice." He paused. "Really, Siena? I think I can handle picking out a gift. What does that mean? A woman's touch?" He paused again, then laughed.

Leanna was trying not to eavesdrop—no, that's a lie. She was blatantly eavesdropping. *Who is Siena?*

"Okay, fine. Yes. I'll look for something that's not too manly. Do you want to just buy it and say I picked it out?" He paused again. "You're a pain. I love you, too. Okay. Uh-huh. Bye."

He ended the call and went back to writing.

Leanna couldn't see his face, and she wondered *who* he loved. *Who* was a pain? They were boyfriend and girlfriend. Didn't that give her the right to ask? She watched him typing and resisted the urge.

"Leanna?"

"Mm-hmm."

"You're burning a hole in my back." He rose from the table and moved her hip over, then squeezed in beside her on the lounge chair. "Siena is my sister. My family always says, *I love you*, and she was giving me a hard time about buying my brother Jack, who is getting married, a wedding present."

"You didn't have to tell me who you were talking to."

"I didn't have to, but I felt you worrying." He ran his finger along her thigh, and it sent goose bumps down her leg.

"You felt me worrying? I didn't even say anything."

"You didn't have to. We're in sync, remember?"

Chapter Fifteen

THE SUN SET, leaving a warm streak of blue against the night sky. An evening breeze swept across the deck. Kurt had been writing all afternoon, and it had taken all of his focus to continue writing with Leanna wandering around in her little pink bikini, touching his shoulders as she passed by. He liked knowing she was there with him. He heard the French doors open, and her sweet scent surrounded him. He glanced at his word count: *8,289. Not bad.* He just wanted to finish this one paragraph; then he'd put the computer away for the night.

Leanna leaned against the table, and Kurt's eyes slid from the keyboard to the curve of her hip. He continued typing as his eyes followed the line of her body up to her breasts, then to the playful smile on her full lips.

"I missed you." She leaned forward and kissed his neck.

Her hair tickled his bare chest, causing his fingers to still on the keyboard. *Two. More. Sentences.* She slid her hand down his chest to his thighs. He held his breath.

She flicked his earlobe with her tongue. "I missed you a lot." Her lips grazed his cheek, and then she pressed kisses along his lips as she moved in front of his computer and pushed his legs apart, then seductively positioned herself between them, looking at him through heavy eyelids, hair falling loosely over her breasts. She leaned in close and ran her hands down his chest. Kurt saved his work and pushed the laptop back, unable to even remember what he had wanted to write. Her breasts lifted and fell with each desire-filled breath. He kissed the warmth of her deep cleavage and ran his hands down her ribs to her rounded hips. God, he loved her hips. She sank down on her knees, and his pulse kicked up. He shot a look at the empty beach despite knowing they were too high up to be seen.

"Leanna," he whispered. "You don't have to—"

"Shh." She pressed her finger to his lips as she unzipped his pants and set his erection free; then she lost her balance and toppled to the right. He caught her midfall with one strong hand and helped her find her footing again. She covered her face with her hands.

"I am so bad at this whole seductress thing."

He caressed her cheek. "You're amazing at the whole seductress thing." And she was. He couldn't have been more turned on by the way she looked at him, her tentative movements, or her sensuous body.

"Let's pretend that didn't happen."

"Already pretending." He had no idea that a woman could be so hot and so goddamn cute at the same time, but she pulled it off perfectly. Every muscle corded tight at the sight of her between his legs.

She nodded and closed her eyes for a beat—long enough for Kurt to take a deep breath and try to calm his racing heart. When she wrapped her hand around his throbbing arousal, then took him in her mouth, he didn't have a chance in hell.

"Good Lord," he said in one long breath.

Her hair curtained her face and he moved it to the side so he could watch her take him in. She stroked him with her delicate hand, loving him with her sexy, hot mouth. He untied her bathing suit top and watched it fall away, exposing her milky-white breasts, strikingly beautiful against her deep tan. She licked the tip and met his gaze from beneath her hair, sending heat searing through him. She licked him from base to tip, never breaking their eye contact. He clenched his teeth against the urge to come. She was taking him to places he'd only fantasized about but never allowed himself to enjoy. He pulled her to him and kissed her hard, stroking her mouth with his tongue while drawing her bikini bottom down. He needed more of her. He filled his palms with her heavy breasts, loved them with his mouth, sucked them until she fisted her hands in his hair, tilted his head up, and set a dark, hungry stare on him.

"I want more," she whispered.

A groan rose from deep within him as he lifted her to the table and laid her back, spread her legs with his, and lowered his mouth to her moist, hot center. She sucked in a breath as he stroked her with his tongue, tasting her sweetness as she arched against him.

"More, Kurt," she pleaded.

He slid his fingers inside her and licked her sensitive folds. She clawed at the table, moaning with pleasure, and shaking her head from side to side as her insides squeezed tight, pulsing against him.

"That's it, baby. Come for me."

Jesus, she was beautiful when she came. He spread her legs farther, and she tensed against his efforts, still in the throes of her orgasm. He withdrew his fingers, and she cried out.

"No. Please. More."

He brought his mouth to her once again, devouring her as her body eased down from its peak, and he could wait no longer. He lifted her hips and brought her to the edge of the table, then drove into her. She gasped a breath—he groaned with the intensity of their passion, thrusting harder, deeper, faster.

"Yes. Oh God, Kurt. Yes!"

She reached for his hips, and he captured her cries in his mouth as another orgasm clutched her. Her body shook, and her hips bucked wildly against his. He slowed her sinfully sensual hips and found their rhythm again.

"There we go, babe. Let it go."

She cried out again, grabbing his wrists and digging her nails into his skin. The intense pleasure and pain impassioned him. He was unable to hold back any longer. Every muscle was strung tight, his legs burned, and with two more powerful thrusts, he surrendered control and followed her right over the edge with his own ardent release.

He drew Leanna to him and held her tight, still buried deep, breathing hard. Three words lay on the tip of his tongue, and he held them back. Trapped them in his mind like butterflies under glass, where they flapped and fluttered, trying to set their magnificence free. They hadn't known each other long enough for him to even think the three words that, when strung together and spoken from the heart, were the three most significant words in the English language, yet they were there, as clear and present as he knew his own name.

THE BRISK EVENING air whipped through Leanna's hair as they drove toward Provincetown with the top down. They'd stopped by her cottage to pick up clothes for the evening, and Leanna stored the new batch of jam in the room off the kitchen. Now she and Kurt were on a mission to find the perfect gift for his eldest brother, Jack, and his fiancée, Savannah, who were getting married at the end of the month. Pepper sat at her feet with his head on her lap, happy as could be. She couldn't believe Kurt had accepted Pepper into the fold of their relationship, but he had insisted that leaving Pepper at home would just make the pup feel bad and that dogs who felt lonely tended to act out. How did he know? She imagined that, as with the stain, he'd Googled it. She imagined him researching how to properly care for a misbehaved, needy dog. The thought brought a smile to her lips.

As they passed Pilgrim's Lake on the right, nestled

between mountainous dunes and rows of beachside cottages on the left, Leanna felt as though she was moving forward, and surprisingly, felt more fulfilled. At the same time, what she'd been doing with her life had hardly changed—except for the addition of Kurt.

Kurt reached for her hand. "You're quiet. You okay?"

"Better than okay." She watched the edges of his lips curve up and wondered if he was thinking about their intimacy on the deck. She had never before even attempted to be a seductress. *A seductress?* She was more like Lucille Ball in *I Love Lucy*. She didn't know what she had been thinking, except that she wanted Kurt so badly that she couldn't get enough. She wanted to be closer, to taste him, to knock him off balance and see him with all defenses down, and she'd knocked herself off balance. She thought of the way he'd caught her on the deck and how he brought out the confidence that she exuded in every aspect of her life except relationships. He helped her bring that confidence to their relationship in the most loving and tender ways, but there had been a moment in their passion when she saw everything else in his eyes fall away. And in the space of a breath she could tell that he wasn't thinking either. He'd dropped all his defenses. He was touching, tasting, moving, driven by the sizzling connection between them, just as she had been.

"Nervous about tomorrow's meeting?" He turned off the main highway and followed the road into Provincetown to the parking lot by the pier.

"Not really. I will be when the time comes,

though."

"I envy your ability to be so relaxed about things." He parked and put the top up, then came around and opened the door for her. Pepper ran around his feet, tangling the leash as if he were a tree. He looked down at him and shook his head.

"Sit."

Pepper plopped down on his butt and whined while Kurt untangled the leash. "Aren't these meetings huge for your business? I mean, they must be the equivalent of my signing with a publisher for my books, right?"

"I guess. Yeah, probably about the same."

A gust of wind swept through the parking lot and followed them toward one of the busiest streets on the Cape, Commercial Street. Commercial Street was lined with colorful stores, artists, restaurants, and all types of musicians. Provincetown was an arts community with a year-round population of around three thousand, but in the summer it was *the* vacation destination of gay men and lesbians, as well as tourists from all over the world, bringing tens of thousands into the small town. The streets held the aroma of salty sea air, baked goods, and patchouli. It was an assault of the senses, an explosion of colorful people, artistic efforts, and one-of-a-kind experiences—and one of Leanna's favorite places on earth.

A young man playing a guitar sat on the ground outside a restaurant, and they stopped to listen for a few minutes. Kurt threw a few bucks into the guitar case before they continued on their way, passing families with children, men and women of varying nationalities, cross-dressers, transvestites, and a wide variety of leashed dogs. A man whose entire body, including his clothing, was painted silver stood on a crate, still as a statue. Nearby, a tall, thin man with long brown hair sang in front of the Town Hall, dressed in a green minidress and spiked heels, surrounded by onlookers, who applauded and tossed money into a box on the ground. The diversity of Provincetown was just one of the reasons Leanna loved the area. The widespread acceptance seemed to go hand in hand with interesting, creative shops and people.

"There's something about P-town that makes me happy." She smiled up at Kurt.

"There's something about P-town that makes everyone happy. That's the best thing about this place. Everyone fits in." He kissed her temple.

Another surprise. She'd wondered if he was comfortable with the crowds and diversity. Now she knew. And she added his appreciation of Provincetown to her mental Like List, which was getting pretty darn long.

At the main intersection, they walked past a gray-haired, paunchy policeman who made traffic direction an art form. He swayed his hips to silent music, bowed as cars passed, and blew his whistle at the throngs of onlookers. Throughout the years, Leanna had danced with that policeman, and now she had an urge to run into the street and do it again.

"I love that guy," Kurt said as they walked past.

Leanna threw caution to the wind and let go of Kurt's hand. "Be right back." She kissed his cheek and ran into the road. If he was going to like her for her, he had to know the real her. And she wouldn't be Leanna if she didn't mimic the policeman's moves and dance with him.

Hands on hips, the policeman blew his whistle at her. She mimicked his actions with a smirk and an *oh-yes-I-am* shake of her head. He turned his attention back to the line of cars waiting to pass, and as he waved them by, so did she. She had seen many people join him in the street throughout the years, and though he kept a stern face, he always bowed in appreciation when they parted. When he spun in a circle, motioning for the cars to cross the intersection, she was right behind him doing the same thing, and caught sight of Kurt holding his phone up and snapping a picture with a wide smile that reached his eyes.

He wasn't embarrassed.

He wasn't acting like he didn't know her.

He definitely likes me.

Kurt crouched down beside Pepper, one arm protectively around the dog's shoulder as he pointed to Leanna and said something she couldn't hear. It wouldn't matter what he said. Just seeing him embrace Pepper tugged at her heart.

She mimed a thank-you to the policeman, who bowed and made a rolling motion with his hand; then she rejoined Kurt.

"Now, that was priceless. If your Sweet Treats falls through, you could definitely go into the dancing traffic directing business." He pulled her close and kissed her.

"Sorry. He's been there since I was little, and I always used to dance with him. I had to do it." She wiggled and tugged at her T-shirt and cutoffs, adjusting them so they weren't askew from her walk on the wild side.

They walked hand in hand, weaving in and out of the crowd with Pepper in tow. They browsed a leather shop—where Kurt joked about buying matching leather chaps for Jack and Savannah. They meandered through two art galleries, a kitchen shop, and they came out empty-handed from each.

They stopped at Shop Therapy, a hippie clothing store downstairs and adult toy store upstairs. Dresses and tie-dyed tops hung in the front windows. A basket of sage incense blocked part of the entrance. The shop smelled like marijuana, which the employees claimed was the sage incense they burned. Leanna had her doubts.

Kurt led her to the stairs in the back of the shop with a hint of mischief in his gorgeous eyes.

"Wanna go up?"

Her heartbeat sped up, and she felt her cheeks burn. With Bella and the girls? Sure. But with Kurt? Even the idea of looking at adult toys with him made her a little dizzy.

"Um...How about...?"

He laughed a little under his breath and kissed her forehead. "Don't sweat it. I only know what you're into by asking." He led her safely back through the shop to the racks of women's clothes. "Show me what you like."

Oh God. You think I'm a prude. "I don't mind...that

stuff."

"The dress?" he asked, holding up a dress.

She rolled her eyes. "No." She pointed at the ceiling.

"Babe, I was teasing. You're enough for me. I was just giving you the option." He pressed his cheek to hers and whispered, "I didn't want to stifle your pleasure."

Her stomach fluttered, and she felt herself getting aroused.

He touched her cheek and grinned. "Better change the look on your pretty little face, or I'm going to have to take you right here."

My good boy is a naughty boy. I love that. For a second she considered his words. *No, no, no.* She took a deep breath and focused her attention on the dresses. He held up a dozen, and she loved all of them, but there was one particular aqua tank dress that was just her style. It was cotton, short, had a scoop neckline and a zillion tiny buttons down the front.

"The last thing I need is another summer dress. The summer's almost over."

"You sure? You'd look beautiful in it."

She wanted the dress, but she was being careful with her money until she knew where she was headed after the summer. "Nah. I have enough."

He took one last look at the dress before they left the store.

They stopped for gelato at the Purple Feather—and bought Pepper a doggy dish of gelato, too—and sat outside on the brick patio while they ate.

"Do you have a gift in mind for Jack and

Savannah? What are they like?"

"Savannah is strong and confident. She's an entertainment attorney in New York City. She's funny, she adores Jack, and she challenges everyone. Him, her brothers. She's a lot like my sister, Siena, in that way, and Jack's a strange combination of big, bad, and sensitive." Kurt ran his hand through his hair and smiled a little, as if he were thinking of his brother.

"Are all the Remington men like that?" She watched a group of men dressed as women, heavily applied makeup on their faces, hand out cards, and knew they were part of a show taking place at one of the bars. She'd give anything to have killer legs like the dark-haired man had.

"Well, considering I'm a Remington man, I'd have to say no."

"Why?" She leaned in close and lowered her voice. "You're big and bad, and you can't even tell me you're not sensitive."

"I might be big size-wise, but I'm not *bad*. Jack would rip apart anyone who bothered Savannah. He's ex Special Forces, and he also runs a survivalist program. I'm a writer, not a fighter, and I'm not sure I'd ever want to live in a tent in the woods. I like my creature comforts."

She leaned back. "Hmm."

"Hmm, what?" He picked up Pepper's empty dish and set it on the table.

"I think you're wrong. I think if someone hurt me, you'd be all over them, and I would bet you my van, which I love, that if I asked you to go camping with me, you would go."

Kurt got up and threw away the empty ice cream dishes. When he came back to the table, he held a hand out to her. "It's scary that you might know me better than I know myself."

Chapter Sixteen

KURT DROVE LEANNA home Thursday morning to prepare for her meeting with Mama's Market. She'd gathered samples of each jam in a pretty basket and, dressed in a sundress and sandals, wore her hair loose. Traffic was light on the way to Yarmouth, and she arrived early. She hadn't been nervous on the way, but now, as she entered the one-story office building, her stomach coiled tight. She felt Al's presence, as if he were right there with her, and she drew confidence from the feeling. She had envisioned a sweet old couple sitting on a couch in a house set off the beaten path, with a garden out front and cats romancing the property. After all, the Mama's Market in Wellfleet was run out of a small house at the end of the parking lot behind an old white church off of Main Street. The produce and breads were sold out of baskets perched on long wooden tables with tablecloth coverings. They didn't even use a cash register. The staff calculated customer totals with paper and pencil.

Simple. Efficient. Friendly.

That was one of the reasons Leanna had decided to try to meet with them first. She figured that they'd be an easy sell. She was simple, efficient, and friendly. It seemed like a good match.

She walked through the glass door and into their office. A red and white hand-painted sign that read MAMA'S MARKET hung above a reception desk. The pretty blonde behind the desk smiled as she greeted Leanna.

"Welcome to Mama's Market." She glanced briefly at her computer. "You must be with Luscious Leanna's Sweet Treats."

"Yes. I'm Leanna Bray. I have a meeting with Leslie Strobe."

The blonde nodded. "I'll get him for you. You can have a seat if you'd like." She picked up the phone and notified someone of Leanna's arrival.

Him? Leanna had pictured Leslie as Mama, the elderly wife of the couple she'd envisioned.

A man about Kurt's age, wearing dress slacks and a white button-down, short-sleeved shirt, appeared in a doorway behind the reception desk. He had closely shorn dark hair and squinty dark eyes.

"Leanna?"

And a voice as soft as butter. The muscles in her neck tightened as his eyes slid to the basket she carried. She felt underdressed and underprepared. "Yes. Hi."

"Leslie Strobe. Nice to meet you. Come on back, and we'll get started."

She followed him through a hallway lined with photographs of Mama's Markets—several of them, not just the one in Wellfleet. She swallowed hard. *Breathe. Oh God, breathe. I can do this.* She remembered a story Al had told her about the first time he brought his jams to the flea market, and she drew on the memory. *They were good, Leanna. That's all I had to remember. It wouldn't matter what I said, as long as I could get customers to taste them.*

He led her into a conference room where three men and a woman, all dressed in business attire—starched collars, dark suits—sat around a large conference table. The woman wore high heels and lipstick. *Lipstick?* No one wore lipstick on the Cape. No one wore business suits, either, at least not that she'd ever witnessed in Wellfleet and the surrounding small towns. *I'm so out of my league.* She ran her hand down her dress, smoothing nonexistent wrinkles in an effort to calm her nerves.

"Leanna Bray, this is Teddy Strobe, my sister and partner in Mama's Market; Chester Magnus, our CFO; and Brian Warren, our marketing manager. You probably already know that we cover fifteen states and thirty-seven cities, and as of next week, we'll be in two additional locations."

She contemplated telling them the meeting was a big mistake and leaving, but if she was ever going to make her mark, she had to at least try. Al's words pulled her forward. *It wouldn't matter what I said, as long as I could get customers to taste them.*

"Hi. It's very nice to meet each of you." With her heart in her throat, she set the basket on the table and did her best to envision them wearing shorts and T-shirts and sitting around a picnic table. It didn't work. They sat with their hands politely folded on the expensive conference table in a room that smelled of success and intimidation.

In the space of a breath she thought of Kurt—*You're perfect*—and used his faith to anchor her confidence.

"Thank you for meeting with me today." To settle her nerves, as she spoke, she emptied her basket of the samples, plates, and silverware she'd brought. "I make all of my own jams, and I've got a number of flavors that I think you'll find unique."

She opened the jars and the bread she'd baked and sliced and set them in the middle of the table. Leslie reached for a slice of bread and spread jam thickly over the top. The others followed.

"I work with fresh berries during the summer, and I plan on using frozen berries in the winter. There's no difference in the final product, as the frozen berries will be whole and packaged without sugar or syrup."

Leslie took a bite of the bread and his eyes widened. He glanced at Teddy, who smiled and nodded as well; then they both turned their attention back to Leanna.

With her confidence bolstered, she continued. "I make my own pectin, and I only use it when making low-pectin fruit jams, such as apricot, blueberry, peach, or pear. With higher-pectin fruits like ripe apples, cranberries, plums, or gooseberries, there's no need for added pectin. If they're not overripe, of course, then they have enough natural pectin and acid for gel formation with only added sugar."

"Leanna, this jam is remarkable. Very sweet, perfectly textured, and the bread is delicious. You made the bread as well?" Leslie's voice was serious, and as he wiped his mouth with a napkin, he held her gaze.

"Yes. I make the bread and the jam." *Breathe. Breathe.*

"And where are you manufacturing the product?" Teddy asked.

The word *product* threw her off. "The jam? I make it in my cottage, which is in Wellfleet— another reason I thought this might be a good fit."

"And do you have backup for power outages during the winter?" Teddy asked.

"Backup? No. I'm afraid I don't, but my kitchen has been certified by the town of Wellfleet for summer production." *Has the cottage ever lost power in the winter? Will I be here in the winter?*

"How do you handle returns? If we were to purchase a batch of jam and it was found to weep, we assume that would be easily and expediently replaced." Teddy glanced at handwritten notes in a notebook on the table and then met Leanna's gaze again.

"Weeping? I control weeping with the acidity of the juice and ensure that the jars are properly stored. Without temperature fluctuation, there should be no loss of liquid, or what you refer to as weeping." *Aw, crap. I don't control the temperature of the cottage. I don't even use air-conditioning.* She made mental notes about their concerns to address later.

"If weeping were to occur, how quickly would we see the replacement stock?" Teddy made a notation in the notebook.

Leanna's pulse raced. "I could have a batch ready in twenty-four hours, assuming I had the appropriate ingredients in stock."

"Do you have an ingredient list, product list, and preparation outline that we can review along with prices and delivery times?" When Teddy asked the questions, Chester and Brian leaned forward and picked up their pens.

"I...um...No. I'm sorry. But I can get that to you next week."

Brian and Chester made notations on their notepads, and Leanna felt as though she were being sucked into a dark hole and clamoring to remain on level ground. *I can do this. I can do this. I'm perfect.* She took a deep breath. *Okay, clearly not perfect, but good enough to do this right.*

"I apologize. I wasn't sure what to expect when I approached your company with the proposal. To be honest, I thought I'd be meeting with an elderly couple in their home. They'd sample my jams and bread and maybe agree that we were a good match." She crinkled her nose out of habit and silently chided herself for doing it. She knew it made her look young and inexperienced.

"Then our branding worked perfectly," Brian said as he clasped his hands behind his head and leaned back in his chair. When he smiled, it softened his chiseled features, and instead of looking fifty-something he looked to be in his late thirties—and maybe not quite so stoic.

Leslie laughed. "That it does, Brian. Mama's was actually named for our great-grandfather's cow. It's a long story. It started out as a milk market, but by the time we took it over, the name was well known and respected." He shrugged, as if that was all the explanation she needed.

Which it was.

Lesson learned. Research is important. She made a mental note not to take Bella's word for anything ever again. *Mama's Market is owned by this old couple out in Yarmouth.*

Leanna drew her shoulders back and began gathering her supplies, leaving the jams and bread for them.

"I believe in my products, and though this business is quite new to me, I plan on making a career out of it." She hadn't realized how certain she was, or that she even had a real *plan*, until that very moment, and she was as sure of it as she was about loving Pepper, which spurred her to continue.

"I will address each of these issues, and if you liked my product, then I'd appreciate the opportunity to discuss this with you further in the near future, when I have addressed your concerns." She surveyed their expressions as they exchanged looks she couldn't read any better than she could sweep a sandy deck.

"Your products are excellent. We'd welcome a future meeting with you." Leslie and the others stood, indicating a clear end to the meeting.

"Thank you." She breathed a sigh of relief and tried to hide her trembling hands by holding the basket against her hip as she shook hands with each of them.

"The first bite of the strawberry-apricot jam has a strong strawberry taste. How do you achieve such a smooth apricot finish?" Leslie asked.

"Leslie." She flashed her sweetest smile. "You're not asking me to give away my secrets, now, are you?"

A smile found his serious eyes.

"If you thought that flavor was interesting, wait until you try Frangelico Peach." She pointed to the jars of jam on the table. "The one with the peach ribbon around the jar. Try it. I'd love to know what you think."

He nodded. "Thank you. I'll drop you an email and let you know. In the meantime, good luck. I think you'll have a killer business on your hands once you see it as a business rather than a hobby."

Ouch.

"Honesty. I like that." Leanna shook his hand again, trying her best to mask the pain of his comment. "I assure you, this is far more than a hobby. I'll be in touch."

Chapter Seventeen

KURT LOOKED AT his watch for the hundredth time that afternoon. He tried to concentrate on writing, but climbing into the dark recesses of his mind proved to be problematic when he was so excited and worried, in equal measure, to hear how Leanna's meeting with Mama's Market went. He finally gave up on hammering out more than five thousand words and drove over to wait for Leanna at her cottage.

He parked in the driveway, and even before he turned off the car, he heard Pepper barking. His nose was pressed against the window screen, and when Kurt stepped from his car, Pepper began whining.

"I hear you." He went to the window and touched his finger to Pepper's nose. The dog licked the screen and whimpered. Kurt tried the door and wasn't surprised to find it unlocked.

"So now you're breaking into her house?"

He spun around at the sound of Bella's voice and

found all three of Leanna's girlfriends standing in their bikinis with their arms crossed and their mouths pressed into tight lines.

"No. I came to wait for Leanna and heard Pepper barking."

As if on cue, Pepper barked.

"And I thought I'd see if it was unlocked, so I could take him for a walk."

Amy was the first to lose her scowl. She burst into laughter. "If you could only see your face."

Bella and Jenna laughed with her.

"We know you're not breaking in." Bella opened Leanna's door and walked inside.

Kurt and the others followed.

Amy crouched down to love-up Pepper. Pepper's tongue hung from his mouth as he rolled around on his back.

Kurt found Pepper's leash on top of the pile of shoes beside the door. "Why aren't you guys at the beach?"

"And miss Leanna's big news? No way. You know there's no cell reception on the beaches." Bella grabbed a beer from the refrigerator and held it up. "Anyone?"

"Not me, thanks," Amy said as Pepper wiggled from beneath her hand and began pawing at Kurt's feet.

"No thanks, Bella. Sit, Pepper." He hooked his leash. "I'm just going to take him for a walk."

"I want to go," Jenna said. "And I want a wine cooler please, Bell."

"She has none. Beer or jam?" Bella held up both.

"We'll stop at my place for a cooler." Jenna looped her arm into Kurt's. "Shall we?"

"We're coming, too." Amy and Bella followed them out.

For a guy who was used to spending almost every waking hour alone, Kurt wondered how the hell he'd ended up walking around a complex with a dog and three women pawing at him. Strangely, he didn't have the urge to run back to his keyboard, which would have been his reaction a week earlier. These were Leanna's friends, and Pepper was Leanna's dog, and for that reason, he wanted to be near them all.

His cell phone rang, and he had to disengage from Jenna's hand on his arm to dig his phone from his pocket.

"Is it Leanna?" Bella asked.

"No, Leanna and I haven't exchanged numbers." He hadn't realized that until this moment. "It's my sister." He answered the call. "Hi, Siena."

"Hey, Kurt. I had an idea of what you could buy Jack and Savannah."

"Give it to someone else. I've already bought them something." On their way out of Provincetown, he and Leanna had stopped into a gallery and picked out a nice marble sculpture depicting a couple embracing. It was perfect for Jack and Savannah, and even more perfect because Leanna had helped him pick it out. They walked by the pool, and the women began laughing about chunky-dunking.

"Where are you?" Siena asked.

"Walking a dog with three beautiful women." He knew that would throw her for a loop.

"That's right; he is," Jenna said.

"You know it," Bella added.

"Shh. He's on the phone." Amy waved her hands at them.

"Oh my God. You're not lying. How did they get you to leave your house? You won't even stop writing for me."

He imagined her eyes narrowed, and where any other woman might stick out her lip and pout, Siena would be more likely to shoot steam from her ears.

"I stopped writing when we all got together for your Gunner Gibson intervention, didn't I?"

"Gunner Gibson?" Bella asked. "Oh my God, he's totally hot."

Kurt lowered the phone away from his mouth. "And he's also an ass."

"Are you really out walking a dog? Whose dog?" Siena asked. "I wish I was there so I could see it for myself. Take a picture. Text it to me."

"You're so weird. Okay. I will. My girlfriend's dog."

Siena squealed so loud he had to pull the phone away from his ear.

"Wow, seriously?" Bella laughed.

"I've never heard you use that word before," Siena said. "Is it serious? I guess it has to be if you're walking her dog. You. A dog. A girlfriend. Oh my God. Kurt?"

"Yes, Siena?" He had no idea why, but he enjoyed her reaction.

She sighed loudly. "You know girlfriends need attention. We're not like plants that you can water once a day and then ignore. We like when guys think about us, and we love to talk, and we—"

"Siena, I'm thirty years old. I think I know how to treat a girlfriend."

"Yeah, he does," Jenna yelled toward the phone.

"Who's that? Is that her?" Siena asked.

"That's one of Leanna's friends, Jenna."

"Leanna? Is that your girlfriend?"

He knew that Leanna's name would be on the tongues of every one of his siblings within the hour. "Yes. Leanna Bray."

Another call beeped through on Siena's phone. "I've got to take that. It's my agent. Love you, Kurt. You sound happy. I'm happy for you."

"Love you, too." He ended the call to the tune of the three women saying, *Aw*. They circled up to Leanna's cottage.

"Let's sit on my deck and wait for her," Amy offered.

"I want to get a cooler. I'll be right over." Jenna hurried across the grass to her cottage.

"I'll see you guys later," Kurt said as he headed for Leanna's deck.

"What?" Bella grabbed his arm. "Come on. You can wait with us."

There were worse things than sitting around with three bikini-clad women waiting for the woman who had made quick and efficient work of stealing his heart. He followed Bella up to Amy's porch.

LEANNA SANG ALONG to the radio as she pulled into Seaside and parked by the laundry room. She was still singing as she crossed the grass and heard Kurt's laugh, followed by Bella's and Jenna's. Her stomach fluttered as she picked up her pace in anticipation of seeing Kurt. She followed the sound of their voices to Amy's deck, where she found them eating chips and dip and drinking wine coolers. Her heart squeezed a little at the sight of him sitting so comfortably with her friends.

"What are you doing here?" She lifted up on her tiptoes and peered over the deck railing. Kurt rose to greet her with Pepper's leash in hand. She reached through the railing and petted Pepper's head.

"I couldn't concentrate. I was so busy wondering how your meeting went that I decided to come wait here instead."

She came up on the deck, and he took her hand as he pulled out a chair for her.

"How did it go?" he asked.

"Good." She watched their hopeful eyes widen. "And bad." Their smiles faded. "But overall I think I'd say it was a really good first meeting."

Kurt reached for her hand. "*Really good* sounds promising. Do you want to share any of it with us, or do you need time to process it all?"

"Oh, hell no, Kurt," Bella said firmly. "We don't work that way. We're women. We process *by* sharing."

"I've already processed most of it. You were right, Kurt. I needed to be far better prepared. I should have researched Mama's Market, prepared a product brochure, ingredient list, price list, expected turnaround times, come up with a sound refund policy, a contract." She shook her head.

"Oh, babe. I'm so sorry." Kurt's eyes filled with compassion.

"Sorry? You were trying to help, and I should have listened." She glared at Bella. "By the way, Bella, Mama's Markets are in fifteen states and thirty-seven cities. How could you tell me the business was run by an old couple in Yarmouth and they only had the Wellfleet location?"

Bella pointed at Jenna.

"I'm sorry. That's what I'd heard," Jenna explained. "Or I read it somewhere."

"Or you made it up." Amy rolled her eyes. "Do you want a cooler, Lea?"

"Yes, please. Make it twelve."

Kurt reached for her hand. "So what now? We prepare better for next week's meeting?"

We? I love that. "Yes, but I have other decisions to make, too. I think I should delay next week's meeting until I have a better handle on things. They asked about things I haven't even thought of, like backup services in case the electricity went out and turnaround time on replacement stock if there are issues. And as Leslie, the owner, walked me out, he said that if we decided to work together in the future, it would likely involve more than just the Wellfleet store, which means I'd need a bigger kitchen with more stovetops, maybe a real facility to work in." She took a long drink of the wine cooler.

"Is that what you want?" Kurt asked.

"You know what? I wasn't sure when I went in how committed I was, but once I was there, talking about it and thinking about what I wanted, I realized that yes, that is exactly what I want." She assessed her friends' faces and thought she saw a combination of surprise and support. When her eyes met Kurt's, there was no doubt about what she saw in those pools of blue. Depths of support and maybe even a little pride. "I love making jam and jelly, and baking breads, and I'm even thinking that at some point I can expand into making tarts and other baked items that work well with jam. I know it sounds crazy, and I know I'm the most unorganized, forgetful, whim-seeking person on earth, but I think—"

Kurt interrupted her. "I don't think it sounds crazy at all. I think it sounds like you just found your passion, and when it comes to something that means that much to you, the rest will fall into place."

"Kurt, I have a clone machine inside. Could you please step inside my cottage for a minute?" Amy opened the glass door. "Pretty please?"

He laughed and brought his eyes right back to Leanna. "I'm so happy for you."

"Will you help me figure out the organization side of things? I mean, I really suck at research and, well, anything that requires structure." *Maybe I can't do this.*

"Of course." Kurt pulled her onto his lap. "But you don't suck at anything. You just haven't gone down that path yet."

"Um, have you forgotten little miss OCD here?" Bella nodded in Jenna's direction. "Jenna can organize your ingredient lists, turnaround times, etc. And I kick ass on PowerPoint, so I can help you make the brochures pretty."

"And I can help you look into locations if you need more space to work. I'm good at haggling." Amy went inside and came back out with a newspaper.

"Thanks, you guys. But I need to decide where I'm going to live. I mean, I'm not even sure where I'm going to be after the summer, and if I really do this, I have to settle that end of things before looking for a better facility to work in. Gosh, I also have to decide if this is a summer business or a year-round endeavor."

"Which way are you leaning?" Kurt asked.

She shrugged. "I guess when I first started, I thought it would be kind of part-time and year-round. You know, work the flea markets in the summer, maybe indoor fairs in the winter, and see how it goes. Then I had the idea of trying to connect with grocers. I never thought I would have a chance, but now I'm not sure that I don't have a chance. Then again, I don't even have one contract, so maybe I should just stick to my plan of working from the cottage, at least for the summer, and then, if I am able to secure enough to keep me busy during the winter, I can always put more time into it and look for a better facility at that point. I would love to see this become a *real* business."

"That's what I would do," Amy said. "It seems like a big jump to plan for a full-time, year-round business based on what you *hope* you can do."

"But how can you ever accomplish more if you don't hope and plan for it?" Kurt touched her hand. "Not that Leanna has to do more. I'm just curious about your thought process. If you build a business based on a three- or four-month schedule, then you're winding down at summer's end, whereas if you are trying to really build a brand, and a business, you're marketing and moving forward in the fall, and I wonder if it affects cutting deals with suppliers?" He had that serious look in his eyes again. "Maybe I'm way off base, and I am definitely not trying to push you to do more. I'm just playing devil's advocate. When we first met, you told me how much you loved what you were doing and that you hoped this would be the thing that fit your personality best. Why not plan for it?"

"I hadn't thought that far out, but I'm not sure I want to be locked into a facility for twelve months out of the year. What if I take a twelve-month lease and...? I don't know. Something in my life changes? Or I don't have enough contracts to cover the rent? That would be awful." She bit her lower lip. "I need to think about this, but we can still work on everything else, if you're sure you guys still don't mind helping."

"I'm in," Bella said.

"Definitely in. Why don't we plan on working together Saturday after the flea market closes? That gives you a few days to think about it before we get started."

"Suits me!" Amy said as she finished her wine cooler.

Leanna felt Kurt's arms tighten around her waist, and she leaned her forehead against his. "How much of your day did I suck away from you?" She saw a glint in his eyes and wondered if he was thinking about the evening before on his deck, just as she'd been when the word *suck* left her lips.

He cleared his throat. "Not much. I'll have to write tonight for a while to catch up, but that's okay, and Pepper was happy to see me."

She wiggled her butt on his lap and whispered,

"Not as happy as you are to see me, I hope."

Chapter Eighteen

LEANNA AWOKE EARLY Friday morning and peeled her arm from Kurt's chest carefully, trying not to wake him or Pepper, who was curled up at his feet. After barbequing with the girls last night and celebrating her first big decision with margaritas, they'd stayed at her cottage. She worried about how much writing time Kurt was giving up to be with her, but he assured her that he was capable of managing his time and his deadline.

She loved seeing him in her bed, and waking up to him now felt like something she expected, rather than hoped for. *How the hell did that happen so fast?* They'd closed the windows last night when they made love so the others wouldn't use their sounds as entertainment—and tease her about it later. She wasn't exactly a quiet lover, but Kurt didn't seem to mind. Last night he'd whispered everything he was going to do to her before he did it, and hearing those naughty things in his gravelly whisper aroused her almost as much as the dirty things they'd done.

She lifted up on one elbow and whispered, "I've fallen hard for you, Kurt Remington." She lay back down and closed her eyes. "Yup. I feel it in my crazy-ass heart. I love you."

Leanna got out of bed and padded quietly into the kitchen in her cami and boy shorts skivvies and sent an email to Daisy Chain, requesting to reschedule their meeting. She needed time to prepare so she didn't blow that meeting, too. *A hobby.* She thought about the comment Leslie had made and realized now that he'd seen right through her. She *had* been thinking of the business as a hobby, even if she'd been verbalizing something else. She knew the minute the rebuttal left her mouth that a hobby was not what she was looking for, and she was determined to make this business work.

She took a deep breath and began typing a list of the things she needed to do in order to move forward with her plans.

> *Figure out where I want to live in the fall! Cape?*
> *Kurt?*
> *Product list*
> *Ingredient list*
> *Delivery timetable*
> *Backup generator? Cost? Facility cost? Share space? Check out bakeries?*
> *Talk to an attorney about contracts and insurance liabilities*

Employees?

Then she began another list, a list she'd never before contemplated, a list that she'd made fun of other women for creating. Nonetheless, she began typing.

> *What I want in a boyfriend:*
> *Kind, considerate, empathetic, fun, interesting, careful, smart! Has to be willing to listen to me talk. A lot. Can't get mad about my awkwardness in bed. Good in bed. Really good. Maybe even helpful. Encourage me in every way. Sexy. Very sexy. Good body. Likes my friends.*

She pulled back from the computer and realized that she wasn't just creating a list of what she wanted in a man. She was describing Kurt. With pinpoint accuracy.

She sighed. *I've got it bad.*

"You're up early."

Startled, she closed the laptop and spun around. Kurt's hands were stretched above his head as he used the doorframe for support and arched his broad chest forward in a stretch as slow and graceful as a Cheshire cat, wearing nothing but his boxer briefs and a morning woody.

"You should have a warning sign on that body." She rose, and he folded her into his arms.

"If I had a warning sign, you might not come near me. That was nice last night. I love being close to you."

He kissed the top of her head.

She pressed her cheek to his warm chest. "Me too." *And, by the way, I think I'm falling in love with you.* "Would you like some coffee?"

"No, thanks. I know you have to go to the flea market today, so I'm going to head home and go for a run. You know my morning routine. Hopefully, I can make up for the writing that I skipped last night. My deadline is coming up fast, and I need to catch up to meet it."

"I'm sorry that I'm such a distraction."

He pulled back from their embrace and kissed her. "You are the best distraction I could ever imagine and worth every moment away from my writing. Want to come by after you're done at the flea market?"

"Yeah, that sounds good."

Kurt pulled on his shorts and picked up Pepper's leash. "Come on, Pep."

"Where are you taking him?"

"I was going to walk him since you're not really dressed for it." He ran his eyes down her body with a hint of appreciation—but his offer was more than sweet assistance; it held a flavor of possessiveness.

It was so different from what she'd seen from him that it took her by surprise. And she liked it.

"I can do it. He's used to waiting for me to throw on shorts and a top. Besides, the last thing you need is more time away from your writing." She reached for the leash.

"Would you mind if I walked him? We've sort of bonded."

Pepper whimpered.

"I can't even believe you're the same guy who scowled at him when we met."

Kurt paused on his way out the door. "I'm not sure I even know who that guy is anymore."

KURT PULLED INTO his driveway still thinking about Leanna. He seemed to always be thinking about Leanna. When he stepped from the car, he looked for Pepper out of habit, then reminded himself that Pepper was with her at the flea market. He never understood how his siblings had fallen in love with their significant others so quickly, but now he was beginning to understand. He couldn't deny his feelings for Leanna if he had a gun to his head, and hearing her whisper that she loved him when she thought he was sleeping had sent a chill right through him. Fear and happiness had collided, paralyzing him for a minute or two, until he'd been able to breathe again with the relief that she had the same strong feelings for him as he had for her.

He walked around the cottage and crossed the grass to the studio. It was surrounded by an umbrella of trees. The real estate agent he'd bought the property from had told him that the previous owner had planted the trees, as he preferred natural cooling to air-conditioning, although the studio as well as the cottage had central air, which was uncommon on the Cape. He hadn't been in the studio since he'd arrived a few weeks earlier, and he'd been thinking about it since Leanna mentioned needing a larger place to work. He unlocked the heavy wooden door and pushed it open. The inside was cool despite the warm summer days. An industrial-sized sink and built-in cabinetry lined the wall to the right. The ceramic floor was in good shape, and the cathedral ceiling allowed most of the heat to rise away from the living space. He crossed the floor to what had been a supply closet in the back of the building. It was cool and dry, and the deep wooden shelves would be perfect for Leanna to store her products. There were three windows on either side of the studio as well as a skylight in the roof, allowing for plenty of natural light. He contemplated adding stovetops, cooling racks, and whatever else Leanna might need.

I'm getting ahead of myself.

Her voice sailed through his mind, bringing another chill down his back. *I feel it in my crazy-ass heart. I love you.* Maybe he wasn't getting ahead of himself after all.

Chapter Nineteen

LEANNA HAD BEEN worried about how Carey would treat her after she'd turned down his advances, but he had acted no differently all day, and she was relieved. She'd brought her laptop with her and worked on creating product and ingredient lists when she had a few minutes without customers. It had been a productive day, and even Pepper had been better behaved, allowing her to walk him instead of taking off running as soon as he was untethered from the table.

As she climbed into her van at the end of the day, Carey came to the open window.

"Wanna hit the beach?" Carey asked.

"Thanks, but I can't."

He ran his hand through his hair and looked away, then drew his eyes back to Leanna. "So, it's cool that you weren't into me, but I'm wondering. Was it because you're into the writer? I'd totally understand. I'm just curious."

He looked so sincere, and for some reason, vulnerable. She hoped she hadn't hurt his feelings. "I wasn't dating him the night you and I went to the Beachcomber, but I'm seeing him now."

Carey nodded. "That's cool. He's a nice guy. If you guys don't work out and you want to hang, you know where I am."

"Thanks, Carey. I really enjoyed the time we spent together, and you made the flea market a lot more fun."

He smiled in that easy way of his. "So did you. Your dancing? Priceless."

She watched him walk away and breathed a sigh of relief. Her stomach fluttered again as she drove toward Kurt's cottage. It had been doing that a lot, fluttering, tightening. Her entire body reacted to Kurt—his touch, his voice, his facial expressions, his scent—in ways it hadn't reacted to any other man. She was a little frightened by how fast she felt her heart becoming his, but at the same time, she'd never known anything to feel so right.

When she arrived, she didn't bother going to the front door. Instead, she followed Pepper down the path to the back deck, where she found Kurt, shirtless again and typing a mile a minute.

"Hey, babe. I'm glad you're here. I missed you." He didn't shift his eyes from the computer screen as his fingers sailed across the keyboard. Pepper lay down at his feet with a loud sigh. "I'll be done in a few minutes. This has been an incredible day for my writing. How was your day?"

She kissed his shoulder as she walked by and sat

at the table. "I missed you, too. My day was surprising. I had three people come by and place orders. Orders! I never saw that coming. One was for a bridal shower, and the other two were for families. They were customers who had bought from me earlier in the summer. You know what that means."

He kept his eyes trained on the computer. "They loved it?"

"Yup. That's got to be a good sign."

"Mm-hm." He saved his work, and in one swift move, he cupped the back of her head, then met her in a sensuous kiss. "I really missed you."

"Me too." She settled back in the chair and took a deep breath, then let it out slowly. She was getting used to being there with him, and she took comfort in the familiarity that had settled in between them.

"I'm excited for you. That's really good news."

"Yeah. And you know what? I've never felt so excited about anything in my life." *Except you.* "I have no idea what's changed, but this feels like what I've been searching for. I can control who I work with and how many clients I take on. If I decide to work with only one grocer, or none, then that's fine, as long as I can make rent or whatever, depending on where I end up living."

Kurt pulled her onto his lap. "Talk to me. I know you're not a planner, but where are you heading in your mind with all of this?"

I want the business and you. She didn't want to put Kurt on the spot, so instead she swallowed her thoughts and shrugged.

"Are you thinking you'll stay in your parents'

cottage for a while and plant your business roots here at the Cape?" He tucked her hair behind her ear.

"I'm not sure. I do love it here, but here on the lower Cape, everything is so expensive. I'm not sure I'd make enough money to be able to afford a bigger place in the first year or two, and I don't want to use my great-grandparents' money."

"I don't blame you, and I love that you feel that way."

"So I have some thinking to do."

"I want to show you something. I don't know much about your business, but I was doing a little research today, and I found this drawing. Is this what you have in mind for your facility?" Kurt pulled up a picture of the interior of what looked like an enormous kitchen. There were four stainless-steel stoves against the west wall and a sink and counter space along the east wall. Large stainless-steel tables formed a U-shaped workspace in the center of the room. He clicked on another image that showed an open door. The walls beside the door were lined with stainless-steel shelves. He pulled up a third picture, which showed a large storage area with deep wooden shelves. There were plenty of windows and what looked like ceramic or tiled floors. Easy to clean. Even for her.

"I hadn't really thought about it in detail, but that's amazing. The only things that are missing are freezers and refrigerators. Other than that, that's a dream workspace for any jam maker. Or baker, really." She searched the images and realized they were individual photos, not a website. "Where is that place?"

He shrugged. "Found it online. I just thought I'd see if it was similar to what you had in mind."

"Amazing, and way too expensive." She closed the laptop. "Did you catch up on your writing?"

"Yeah, and then some. My muse was sitting on my shoulder, whispering in my ear."

"Thank God. I was so worried that I was ruining your career. I thought for sure you'd want to break up with me when you realized I was not a quiet girlfriend but an annoyingly loud one."

"Annoyingly loud?" He laughed.

"Yeah. Don't you think so? I mean, I talk a lot. And I'm a little mouthy, and I question everything. And now I'm running down a career path I didn't really see coming. I mean, I hoped, but..." *And I'm in love with a man I didn't see coming.* "In a week I've turned your very organized and well-planned life upside down."

"Upside down?"

"Yeah. Think about it. You dragged me from the sea, saved my dog, you've written less this week than you probably have any other week of your professional life, and—"

He covered her mouth with his, her words muffled against his tongue as he stroked her worry away. She closed her eyes and melted against him, and when he drew back, she was breathless.

"Wow."

"I've written less, but I've never enjoyed my life more than I have this past week with you, Leanna. If this is what it feels like to live in an upside-down world, then I never want to be right-side up."

ON THE WAY into town, they dropped Leanna's van at her cottage. *"That way you have to drive me home tomorrow and I get more time with you,"* she'd said. He loved the way her mind worked, and he couldn't have agreed more. With Pepper in tow, they had dinner at Mac's Seafood by the Wellfleet Pier. Leanna's hair whipped across her cheeks, and Pepper's fur flattened against the wind. She zipped her hoodie and curled her shoulders forward to ward off the breeze.

"Let's walk down to the park." Kurt draped an arm over her shoulder as they walked away from the water, leaving the gustier wind behind.

Every summer an awning was constructed across from Wellfleet Harbor, where community plays and local bands put on free shows. Tonight there was a blues band playing. There were several rows of metal chairs beneath the awning, most of the seats taken. They claimed two free seats in the back row, and Pepper settled in between their feet. Beside the awning were tennis courts, and beyond that a small, colorful park. Children played on the metal playground equipment while parents stood nearby, enjoying the music. The scene reminded Kurt of his college days. He'd spent time with friends, hanging out at bars and going to concerts at local parks. Before he'd focused on writing as a full-time endeavor, he'd been more relaxed about how he spent his time. During summers and school breaks, he'd worked at a literary agent's office, learning about the publishing industry and penning his first novel in the evenings and on weekends. After graduation he'd attended a writer's conference, where Jackie Tolson asked to see his work. He never expected to be signed two weeks later, or to have a six-figure, two-book deal five months after that. His father was the driving force behind his determination to be the best damn thriller writer imaginable, and he would never stop trying to outwrite other authors or his own last novel. *Do more than you think you can; be better than everyone else*— his father's words had served him well. What he'd never learned was how to apply the same standards and determination to a relationship, and in the days since he'd been with Leanna, he realized that he needed, and wanted, to find a way to strike a balance.

Leanna moved to the beat of the music, a contented smile on her lips. Her shoulders swayed sexily, and as he watched her, Kurt hoped that he was doing enough. That, as Siena mentioned, he was giving her enough attention, thinking about her enough, letting her know how much he cared for her. How could he be sure he was? His mother was the yin to his father's yang. She softened the rough edges of his father's lessons with unconditional love and understanding. She wasn't a pushover. No, Joanie Remington believed that children needed to learn from their mistakes and take responsibilities for their actions, but she also exuded warmth and love like others exuded confidence or insecurity. He hoped that he'd learned enough from her to allow Leanna to feel the same emotional comfort from him.

He reached for Leanna's hand as the band played a slower song.

"Dance with me."

"Here?"

He pointed to the grassy area between the tent and the tennis courts. "There."

He held her close and closed his eyes against the discomfort of feeling like a spectacle. He wanted to hold Leanna, to dance with her, and he'd learned from watching her that there were some urges a person should just give in to. This was one of them, and it felt damn good, even with Pepper's leash around his wrist and Pepper looking up at them with wondrous eyes.

An elderly couple joined them on the grass and danced a few feet away.

Kurt focused on Leanna's heart beating against his, her arms around his neck, and the feminine, sweet, scent of her skin. Her fingers ran lightly over the back of his neck. He felt the curve of her lower back, right above her hips, the dip at the center of her spine as he pressed his palms to hold her closer. He brought one hand up and buried his hand in her silky hair, and without thought, he lowered his mouth to hers. He didn't notice when the music stopped, or when the elderly couple returned to their seats. He didn't notice the fast beat of the band's next song or the child who was pointing at them as they kissed. His focus was only cocooning Leanna in his love until she couldn't help but feel how much he adored her, until she felt it with every breath and trusted it would be in every touch. As he held her with the bay breeze at his back, he realized that Leanna had become his *more*.

"Come to my brother's wedding with me."

Leanna looked up at him and crinkled her nose. "Now?"

She was so damn cute. He felt a soft laugh slip

from his lips and quickly covered it with a cough. "It's next week in Colorado. I'll take care of the flight arrangements and everything."

"But it's a wedding. There are invitations and place settings, and your brother might not want me there." She ran her finger in circles on the back of his neck.

"I want you there, and Jack wants me there. He won't mind. They're getting married at Savannah's father's ranch, so it's not like there's a formal seating chart or anything. Please go with me. I leave straight from Colorado to go back to New York, and I want every second with you that I can get." He hadn't realized how quickly his time at the Cape was coming to an end. A sharp pain seared his heart at the thought of not being with Leanna.

"Okay. Yes. I will. I want to. But promise me you'll ask Savannah and Jack if they'd mind before we make arrangements." She reached up and touched his cheek. "I'm so glad you asked me to go with you."

"You are?"

She nodded. "You're really leaving next week? I didn't realize..." Her eyes filled with sadness.

"Neither did I until just now. I hate the thought of going anywhere without you. I know that makes me sound weak, or wimpy, or something bad, but..." He shrugged.

Her lips spread into a wide smile. "I think it makes you even hotter."

"Hotter? Well, there's more where that came from." He took her hand, and they headed back toward the car. Pepper hurried along beside them.

They stopped every few steps to kiss, and by the time they reached the car, Kurt's body was thick with desire. Leanna wrapped her arms around his neck and rocked her hips into him. She drew his mouth to hers and moaned seductively.

He narrowed his eyes. "You make me crazy when you do that."

"That's the point." She rocked into him again and settled her mouth over his neck, sucking and licking until he was ready to explode.

He reached behind her and opened the car door. "In."

She slid into the seat, and Pepper jumped in at her feet. Kurt climbed into the driver's seat, and as he started the car, Leanna reached between his legs and rubbed his hard length, hungrily licking her lips. *Dear Lord.* He threw the car into drive and drove directly to the darkest corner of the lot. By the time he put the car in park, Leanna was halfway across the center console.

Pepper jumped onto the passenger seat and cocked his head, watching them with his big, dark eyes.

"God, I want you." He tangled his hands in her hair and tilted her head back, then teased her the same way she'd teased him, sensually sucking on her neck until she climbed right onto his lap and began working his zipper.

Their lips never parted and the strokes of their tongues never slowed as Kurt reclined the seat, drew his pants down, and pushed Leanna's panties to the side. She gazed deeply into his eyes as her body swallowed every inch of his hard length and drew another moan from her lungs. At six foot two, Kurt didn't have much room to play in the front seat of the Mercedes. He held tightly to Leanna's hips and helped her efforts, but his cock was throbbing and he needed to move, to drive into her, to feel her body against his. He drew her close.

Pepper barked.

They both stilled, then laughed.

Pepper climbed across the console and licked Leanna's arm.

"Home." Kurt lifted Leanna back onto the passenger seat, pulled his jeans up but left them unzipped—there was no way he was trapping his erection behind a hard, metal zipper.

He'd never driven so fast in his life.

Chapter Twenty

THEY RAN UP the steps to the cottage like two teenagers stealing away. Leanna was hot, and wet, and she wanted Kurt so badly that her insides ached. They'd forgotten to leave the porch light on, and Kurt fumbled with the keys, cursing under his breath.

She slid between him and the door and lifted his shirt, kissing and groping his hard muscles and warm skin. He pressed his hips into her and the door pushed open. Leanna stumbled backward, her arms flailing. Kurt caught her with one strong arm. They kissed and groped their way to the couch, kicking off their shoes. Kurt dropped the keys and Pepper's leash; then he lifted her shirt over her head and tossed it away and did the same with his own. Leanna hooked her hands in his pants and drew them down, licking his hard length on her way back up, and felt his body shudder as he wrapped his strong hands around her ribs and laid her on the couch.

"You're impossibly beautiful," he said in a husky voice.

She drew his hands to her breasts. His mouth followed, and the feel of his tongue on her hot skin was almost too much to take. She whimpered for more. She needed all of him, and she pulled his hips toward hers, arching into him.

"Let me make you come first," he whispered.

"No. Need you. Now," was all she could manage, and in the next breath, he slid gently, lovingly, into her. Her body went white hot, and she went a little wild. She didn't want loving—she wanted hot, dirty, fun sex—the kind of sex she'd read about and her friends talked about, and she wanted it now. She pressed her palms to his cheeks and looked into his eyes with what she hoped was a serious stare.

"Take me. Love me. Fuck me," she whispered. His eyes narrowed, and she recognized his hesitation. Her body vibrated with anticipation. Kurt was kind, generous, loving, everything a woman could want, but she knew he had more to give. His tight muscles told her he was holding back. She could see it in his eyes when they were in the throes of passion, and she wanted to experience it. Him. All of him. "I want more of you," she assured him.

He narrowed his eyes and held her gaze.

She nodded, and in the next second, his eyes went almost black. When his lips found hers, the intensity of everything changed. It was a rougher, harder, scratch-her-face-with-his-stubble kiss that made her tingle all the way to her toes. His tongue didn't just stroke her mouth. He consumed it. His hands moved hard and fast, pinching her nipples and groping her breasts as he thrust into her deeper, with more force and more passion than she ever imagined. Every thought fell away. She was enveloped in their heat. He never broke the kiss as he lifted her hips with one hand and pushed a cushion beneath them, then penetrated her deeper, harder, grunting with each powerful thrust. Her toes curled under, and her skin went so hot it felt icy cold. She clawed at his back, crying out so loud that Pepper whined. Kurt grabbed her knees and brought them up to her chest, driving into her from a new angle, bringing heightened arousal and new sensations rippling through her.

"More," she managed.

He shifted his hips, and she gasped for air as another orgasm ravaged her, causing her inside muscles to clench tightly around him, over and over, but he still didn't relent. Kurt pushed her legs farther back. His dark stare locked with her, sending heat through her tingling body.

"Holy…crap. You're…a-amazing," she said through heavy breaths.

Kurt lifted his hips, and her legs fell free.

"No, no. That was so good." She reached for him.

The right side of his mouth lifted. "So is this."

He repositioned her legs. The backs of her legs rested against his chest, and he entered her again, slow and deep. Leanna gripped the edge of the cushion and slammed her eyes shut as lights exploded behind her lids. Kurt drove into her again and again at the same slow pace. She'd never felt so alive. Every nerve reached for him, and when he teased her with just the tip of his hard length, she nearly crawled out of her skin.

"More. Please, more." *Oh my God. I'm begging for sex.* She pushed the embarrassment away. She was with Kurt, and this was so much more than sex. Her heart was so full of Kurt. She wanted to experience everything with him. Sweaty, steamy, sticky, I-can't-breathe lovemaking—and he obliged, taking her right up to the crest again and holding her there as he pushed into her slowly until he was buried deep. Then he lowered her legs and moved the cushion from beneath her hips. With eyes full of love and every motion laden with tenderness, he came down on top of her and pressed his chest to hers.

"I have to love you."

"Yes. Yes, love me."

Their hips collided with every impassioned movement.

"Open your eyes," he whispered.

"Can't," she said in one long breath.

He kissed her closed eyelids. "Try."

She did, and the love in his eyes seared a path to her heart. He tilted his hips up, sending a frisson of pleasure through her entire body, and then he took her in another intimate, loving kiss. She felt his thighs flex in perfect time to her own magnificent climax, which was seizing her body. He held her tightly as they rode out their love, barely breathing and clinging to each other as their bodies trembled and shook, until they collapsed beside each other, sated and spent.

Chapter Twenty-One

THE NEXT MORNING Kurt drove Leanna home before going for his run so she could prepare for her day at the flea market, and when they got there, he didn't want to leave. Hell, he never wanted to be apart from her.

Leanna flitted from room to room, packing up what she'd need for the sunny afternoon. Sunscreen, paper towels, bottles of water. She stopped in the middle of the kitchen floor, looking cute as hell in her shorts and tank and tapping her lips with her finger as if it might bring forth whatever she was looking for.

Kurt folded her into his arms. "Have you thought any more about how much time you want to commit to your business or where you might want to set up shop?"

She ran her index finger down the center of his chin to his chest. "Mm-hm."

"And?" His heart raced. He didn't want to put

added pressure on her, but damn if he didn't feel like he'd go crazy if they weren't together.

She looked up at him, and he saw the answer in her hazel eyes. "I think I want to keep the business as a summer business. That's when fruits are freshest, and I can specialize in gift baskets or something similar and equally as fun, the rest of the year. And..." She lifted up on her tiptoes and kissed his chin. "I want to be near you."

Near me. Kurt could hardly believe it. He filled the silence with an embrace.

"Near me. You're sure?"

She nodded.

"I live just outside of New York City. Is that someplace you would really consider moving to?"

"If that's where you'll be, then I want to be there, too. Unless you don't want me to. I'd totally understand if you didn't, I mean, we haven't known each other that long, and I can be noisy, and you like quiet, and I can be a little messy, and you're neat, and—"

He pressed a soft kiss to her lips. "I want you there with me. In my house. By my side. Talking while I try to write and making messes that I have to clean up."

He felt her heart beating fast and hard against his chest.

"You want me to move in with you?"

"Yes."

"You don't have to feel pressure or anything. I can find an apartment nearby." Her voice shook. "I have some money saved from my *real* jobs, so I can manage for a while without dipping into my trust fund."

The love in her eyes betrayed her offer. "Leanna, *I feel it in my crazy-ass heart.* I love you."

Her cheeks flushed pink, and her finger made quick work of tracing the edge of his triceps. "You heard that?"

He kissed her. "I love you, and you love me. It's fast, but I trust my instincts. Hell, when you're not with me, I'm looking for you."

Pepper pawed at his leg.

Kurt glanced at Pepper. "Yes, you, too, Pep."

Her eyes welled with tears.

"Is this too fast? I'm sorry. I'm a pretty focused guy, but if it's too fast—"

"No." She gripped his waist. "No. I want to be with you more than anything in the world."

"Then what is it?"

A tear slipped down her cheek. "It's just..." She buried her face in his chest. "You fill my empty spots."

He loved her so much that his heart ached. He wiped the tear with the pad of his thumb and held her close. "You fill mine, too. Even the ones I never knew I had." They hugged until Leanna pushed him playfully away.

"You need to go for your run or I'll steal your writing *and* your running time, and then you'll rethink my moving in with you."

"I'll probably need to write pretty late tonight. Want me to come over after I'm done, or would you like a break from me for a night?"

"Break? No way. I'm working with the girls on organizing the brochures and stuff. Just come over when you're done."

"It might be pretty late."

"I'll leave the door unlocked." She kissed him and patted his butt on the way out the door.

"Careful or I'll miss my run and you'll miss the flea market."

On the way back to his cottage, Kurt's pulse raced. He'd never felt so aware of everything around him or so alive. The trees looked more interesting, the wildflowers on the side of the road more vibrant, the grass greener; the air even smelled clearer. His mind ran in a hundred different directions, and every one of them circled back to the studio. Leanna. Forever.

He called Siena on the way back to his cottage.

"You realize it's the ass crack of dawn, right?" Siena yawned.

"No, it's not. It's seven. Listen, isn't Cash's brother a contractor in New England?"

"Yeah. Blue. He's good, too. I've seen pictures of his work."

"Think he'd do work for me on the Cape?" Kurt's mind was going a mile a minute. He had a plan in place, and surprising Leanna with the studio was the tip of the iceberg.

"I guess." She yawned again. "Hold on."

He heard her talking to Cash. A minute later, Cash came to the phone.

"Hey, Kurt. You need a contractor on the Cape?" Cash sounded far more awake than Siena. He was a firefighter and used to waking up fast.

"Yeah. I have a studio that needs to be renovated."

"He's doing some work at the Kennedy compound in Hyannis, I think. I'll text you his number. I'm sure if he can fit it in, he'd love to do it."

"Thanks, Cash. We'll see you at the wedding?" Kurt pulled into the driveway and walked around the house until the studio came into view.

"Yeah. Are you bringing Leanna?"

Kurt laughed. "That old Remington grapevine."

"Oh, Siena made quick work of that. Burned up the cell lines. Everyone knows, and I think they expect you to bring her along."

He heard Siena holler in the background. "It's a big deal that Kurt has a girlfriend!"

"Tell my sister it *is* a big deal. Yeah, she's coming with me, and thanks for texting Blue's number. I'll get in touch with him as soon as you send it over." He ended the call and gazed at the studio, feeling the pieces of his heart falling into place. *No wonder I didn't know what to do with you. You were waiting for Leanna.*

Maybe I was, too.

Chapter Twenty-Two

AFTER SHE ARRIVED home from the flea market, Leanna checked her email and confirmed the meeting with Daisy Chain for the twenty-eighth, the only day every member of their executive staff would be in town in the next four weeks. She fed Pepper, and for the first time, wished she had Kurt's phone number. She'd like to hear his voice. Although that would require remembering where she left her phone. She took out her notepad and wrote FIND PHONE across the top of the page.

"Ready to get to work?" Jenna walked into the cottage armed with her iPad, a notebook, and a six-pack of wine coolers.

"As ready as I can be, I think."

"Hey, girlies." Amy held the door open for Bella; each of them carried their laptop and a plastic wineglass. "We're ready to work, Leanna. Just tell us what you need."

"You guys are the best. Let's set up outside, though. That way we can scarf the Internet from Clark and Vanessa's cottage. Their connection is so much stronger than mine." She set her computer on the table, and Pepper settled down in the corner of the deck. Leanna couldn't wait to tell them about her decision to move in with Kurt, and she knew just how she wanted to reveal her news.

"I made a list." Jenna pulled out a notebook.

"Of course you did." Bella rolled her eyes.

"Someone had to." Jenna poured a wine cooler into her plastic cup.

"I made one, too." Leanna pulled up her list, and the girls looked over her shoulder while she put a slash through the items she'd already taken care of.

> ~~Figure out where I want to live in the fall! Cape?~~ New York/Cape Cod!
> ~~Kurt?~~ Definitely!
> Product list
> Ingredient list
> Delivery timetable
> Backup generator? Cost? Facility cost? Share space? Check out bakeries?
> Talk to an attorney about contracts and insurance liabilities
> Employees?

"New York and Cape Cod?" Before Leanna could answer, Bella screamed. "New York and Cape Cod? Oh my God. You and Kurt? Leanna!"

Jenna and Amy shrieked, and they wrapped her

into a group hug.

"I was just about to tell you." She couldn't stop herself from smiling. "I'm moving in with Kurt after the summer."

Jenna and Amy squealed again.

"Oh my God. You're really moving to New York? With Kurt?" Bella held Leanna's forearm. "You and Kurt Remington? That gorgeous creature who looks at you like you were dropped from the clouds just for him? Holy crap, Leanna. I thought you were the *unlucky* Seaside girl!" She wrapped her arms around Leanna again and squeezed so tightly that Leanna had to push free just to breathe.

"I know." Leanna shook her head. "I can't believe it either. I know it's crazy fast, but it feels so right! I feel like even if everything fell apart tomorrow, as long as we were together, everything would still be perfect."

"I want that." Amy leaned across the table. "Please tell me he knows about your penchant for laundry piles."

Leanna laughed. "I haven't hidden a thing. I'm sure we'll both have to make concessions. I mean, he's already accepted Pepper. He wouldn't even smile at him when we first met, and I can't believe he's taking time away from his writing for us. But he is, and he says it's what he wants." She took a sip of her wine cooler. "Maybe my luck is changing. Speaking of which, if we don't get to work, we'll be at it all night."

"From what I've seen, you're good at going at it all night." Bella raised her cup. "To Leanna and Kurt."

They all clinked glasses. Not for the first time, and certainly not for the last, Leanna silently thanked God that she had Bella, Amy, and Jenna in her life. When she thought of the people who would always be there for her, they were the only ones who came to mind. She never thought anyone else outside of her family could measure up to the safety and love that her friends gave her unconditionally, and now that she'd met and fallen in love with Kurt, she knew just how wrong she'd been. And how lucky she was.

"Wait. Are you getting married or just living in sinful pleasure?" Amy asked.

"Marriage? Sinful pleasure, thank you very much." *Marriage?* She had trouble moving past the idea, but she pushed herself to focus. "Can you believe it? I'm so excited that I can barely stand it."

"Lea, you'll live close to me! We can get together during the year. New York and Connecticut aren't far apart." Bella hugged her again.

"I know. The whole thing has my heart going crazy. *He* has my heart going crazy."

"That's what love is," Amy said as she patted Leanna's hand. "Enjoy every second of it, so we can envy you."

"Oh, I plan to." Leanna let out a loud breath. "Okay, we need to focus because I can talk about Kurt all night. Come on. Let's get Sweet Treats off the ground so I'm not a moocher, too." She pointed to the list on her computer. "Jenna, I put together the product and ingredient lists. Can you make them organized and presentable? I really stink at that."

Jenna saluted. "Aye, aye, Captain. I've got this."

"Bella, I know nothing about brochures or anything like that. Maybe we can work together to figure out something?" Leanna took an elastic hairband from her wrist and put her hair up in a ponytail. "That's better. It was a little warm."

"I was looking at facilities, and they're superexpensive, Leanna." Amy pulled up a website on her computer. "I was thinking that you could just sublet someplace for a few months, or work from your cottage, and if you need a backup power source, I looked into a few generators. Your place is so small that you wouldn't need much. It might run you a couple grand, but at least you wouldn't be locked into a lease."

"I was actually thinking along the same lines. If I'll be in New York in the fall, then I don't really need another facility. I can work from the cottage in the summer and find a place in New York in the fall if I have to. We don't lose power in the summers. Ever." She sat back and blew out a breath. "Do you guys think I'm nuts? I mean, I want this to work so badly. I love what I'm doing, and next summer I'll do the flea market in Dennis, too, which is during the week, so that works out perfectly."

"Next year you won't need to make jam." Jenna looked up from her keyboard as she typed. "You'll be married to a wealthy writer."

"Married?" *Married!* "I'm not getting married, but even if I were, I'd still want to make jam for as long as I'm enjoying it. I can't sit around and do nothing." She shot a look at Jenna. "Married?"

"Probably. Don't you think?" Amy nodded in agreement. "Jenna said every article she read about Kurt mentioned how important family was to him."

"That's right." Jenna drank her wine cooler. "The article on the Huff Post said that he and his family get together every month for family dinners. I think that's so sweet. I mean really, how many attractive, single guys make time like that for their family?"

"None that I know. I guess it's a good thing Leanna's going to move in with him. It would probably be hard to get him to move away from his family if they're that close. And then you have the whole, is he a mama's boy thing to worry about." Bella stared intently at her laptop. "I'm working on a great logo idea for you."

"Thanks, Bella." Leanna ran her finger in circles on the table. "Should I worry that he's a mama's boy? I mean, I don't know his family, but he sure doesn't seem like one."

"There's one sure test." Bella met Leanna's gaze. "Mama's boys have sex one way. Missionary, in a bed. That's it. At least that's been my experience."

Amy went into the cottage and came back out with a bag of pretzels. "You know, I think you might be right about missionary-style sex and mama's boys. Even nice guys like to taste the fruits of our loins once in a while, but mama's boys..."

Leanna burst out laughing. "Fruits of our loins?"

"You know what I mean. Mama's boys don't do that. They're all repressed and afraid their mothers will tell them they're being dirty." Amy leaned in close. "So, is he a mama's boy?"

"No! God. He's anything but a mama's boy by your standards."

"Ha! You owe me ten bucks." Bella held out her

hand.

"You bet on him?" Leanna ran her eyes between Amy and Bella.

"Not me. I pegged him as a down-and-dirty boy under the sheets," Jenna said as she primly tucked her hair behind her ear.

Bella raised her hand. "Me too. Total alpha in the bedroom was my guess."

"That's not fair." Amy crossed her arms over her chest. "I didn't say he was a mama's boy. I said he seemed refined and that guys who were refined weren't as adventurous as other guys."

"Well, my dear Amy, you're sorely mistaken. I happen to have an adventurous, refined, alpha hottie who doesn't mind that my rhythm is off or that I have piles of clothes on the floor and can't clean worth shit. And you know what?" She finished her wine cooler. "I have no idea what he sees in me. I'm so flaky and he's so not."

"You are not flaky. You love life. You don't settle for things that don't make you happy, but you're definitely not flaky." Amy handed Leanna a pretzel. "Eat a pretzel and let's get this stuff done. He knows he's lucky to be with you, as he should."

Leanna put her head on Amy's shoulder. "See why I love you guys? You'll totally lie to me when I need you to."

They spent the next few hours hammering out product and ingredient lists, brochures and order forms, and Amy even came up with an outline for a delivery schedule. Amy also offered to go with her to the print shop as soon as Leanna had finalized all of the documents.

"Thank you. I want to go over everything with Kurt, too. He might have some ideas. Bella, this logo is perfect. How did you come up with the idea for the grapevine interlaced with the Sweet Treats? I love how you put Luscious Leanna's arched over it, too. It's simple and elegant."

"I'm glad you like it. It just came to me as we were talking." Bella pointed to a few other examples she came up with.

"I love the first one. It's clever and clean, and with Luscious Leanna's in the title, it's sexy, too, and sexy sells." Jenna stood and stretched, wiggling as she tugged at the bottom of her shorts. "Are you guys hungry? Want to go out for pizza?"

"Starved. I'm not sure when Kurt is going to be here, and I don't have his phone number. Not that I know where my phone is." *Where is that damn thing?* "Why don't I drive over just to touch base with him and then I can meet you guys? Where are we going?"

"Let's take one car. We'll stop by Kurt's—unless you plan on dragging his ass into bed, in which case we'll take two cars. I can drive," Bella offered.

"I'm not dragging his ass into bed. Jeez, Bella. I've had more sex in the past week than I've had in the past two years." Leanna grabbed a sweatshirt from in the house and leashed Pepper. "Grab your sweatshirts and we can all meet at Bella's in a few minutes."

Bella drove to Kurt's house, and when she pulled up in the driveway, they all got out with Leanna.

"Are you shitting me?" Bella whispered. "This is gorgeous."

"I'm never leaving," Jenna said as she headed up to the front door.

Leanna followed Pepper down the path toward the back of the house. "Come on, you guys. He'll be out on the deck writing."

They found Kurt on the deck, shirtless and writing, with an empty coffee cup beside his computer. Pepper made a beeline for him.

"Hey, Pep." Kurt's eyes remained trained on the computer, and his fingers never stopped typing.

"If it isn't the Seaside girls. Did you *all* miss me?"

"How did you know we call ourselves that? I missed you something awful." Leanna bent to kiss his cheek. He turned into the kiss and met her lips with his own.

"I didn't know, but the name fit. I've missed you, too. You look adorable." He tugged on the bottom of her sweatshirt.

"Thanks. We're heading out for pizza, and I wanted to see when you thought you might be done." It was breezier by the ocean than it was inland. The sound of the waves was soothing, and Pepper claimed his place by Kurt's feet.

"I've got another few hours, I think." Kurt stopped typing and smiled at Leanna. "I'm sorry, but this deadline is coming up so fast. I didn't realize it was due in less than two weeks. I really need to put in a few hours. Go have fun. If it gets too late, I'll just stay here."

"No, you don't need to do that. I don't mind if you come over late." She couldn't even imagine sleeping without him.

"Hey, Kurt, what's that building over by the trees?" Bella asked.

"A studio. This was an artist's home before I bought it, and that's where he worked." He ran his hand through his hair, then pulled Leanna down on his lap and lowered his voice. "I might be writing until eleven or so. Are you sure you still want me to come by?"

"Absolutely. That's not late. I thought you meant, like, two in the morning."

"Sometimes I write that late, but I've had a great writing day. I shouldn't need more than a few more hours."

"Why don't you write in the studio?" Bella zipped up her sweatshirt.

"I prefer to write outside. I find the fresh air and the sounds of the water inspiring." He kissed Leanna's cheek. "You inspire me, too. I came up with a great idea for a villain for my next book. She's a free spirit."

"You did that? I've been so wrapped up in figuring out my life that I haven't even had time to ask for details on what you're writing. I'm sorry." She traced a circle on his chest. "You know I don't like thrillers, or anything creepy like that, but if you want me to, I'll read one of your books. I do care about what you do. I hope you know that."

"You're patterning a villain after Leanna?" Amy sat down at the table. "She's the sweetest person I know. She could never be a villain."

"I'm just borrowing a few traits of hers. It's not really her." He brushed Leanna's hair from her shoulder. "You don't have to read them. I don't want anything to steal your happiness. Not even for a second."

"Jesus, you two are too fricking cute." Bella leaned against the railing and sighed.

"Hey, Leanna," Jenna called from the bottom of the stairs.

"Yeah?"

"I found your phone." She ascended the stairs and handed Leanna her sandy phone.

"Oh my God. It must have fallen from my pocket when you carried me to the deck that first night we met." She laughed and pushed the power button.

"It's not going to work. You were in the water for quite some time." Kurt ran his hand up her calf.

"My brother Colby is a Navy SEAL, and when he found out I was coming to the Cape for the summer, he sent me a LifeProof case for my iPhone." She turned the screen with the illuminated apple toward Kurt. "See? It still works."

"That's crazy, and really good to know for my villains and victims. I'll have to remember that."

Leanna jumped off his lap. "I guess we'll go eat, but before I forget, want to swap phone numbers? That way I don't have to show up and use your writing time. We can text or call."

Kurt picked up his phone and handed it to her. "Have at it."

Bella crossed her arms. "You're just going to let her rifle through your phone?"

"If she wants to rifle, why not?" He rubbed the goose bumps on her legs. "I have nothing to hide."

"Old girlfriend's numbers? 1-900 phone calls?

Come on. Every guy has something to hide." Bella rolled her eyes.

"Maybe you're hanging out with the wrong guys." Kurt laughed. "I have a few women's numbers, but she won't find any recent calls to them—besides my sister—and I've never called a 900 number. Maybe I'm missing out." He squeezed Leanna's thigh.

She handed him back his phone. "Here. I put my phone number in and called my phone from yours, so I have yours, too." She glared at Bella. "And I didn't snoop. Jeez, Bella. Trust much?" She kissed him goodbye, then stopped at the top of the stairs. "I almost forgot to tell you; the meeting with Daisy Chain is rescheduled for the twenty-eighth."

"The twenty-eighth?" Kurt's voice became serious. "That's Jack's wedding."

"Oh no, really?" *Shitshitshit.* "He's getting married on a Friday?"

"Yeah. It was the only day everyone could make it. Savannah's brother and his fiancée are fashion designers, and they had to be in Paris by Sunday."

"Daisy Chain said the twenty-eighth was the only day their executive staff was free over the next few weeks. I guess I can reschedule again for a few weeks out."

"No. Don't be silly. This is what you've been waiting for."

"We'll wait in the car." Bella and the others left them alone.

Leanna took Kurt's hand. "I'm so sorry. We never talked specific dates, and I didn't think twice about accepting. I can change the meeting. Really, it's okay."

"No way. You want to start out on a good foot with them. I'll miss you being there, and I was hoping that you'd meet my family, but we'll have plenty of time for that. I haven't made your flight arrangements yet, so I'll just make them from the Cape to New York. It's an easier flight than going out to Colorado anyway."

"I'm sorry, Kurt."

"Listen, babe. What would life be without the need for revisions here and there? We're fine."

He held her gaze, and even though she knew he was right, it didn't ease the awful tightening in her stomach.

"This is a great opportunity for you, and you've been excited about it. I wouldn't steal that from you, Leanna. I'm not going anywhere. I'll be waiting in New York when you get there."

"You're so good to me."

"You're so good to me," he said with a smile. "My flight takes me back to New York after the wedding. I have a meeting with my agent the following Monday. When do you want to come out?"

She shrugged. "Right after the meeting. Oh, wait. I have to close up the cottage and make all the arrangements for my mail. Gosh, I can't fly. What were we thinking? I have my van, so I'll drive to New York. It's only a few hours. When do you land back in New York?"

"Sunday night." He kissed the back of her hand. "Listen. Go have fun with your friends, and don't stress over this. We'll be fine, and I'm confident that we can handle anything. I'm so proud of you. This could put you exactly where you want to be with your business."

He squeezed her hand. "What's a few days?"

Oh, not much. They'll only feel like a lifetime. "Okay, but I really am sorry." She reached for Pepper's leash.

"You can leave him with me if you want."

"But you need to write."

Kurt glanced under the table. "I think he's pretty used to my schedule. We're okay. Have fun with the girls. Enjoy a leashless night."

Leanna threw her arms around his neck and kissed him. "How on earth did I get so lucky?"

"It was all part of Pepper's big plan. He scoped me out on the deck and then pretended to drown. I didn't stand a chance."

She'd never been more thankful for Pepper.

Chapter Twenty-Three

SUNDAY MORNING KURT awoke to the sound of Leanna typing on her computer. By the darkness of her bedroom, he guessed it wasn't yet six o'clock. Kurt rolled over and caught the scent of her shampoo on the pillow and let his cheek settle into it. He was going to miss her when he left for Colorado. Hell, he'd spent most of Saturday missing her and she was only minutes away. But he'd pushed through the loneliness and was nearing the end of his manuscript—and it was a damn good story. Even better than his last. Jackie would be pleased.

"Hey, babe?" he called into the kitchen.

Leanna appeared in the doorway wearing his T-shirt, which covered up far too much of her gorgeous body. Her hair was tousled, and her eyes were more awake than anyone's should be at that time of day.

"Did I wake you?" She kneeled on the bed and kissed him.

"Nope. I just missed you." He folded her into his arms and pulled her down on top of him. "What are you working on?"

"I had an idea for a few new flavors, and I wanted to add them to the product and ingredient lists. Once I sat down to do that, I started to look for other grocers to submit proposals to." She ran her finger along his chin. "I guess I got stuck poking around on the Internet. I wanted to show you everything we've come up with, too. Maybe tonight?"

"I thought I'd come by the flea market later. We can go over your stuff, and I'll bring my computer and write while you're working."

"Can you write there? Won't the crowds be a distraction?"

"I don't care if they are. I want to be with you." He rolled her over so she was beneath him. His cell phone rang. "Christ? Who would call this early?" He reached for the phone. "It's Siena. I'm sorry. Just a sec." He answered the call with a serious tone. "Is everyone okay?"

"Yeah. I just wanted to ask you if you thought Leanna would want to go out with the girls for dinner Saturday. We'll probably just end up at one of the Bradens' houses with no guys allowed, but the idea is that we women get one last hurrah with Savannah before she and Jack leave for their honeymoon."

He covered the mouthpiece. "Don't move," he whispered to Leanna; then he rolled to his side and answered Siena. "Aren't you the one who complained about me calling at the ass crack of dawn?"

"This is payback." He heard the smile in Siena's

voice.

"Pest. She can't come to the wedding."

"What? Why? Oh no. Did you break up?"

"No, Siena. She has a meeting. Listen, I'm a little busy. Can I call you later?"

Leanna sat up, and Kurt pressed her gently back down to the mattress, smiled, and shook his head.

"Are you sure? I was looking forward to meeting her."

"I know. I'll call you…sometime. Love you, sis. Bye." He ended the call, and Pepper stuck his nose up on the bed and barked.

"She's mine for a few minutes," Kurt said to Pepper.

Pepper whimpered.

"Does he need to go out?" Kurt asked.

"No. He was just out." Leanna pointed to Pepper's tail wagging happily. "I think he wants you, not me."

Kurt nuzzled against her neck. "Too bad. I'm going to miss you in a few days. There's no way I'm giving up one second of our time." He nibbled on her earlobe, and Pepper barked again.

"I think he's jealous," Leanna teased.

"Then let's give him something to be jealous of." Kurt lifted his T-shirt from her body and began kissing his way up her ribs.

She squirmed beneath him, and Pepper barked again.

Kurt pressed his cheek to Leanna's stomach. "Really, Pep?" He turned his attention back to Leanna and took her breast in his mouth.

"Mm." She rocked her hips against his, and Pepper

breathed heavily through his nose and lay down on the floor. "I think you just figured out how to calm him down."

He slipped his finger beneath her panties and touched her damp curls. "And how to rev you up."

"Shh. The window's open."

"Your friends aren't even awake yet."

"It's seven o'clock. It seems later because it's a little cloudy, and Tony got in late last night. He gets up wicked early, and since he's next door, he can probably hear us if he's out on his deck."

"The hot neighbor?" He kissed her neck.

"Mm-hm. That one."

Kurt got up and closed the window. "No need to taunt him. Now, where were we?"

"You were about to drop those sexy little briefs on the floor." Leanna took off her shirt and tossed it toward him.

He caught it midair. "I think I can handle that. I don't have many days left to love you in ways that will make you forget how hot Tony is."

"I think you've already accomplished that."

He crawled onto the bed on all fours and kissed her ankles, calves, and just above her knees, before dragging his tongue along her inner thigh. "I'm an overachiever."

AN HOUR LATER, Kurt was back home and heading out for his morning run. His day would be thrown off by his late start, and again by the interruption of meeting with Blue about the studio renovation. Kurt was such a creature of habit that he expected to be cantankerous because of the upending of his schedule, but an unfamiliar calm settled over him as he ran beneath the thinning clouds.

His thoughts turned introspective, and he took stock of how his life had changed—how he'd changed. He used to work through plot issues and character development in the hours he wasn't writing, and he never understood how writers claimed to turn their writer brains off in the evenings and on the weekends. To Kurt, every day held the promise of a blank page, and he craved the challenge of filling it with meaningful words that engaged the reader to the point of obsession. Now he was beginning to understand the desire to climb out of his characters' minds and turn off the plot formations. As he rounded a bend, he thought of Leanna up early and working on her business. She'd changed, too, he realized. He'd never been a big believer in fate, and as he came to the end of his three-mile run, the sun broke through the clouds, shining brightly on the studio.

Blue arrived right on time. He was a strappingly handsome man with a body built for hard work. He stood eye-to-eye with Kurt, with thick, dark brown hair parted on the side, and smallish eyes, which gave him a mysterious look. In his jeans and a white T-shirt, complete with a five-o'clock shadow at ten in the morning, the man probably turned heads everywhere he went.

"Blue Ryder. It's a pleasure to finally meet you." He flashed a killer smile, and Kurt was surprised when his handshake wasn't a challenge, as he'd expect from a burly guy like Blue, but a gentleman's handshake:

two quick shakes accompanied by a nod.

"Thanks for coming out. You look a lot like Cash." Although Cash's hair was lighter than Blue's, the family resemblance was clear in the strong chin, broad shoulders, and heavily muscled build.

"That's what I hear. Nice place you've got here."

"Thanks. The studio belonged to an artist, and I'd like to outfit it with the materials I noted in the photographs I sent. My girlfriend has a jam and jelly business." They walked across the grass to the studio. Blue eyed the building with an assessing gaze.

"You mentioned that, and this is a surprise, which means you need to be clever about either where she stays or the hours I work."

They went inside, and Blue ran a hand over the countertop. He sized up the ceiling and walls, checked out the storage area, and took notes on a notepad he pulled from his back pocket.

"This place is incredible. There are so many possibilities with the setup. Are you open to a few ideas, or are you set on the images you've already provided?" Blue put one hand on his hip and rubbed his chin. "I think we can make this much more comfortable and elegant, unless your girlfriend really enjoys a sterile feel to the environment."

"She's anything but sterile." He smiled, thinking of Leanna's kitchen, stacked high with dishes the first night he took her home. "I think she'd like something that felt like home but was easy to clean. Jams and jellies make for sticky cleanups, so if you can work with that, then sure. I'd love to hear your ideas."

"I know you want to keep this a surprise, but

renovations like this can be pricey. Are you sure you don't want to run a few ideas by her first?"

Kurt locked the studio, and they headed back to the cottage.

"Do you have images online I can show her? I can work it into a conversation, and she won't have to know about the renovation." Kurt opened his laptop and slid it across the table to Blue.

"Sure." Blue pulled up his website.

"Just save the images to my desktop. That way she won't see your site."

"Smart. So, how long have you two been together?"

"Oh, man, don't even ask. You'll think I'm nuts." Kurt walked into the kitchen and opened the fridge. "Can I get you a drink?"

"Sure, thanks. Water's fine." He saved a number of images and then showed and explained each to Kurt. "And I'll build these cabinets myself, so they'll look as if they were part of the original build. I agree with your using stainless steel for the appliances and a few of the larger workstations, for ease of cleaning, but I think if we mix in some granite and wood along the east wall and in the supply area, then it will give the studio a warmer feel. Maybe warm shades of browns, golds, and beige?"

"Sounds great."

"We need to talk budget, so give me a feel for what you're thinking." Blue turned back to the computer, and Kurt knew he was giving him space to think through the finances. He didn't need to think about it. He had more money than he could spend in the next thirty years, and his father's advice reiterated his thoughts. *Invest in quality—your house, your children's education, your career. Don't skimp on things for the people who matter.* He thought of his mother. She was an artist, and his father had built a studio for her the year Jack was born. He remembered hearing his mother going out to her studio after they'd gone to bed when he was just a boy, leaving their father on "kid duty." Sometimes Kurt would look out his bedroom window and watch her through the studio window. He remembered seeing her dance while she painted. Even now he saw a light in his mother's eyes when she went to work in her studio. He wanted Leanna to have that—a place to call her own that she would still adore twenty years from now. A place where she could create from her heart and that held significance for them.

Kurt gazed out over the ocean, wondering again if he was moving too quickly. For a guy who kept his world close to his chest, he was opening up to Leanna in ways that couldn't be easily closed. He tried to picture his life without Leanna and found he was unable. There was no room for doubt in his very full heart. Fast or not, the only thing in his life that he felt as passionate about as he did Leanna was writing, and even that now took a backseat. He was moving forward, and it felt right all the way to his core.

This is where we met. What could be more meaningful than this property?

"I have a hard time putting a price on love. Work it up, and let's do this."

Chapter Twenty-Four

LEANNA PLACED SIX jars of jam into a bag and handed it across the table to the elderly gentleman in shorts and a polo shirt. He reminded her of Al Black, and a quiet longing passed through her.

"Thank you, and I hope you enjoy them."

"How can I not enjoy something called Luscious Leanna's Sweet Treats? It's all in the name. Do you have a website where I can order throughout the year?" The gray-haired man asked.

Oh no. Of course, a website! She made a mental note to figure out how to create a website. "It's under development right now, but if you leave me your email address, I'll send you the link once it's live." *Note to self: Start an email list, a mailing list, and maybe a newsletter.*

That pushed her total sales for the day over ninety, and it was only noon. Things were definitely looking up. Carey hadn't shown up today, leaving the space beside her empty. The flea market felt strange without his orange van parked behind hers and their friendly banter, but after the first twenty minutes, she'd been too busy to notice. The clouds had cleared and the sun shone brightly on the tented rows of vendor booths, drawing in droves of customers since the flea market opened at nine, and she was thankful for the sales. Several return customers stopped by to stock up on her Sweet Treats in anticipation of the end of summer, when real life took over and the flea market would be a distant memory.

Leanna thought about *real life*. She had a plan for the first time in her life. Not a whim, not a hope, but a solid plan that included a life she wanted, a relationship with a man she adored, and a future full of promise. With Kurt she'd found love, and she'd become stronger, more focused. Happier. Which she found astounding, because she thought she'd always been happy, even if she'd been searching for something more in her life. She hadn't realized that her happiness could triple with Kurt in her life.

Pepper began barking before she spotted her love walking leisurely through the crowd with his computer and notebook tucked under one arm, a small bag and a vase full of flowers in the other. A warm thrill flowed through her. He was incredibly handsome in his khaki shorts and white polo shirt. His hair was perfectly combed to the side, and he hadn't shaved. She loved when he didn't shave. A shiver of anticipation ran up her spine as she thought about the scratchy feel of stubble on her cheek when they kissed. His eyes met hers, and when he smiled, it reached his eyes and brightened her heart.

Pepper fought against his tethered leash. The jars knocked against each other. Kurt stepped up his pace as she came around the table and reached for Pepper's leash.

"Hey, babe." He kissed her and took Pepper's leash from her hand. "Next summer we'll have to figure out a better plan for Pepper."

Her heart warmed at the way he'd come to care for Pepper.

"I'm so glad you're here. I missed you."

He draped his arm over her shoulder, and they sat behind the booth. "I missed you, too. Where's Carey?" He set the vase on the table.

She shrugged. "Not sure. Sometimes vendors don't show up."

"I brought him a few of my books and signed them for him. He seemed like he was into them, so I thought if he didn't want them, he could sell them on eBay or something. I'll put them in your van."

Flowers for me and books for Carey? Could you be more thoughtful?

"Next weekend is the last flea market for most vendors, so I'm not sure if he'll be back or not." She smelled the bouquet of brightly colored flowers and felt a little guilty for not telling him about Carey kissing her. "I need to tell you something."

"Uh-oh. Your voice has that worried sound to it."

She took a deep breath and blew it out slowly. "That night after Carey and I went to the beach, we went to the Beachcomber restaurant, and I drank too much."

"This doesn't sound like something I want to hear." Kurt's eyes filled with worry.

She touched his hand. "It's not bad, and I don't even know why I didn't mention it before, except that it didn't mean anything." She held his gaze. "Anyway, that night, he kissed me." She felt his arm go rigid, and she decided to continue so he understood what really happened. "I didn't kiss him back, I mean, how could I? I had thought about you all night. Anyway, I told him I didn't like him in that way, and he was fine with it. He didn't push for more or try anything else, and when I saw him the next weekend at the flea market, I told him about us."

He had that look of contemplation again.

"I didn't mean to hide it. I honestly just brushed it off and didn't think anything of it." The tension in his hand and arm relaxed.

He pulled her close and kissed the top of her head. "Thank you for telling me."

She looked up at him with a hopeful heart and a storm of worry in her stomach. "Are you mad?"

"No, babe. I'm glad you were honest with me, and quite frankly, he did what any guy would do. How could anyone go to the beach with you and not want to kiss you?" His gaze softened, and the edges of his lips curled up again. "You just scared me for a minute. The worry in your eyes had my mind running in some pretty dark directions."

"Oh God, Kurt. That's because of those dark and scary thrillers you write. I'd never do anything to hurt you. I'm not even the one who kissed. He kissed me." She hugged him around his middle. "Thank you for not being mad."

"I would have been mad if he'd pressured you or if you had done something more and kept it from me. But really, even if you had slept with him, we weren't really dating at the time, so while I might have been jealous, I wouldn't have had the right to get mad."

"Are you always this rational? Because I can tell you with one hundred percent certainty that if another woman kissed you, I'd be mad. Even if I didn't have the right to."

He leaned in close and kissed her. "Then it's a good thing that you're the only woman who has access to these lips. Now, let's change the subject before you convince me that I should be mad."

She had to smile, because that was a very practical, very *Kurt* thing to say. "I love these beautiful flowers. Thank you."

"I thought you might like them." He crouched to pet Pepper. "Does he need to be walked, or do you want to go over your stuff first?"

"Why don't I walk him first? That way we won't be interrupted."

A group of thirty-something women wearing colorful beach cover-ups and big floppy hats browsed the table.

"Don't these look delicious?" said a plump brunette.

"There are tasting spoons in the basket." Leanna pointed to a basket full of tiny plastic spoons. "And these are the tasters." She pointed to six open jars. "Feel free to sample as many as you like, but please take a new spoon for each taste, and when you're done, just drop the little spoons into the trash bin to your left."

"Hey, babe?" Kurt stood with Pepper's leash in his hand. "Why don't I take Pep for that walk? Do you want something from the snack bar?"

What I want, they don't serve at the snack bar. "I've got ice water in the cooler, but thanks." She noticed the women stealing glances at Kurt, and after a second of jealousy, a sense of pride replaced the unfamiliar emotion.

She helped a number of customers, and fifteen minutes later, when Kurt and Pepper returned, she was still answering questions. Kurt sat with his computer on his lap and wrote. She glanced at him a few times and was happy to find him engrossed in his writing. She didn't get a break for another half hour, and she felt a little guilty for keeping him waiting.

"Sorry. Today has been insane." She picked up a pad of paper from the table. "Look at this. More than fifty names and email addresses." She set it back down and shook her head as she sat beside him. "I don't even have a website, so that's on my list now, and I just started collecting names for a mailing list. All these things keep popping up, which means more work, but..."

He closed his laptop and set it beneath his chair. "I love watching you with the customers. You have such a pleasant way with them, and you really listen to everything they say. It's easy to see why your customers return. Besides your jam being luscious, you're warm and friendly, and it's hard not to want to be around you."

She thought he'd been writing, not paying attention to what she was doing. "You see all of that in me?"

"Leanna, I see so much more than that. You had hoped this would pan out, and it looks like it is. *You* did this, Leanna, and it's wonderful."

"I know. I can hardly believe it."

"Let's go over your brochures and everything before you get swamped again."

She pulled up the files on her laptop, and they reviewed them together.

"I started a marketing plan, if you can call it that, but I don't really know what I'm doing. I'm just listing places I can reach out to." She clicked on the document.

He scanned the information. "I'd say you know exactly what you're doing. You've got thirty-two stores here, with real research. Location, staff names, phone numbers, email addresses." His eyes widened. "This is damn good. It looks like you're taking this much further than just flea markets and a few grocers. This could really get big. Is that what you want?"

She shrugged. "I don't know, to be honest. I'm kind of going with the flow of it all. I may get turned down by every place I contact, so it's more of a wish list. I'm just happy to have found something that doesn't leave me wanting more." She leaned against him. "And someone who accepts me for me and doesn't leave me wanting more...or want more than I can give."

"I'm not surprised at all. You're talented and you're smart. I know you like to be a free spirit, but you're also very driven. Look at this, babe." He pointed to the list. "This...This is passion."

Guilt swept through her. Here he was being supportive, and she wanted to respond with, *I'll show you passion,* and kiss the hell out of him.

They finished reviewing the documents, and her mind drifted to thoughts of Kurt leaving and them being separated by all those empty miles.

"I'm really sorry about the wedding."

"I know you are, but there's no need to be. You're going to be so happy when Daisy Chain accepts your proposal. In eight more days, we'll be together again in New York, starting our life together."

She sat back, comforted by the thought, and watched a little boy and his father looking at T-shirts in the booth across from hers. "But you leave in four days, and that seems so soon. Do you ever wish summer could last forever?"

"I don't know. I like the change of seasons. Besides, if it lasted forever, I might spend a lot more time on the Cape, and I like knowing that if my agent needs something, or my publisher, editor, or PR rep, that I can be in their office in under an hour, and my family, too. My parents aren't getting any younger. I live close enough to be there quickly if there's an issue, or if everyone's getting together for dinner or an event. My brothers Dex and Sage and my sister, Siena, and their significant others all live nearby, and we try to get together for drinks or dinner in the city about once a month. And my other brother, Rush, and his girlfriend, Jayla, try to join us as often as they can. They're both competitive skiers, and even during the winter if they can fly in for dinner, they do." He shrugged. "Now I have the best of both worlds."

"I'm looking forward to meeting your family. I love my family, and we're close, but we all live very separate lives."

"How often do you see them?" His eyes were serious again.

"Oh, every few months, I guess. If I needed them, they'd be here in a heartbeat, and I'd do the same for them, but we're spread out in different states, so it's not like we can get together for dinner. Email and cell phones work wonders."

He pulled her close. "Well, you'll love my family, and I know they'll love you."

A young family stopped by her booth, and she excused herself to help them. She couldn't help but wonder what would happen if her business did take off. Could she manage it from two different states? Would she be able to find a place in New York to set up shop? She couldn't very well take over Kurt's kitchen for jam and jelly making. Could she?

If it were easy, it wouldn't be my *life.*

Chapter Twenty-Five

MONDAY MORNING KURT accepted Blue's proposal for the studio renovation. Blue was set to begin working in the evenings after wrapping up his day in Hyannis, and he'd work full-time over the weekends until the renovation was complete. With Kurt leaving on Thursday for Colorado, they were safe from Leanna finding out about the work being done as long as he stayed at her house, and with her friends leaving to go back home soon, he thought she'd enjoy spending more time with them.

Leanna was out with Amy taking the documents to a print shop in Hyannis, which gave Kurt the morning to write without distractions—only he sat staring at his computer screen like it was a foreign object. There was so much to do to prepare for Leanna to move in with him, and he began making a mental list: Clear space in the closet, the dresser, the bathroom. When Jackie called, he was thankful for the distraction.

"Hi, Jackie."

"Hi, Kurt. Are we going to make our deadline?"

"Yes. Didn't you get my confirmation email?" He knew she had.

"And are you on target for our meeting Monday?"

"We're still on. Jack's wedding is Friday, and I fly back into town Sunday. I plan on emailing the manuscript Thursday evening, which will give you the weekend to review and prepare to harangue me." He clicked on his manuscript. *Definitely doable.* With only the final scenes left to write, he should have it done and ready to go before Thursday evening, but he knew better than to shorten a deadline.

"If all my clients were as easy as you, I wouldn't have gray hair."

"You don't have gray hair now."

"And that's the beauty of a good colorist. Can't wait to read your latest."

He ended the call, and when his mind drifted back to house preparations, he gave Leanna's laid-back attitude a test ride as his own. *Don't stress over it. I'll clean out the drawers and stuff when I get home and it'll all be fine.* Kurt repositioned himself in the chair. Sweat beaded his upper lip, and he gazed up at the sky, wondering why it suddenly felt ten degrees hotter.

The hell with it. He felt like he was wearing a sweater two sizes too small and realized—*accepted*—that there were some things he couldn't adapt as his own. The idea of Leanna walking into his house and not feeling at home made him worry, and worrying would hinder his creative ability. He glanced at his manuscript on the computer screen. He needed to get back to it.

Baby steps. Moderation.

He called Siena. "Hey, I need a favor."

"Sure."

"Leanna is moving in with me when I get back home, and—"

"Moving in? So you didn't break up? Good. I was worried. Not that I know her or anything, but you sounded happy, and…Oh, Kurt I'm so happy for you."

"You two will get along great." He smiled at the thought of them spending time together. He was excited for his family to meet Leanna and even more excited to build a life with her.

"Is she coming to the wedding?"

"No. She can't reschedule her meeting, but I won't get back into New York until late Sunday night, and she's coming in Monday. Would you mind helping me to rearrange some things so she has room?"

"You really trust me to go through your drawers and stuff?" Siena asked.

He pictured her thinly manicured brows raised. "I trust you, Siena, and don't worry; you can snoop all you want. I'm an open book."

She sighed. "Like I don't know that already? Jeez, Kurt. I'm not going to snoop. I was just teasing you. Okay. Tell me what you want me to do and I'll do it."

"You're a lifesaver. Mom has an extra key to my house, so you can get that from her."

"Kurt, I've had your key for two years."

He could practically hear her rolling her eyes.

"Right. Sorry. I'm a little sidetracked."

"Do you mind if Mom comes with me? She'd love to help get your house ready for a woman."

"Of course she would." The thought of the two of them working side by side to prepare for Leanna was an amusing one. He pictured them passing comments about how it was about time he found a real girlfriend.

"That's fine. Just don't go overboard. I was thinking about making room in the closet, the bathroom, the dresser. You know what to do."

"Yeah, yeah. It'll be fun. Can we get extra stuff? Do you care if we put some things she might want, like scented soaps, body wash, that kind of stuff?"

He sat back and looked out at the water as the tide rolled back in. "She probably has her own stuff that she'll bring with her, but sure, go for it. Whatever you want. Just don't turn my house into a pink, fluffy chick's place."

"Don't worry. I know you like things a certain way. I'm so excited to finally meet her."

"She's pretty great."

"Can you text me a picture of you guys?"

This gave him pause. He hadn't had a real girlfriend in forever, and he rarely used his cell phone. He felt a step behind in the boyfriend category. He should have thought about pictures before Siena did. "I don't have one, believe it or not, but I'll take one tonight and send it over."

"Good. I can't wait to see it. What's she like? Is she methodical and quiet like you? Does she organize her sock drawer by color?" Siena laughed.

"I don't do that."

"I know, but it's funny."

"Ha-ha. No, she's not methodical. In fact, she's just the opposite. She's a free spirit. She isn't a planner."

"She's a pantser? Wow. How does she feel about Mr. Plan Ahead?"

"She loves me, Siena, and yes, we're a little different, but we're happy." He wasn't sure they were really all that different. Underneath her disorganization and beneath his scheduled lifestyle, they were very much alike.

He and Siena caught up for a few more minutes, and by the time they ended their call, Kurt's mind was ready to focus. He set his fingers on the keyboard and disappeared into the final chapters of *Dark Times*.

Chapter Twenty-Six

KURT'S LAST DAYS on the Cape flew by too fast for Leanna. She wanted to draw them out and eke out every second she could with Kurt. Between preparing for the meeting with Daisy Chain, working with Bella, Jenna, and Amy to figure out how to put a WordPress website together—which was a two-bottle-of-wine job—and spending time with Kurt, she felt the end of summer closing in on her. He'd gone to his house earlier in the day and closed it up for the summer, since he was going back to New York straight from Jack's wedding in Colorado, and when he'd returned, she'd seen a shadow of sadness in his eyes.

    She and Kurt had spent their time at her cottage so she could also have time with the girls, and she appreciated that concession. He seemed content anywhere as long as they were together, and it was one of the things she loved most about him. It was surprising how similar they really were.

They were packing the car with blankets and beach chairs to go to the drive-in theater Wednesday evening when Bella and Jenna stopped by, still dressed in their bathing suits and sundresses.

"Drive-in?" Bella eyed the blankets.

"Yeah. Should be fun. Kurt's never been." Leanna watched Kurt coming up the road with Pepper, and she was touched by how he'd come to care for her dog. "He's a good guy, huh?"

"You're kidding, right? He's amazing."

"Yeah. I know. I'm so lucky."

Jenna sidled up to Leanna. "Why don't you take the van and get down and dirty at the drive-in like a couple of teenagers?"

Leanna laughed. "I swear, we are like a couple of teenagers, but I really just want to cuddle up beside him tonight. I hate that he's leaving tomorrow." She closed the trunk of his car and then whispered, "Besides, we can get down and dirty in the cottage later."

Jenna smirked. "Just remember to close your windows."

Leanna blushed. She and Kurt had forgotten to close the windows on Monday evening, and Jenna had been armed with a litany of jokes the next morning.

"No worries there, eavesdropper."

"Eavesdropper? Please, they heard you in P-town." Bella put an arm around Leanna and the other around Jenna. "I'm going to miss you guys this winter. Maybe we should plan a get-together over the holidays."

"We talk about that every year, but with our schedules..." Jenna reminded her. "Maybe we'll get together for Kurt and Leanna's wedding."

"You guys have it all figured out, don't you?" Leanna reached for Kurt's hand as he approached. *Yeah, I'd so marry you.* Her breath caught in her throat. *Oh God. I would. I really would.*

"Hey, babe. Ready to grab dinner?" He ran his hand through his hair and glanced at Bella and Jenna. "You guys live in your bathing suits."

"Why not?" Bella twirled in her dress. "We have to leave this weekend, so we're making the most of it."

"You'll take good care of my girl, won't you?"

He said it teasingly, but Leanna knew he liked that they were there with her. He'd told her last night that he was glad she had people who cared about her as much as he did.

"You know it," Bella answered.

"If you were dressed and if Leanna didn't mind, I'd invite you to come with us." He glanced at Leanna.

"You would?" She could cuddle with him and spend time with the girls—*a perfect night.*

"I'm sure I'm not the only one who is going to miss you when we leave, so sure, why not?" He shrugged.

Amy came out of her cottage and crouched down beside Pepper to love him up. "Hi, guys."

"Do you guys want to come?" Leanna asked.

"Heck, yeah," Bella answered. "Amy, drive-in with Kurt and Leanna?"

"On their last date night? We can't do that." Amy squinted and shook her head like they'd lost their minds. She was always the voice of reason.

"I'm going to be with Leanna every night after she comes to New York. I'd feel guilty if I didn't share one of her last nights with you guys." He folded Leanna in his arms. "Unless there's something I don't know about the drive-in." He nuzzled against her neck.

"See? I told you." Jenna adjusted her dress over her cleavage.

"Told you what?" Kurt asked.

Leanna felt her cheeks warm. "Nothing. Jenna's being dirty."

"I told her to take the van and make out in the back during the movie." Jenna grinned.

"Now, that does sound fun." He kissed Leanna again, and a shiver ran down her back. "Really, she has very little time with you guys. You decide. I'm easy. I'm going to run inside and grab a drink of water before we go."

"Hear that? He's easy." Jenna watched him walk inside.

Leanna slapped her arm. "Hey, he's taken." She knew from spending time with him that he was anything but *easy*. Whether they were out in public or spending time in private, if he wasn't writing, Leanna was the focus of his attention. She glanced at Pepper panting at the door, watching Kurt. *Me and Pepper.* Leanna had thought that her life would include only her, Pepper, and her Seaside friends for years to come, and she was so glad to have been wrong.

HAVING NEVER BEEN to the Wellfleet Drive-In, Kurt wasn't sure what to expect, but it wasn't kids running around on the playground equipment and families backing their trucks and vans into parking places and piling in under blankets and pillows like one big slumber party, or setting up beach chairs behind their cars with blankets spread out on the asphalt and coolers full of food.

The drive-in played a family-friendly movie at eight o'clock and a movie for adults at ten fifteen. When Leanna had first mentioned that she wanted to watch both movies, he'd questioned the decision. He wasn't exactly a kid movie type of guy. In fact, he couldn't remember ever being into kids' movies, even as a boy, but she said it was part of the drive-in experience, and he'd agreed, because she was, after all, Leanna. He'd brought his computer, and if the children's movie was too painful to watch, he could start outlining his next book while she watched the first movie. He'd sent his manuscript to Jackie earlier in the day, and he'd touched base with Blue and was happy that the work was taking shape. Now he was looking forward to relaxing and watching the second movie, *Prisoners* with Hugh Jackman.

Leanna drove her van so they could all ride together, and she expertly backed into a parking place; then Bella, Amy, and Jenna jumped out of the van and joined her in setting up the beach chairs, complete with pillows, blankets, and bowls of snacks. Kurt and Pepper watched them create a comfortable slumber party of their own, and the whole scene made him smile.

The couple to their right had two small children, both dressed in pajamas. He heard the father tell the children that after the movie, they would go to sleep in the van and they'd drive home after *Mommy and Daddy* watched their movie.

What have I been missing?

He wouldn't have pegged himself as a guy who might enjoy this type of Brady Bunch environment, with the noise and the chaos of lines and crowds hanging out by the snack bar. Now, here with Leanna, he found himself wondering what it might be like to bring his own children there one day. *Their children.*

Kurt left his computer in the van and joined the others on the chairs behind the van. Pepper settled in by his feet. It was a dark night with very few stars, and when the enormous movie screen came to life, it lit up the parking lot. The din of the crowds quieted as information about the theater, including emergency exits from the parking lot and a snack bar commercial that must have been shot in the 1960s filled the screen. Leanna's eyes were wide, and the hint of a smile played across her lips. Jenna, Bella, and Amy sat with popcorn in between them, eyes glued to the previews. The brisk night air carried the scent of popcorn, and every now and again a parent could be heard shushing their child. Kurt probably would have gone forever without seeing a drive-in movie, and it would have been a shame. This...Being with friends and family, coming together without a computer or the Internet, but in real life, in real time...This was more meaningful than the extra hours he'd spent on his manuscript throughout the years. Leanna had opened another door to the world for him. There were probably a hundred things he had scoffed at over the years that, with Leanna, he might see differently, and he couldn't wait to try them all.

Disney's *Frozen* was playing, and by the middle of

the movie, Leanna had moved her blankets in front of Kurt's chair and built herself a comforter platform so she could sit between his legs and lean back against his chest.

And he loved it.

The coconut and berry scent of her shampoo—which he now knew was Aussie Aussome Volume and came in a purple bottle—and the feel of her body pressed against him in a relaxed, completely content manner, was something he'd never forget.

He remembered the picture for Siena and pulled his phone from his pocket.

"Do you mind if I take a picture for my sister?"

Leanna climbed right up on his lap. "Bella," she whispered, then waved her closer. "Take our picture on his phone?"

Bella wore a sweatshirt that looked two sizes too big along with a pair of jeans. Her hair fell thick and wild around her face. She squinted as she lined up the picture. "Okay, smile."

Leanna quickly planted a kiss on Kurt's cheek.

"Perfect!" Bella laughed.

"Sneak," he teased.

Jenna and Amy ran behind Kurt's chair and crouched.

"Take another," Jenna hollered.

"Shh," Amy chided her.

Bella snapped a few more pictures.

"Want me to take one with all of you?" the man to their left asked.

Bella handed him Kurt's phone. "Yes, please." Then she crouched beside Leanna, and the stranger took a few more pictures.

"Thank you." Bella retrieved the phone, and the girls giggled at the pictures.

In each picture, except for the one with Leanna's surprise kiss, Kurt was caught looking at Leanna, and even he could see the love in his eyes.

I'm a goner.

Bella and the girls texted the picture from his phone to each of theirs, and eventually the phone ended up back in his hand. He texted a few pictures to Siena.

"I love you," he whispered to Leanna.

"I saw it in the pictures." She caressed his cheek, and he leaned in to her palm. "Besides, you must to put up with my friends."

She curled up on his lap and wrapped her arms around his neck, then rested her cheek on his shoulder.

"I could stay like this forever."

Forever sounded pretty damn good to him.

THEY RETURNED TO the cottage after midnight, and Kurt wondered how in the hell he was supposed to accept this night as their last night together until Monday. He wanted to wrap himself around Leanna and remain there until, by some act of magic, it was Monday and the days they were apart had passed.

Leanna came out of the bathroom wearing a black lace cami and matching panties. Her hair was mussed, sexily framing her beautiful face.

Okay, maybe around and *inside you until Monday.*

"That movie was really kind of disturbing," Leanna

said as she climbed onto the bed beside him. "The idea of those little girls and all the children before them being abducted. It's terrifying."

He reached for her. "It is disturbing, but it was a movie, babe. It was supposed to be scary."

She traced a vein on the back of his hand. "Do you ever think about having kids?"

"Until I met you, I'd never met a woman I'd want to live with, much less have children with. But yeah, I do want a family. What about you?" Kurt was surprised that he didn't break out into a cold sweat at the mention of having children. Wasn't that what guys were supposed to do when their girlfriends mentioned having children or settling down?

She shrugged and began drawing circles on her thigh.

He wanted to draw circles on her thigh. With his tongue.

"I've never really thought about it in terms of when or how many, but I do want to have children someday." She looked up at him then, the edges of her lips barely curved and her eyes sleepily seductive. "The thought of keeping them safe is a little frightening, isn't it?"

He pulled her close, and she ran her fingers over his bare stomach. "If I ran from things that were terrifying, I'd never have become a writer, and I might never have allowed myself to go out with you."

"I'm frightening?"

He kissed her forehead. "No, babe. You're perfect. The thought of anything coming between me and my writing was what terrified me. But you've made me realize that there's a lot more to life than being the best thriller writer. And with you, I feel like I can enjoy both. You defied the terror, and if you want children someday, then we won't let fear hold us back there, either."

"You know, I came to the Cape expecting to have a fun summer and maybe find a career, but I never expected to find you. Us."

Kurt slid the lacy strap of her cami off of her sun-bronzed shoulder and kissed her silky skin.

"I expected to finish a book in complete solitude." He slid the lacy strap from her other shoulder, and her cami slid down her chest and came to rest on the arc of her breasts. "I never expected to find you." He kissed her neck. "Or us." He kissed the tender skin just below her collarbone. "And now..." He held the edge of her cami between his finger and thumb and planted a trail of kisses across the tops of her breasts. "I can't imagine going a day without you."

Leanna's breath hitched, and he slid his arm around her back, drawing her body closer, her lips a breath away. Her hazel eyes narrowed, full of anticipation; his body ached with impatience. He kissed her lightly. Her tender, warm lips pressed against his; her tongue moved slowly, searching, wanting. Her hips rocked into him, pleading for more. He could feel how much she wanted him in her touch, in the cadence of her breath. He sensed her need, and even stronger, he felt his own need growing thick and hard beneath his briefs and in his heart. He held back, relishing in the desire that drew them closer and made his muscles cord tight. She kissed him harder, urgently seeking his reciprocation. He wanted to please her so badly he ached—but he held back. Kurt's heart pounded inside his chest as he lowered her to the bed beneath him. Her fingers grazed his jawline; then she cupped the back of his head and deepened their kiss. After tonight they had three nights without each other. Seventy-two hours of remembering their last night together. Kurt intended to give Leanna a night she'd never forget.

He drew back from the kiss and looked deeply into her eyes. "Can you feel how much I want you? How much I love you?" He spread her arms out to her sides and held them there, then kissed the inside of her elbow, her forearm, and down to the very tips of her fingers. He lingered there, taking each delicate finger into his mouth and drawing it out slowly, sensually along his tongue. He felt her pulse speed up, saw it in her writhing hips.

"God, yes," she whispered.

"Relax," he whispered back as he moved to her other arm and dragged his tongue along her hot skin, shoulder to elbow. He licked and teased until she fought against his restraint.

"Are you okay?" he whispered.

She nodded. "You're making me crazy."

"I'm loving you. There's a difference." He turned his attention back to her sexy, delicious body. One strong hand on each of her arms held her to the mattress. "If you tell me to let go, I will."

She shook her head. "No. No. Don't stop."

He licked the sensitive skin below her earlobe. "Feel my hot breath on you." He ran his tongue down her neck to her deep cleavage, then blew lightly on her wet skin.

"Oh God," she whispered in one long breath.

Kurt used one hand to hold her and the other to slip out of his briefs; then he pressed his hard length against her thigh. "Feel how much I want you."

"Oh God, yes."

He released her arms, and she remained open to him as he splayed his hands and ran them down her ribs, her hips, and over her lace panties. She fisted her hands against the sheets.

"Relax. Surrender to my touch," he whispered. His hands grazed the front of her legs, feeling goose bumps pebble beneath his palms, and he came down on top of her, pressing his chest to hers, his hips to her center, feeling his balls against the hot, moist lace between her legs. He shuddered with need as he lifted her hands over her head. She was breathing hard, her breasts heaving against his chest as he covered her mouth with his and kissed her greedily, gyrating his hips against her wetness, her desire.

He pulled back, leaving her breathless. "Watch me as I love you."

He slithered down her body and spread her legs, then licked her through her lace panties. Leanna closed her eyes and arched her neck back. He rolled the top of her panties down low on her beautiful, rounded hips, then followed the line of flesh against lace with his tongue.

Leanna moaned, sending a chill down his spine. He ached to be inside of her. She was beautiful, perfect, sweet. She was his.

He drew her cami down her body, gathered her panties with the cami, and tossed them away from the bed. He took her taut, pink nipples into his mouth, flicking her nipple with his tongue, and was rewarded with a litany of sexy little noises of pleasure. He loved them, hungrily sucked them and grazed her flesh with his sharp teeth. She sucked in a breath, rocking her hips into him again and again. He met her hips with his and felt her wetness teasing him, taunting him as she writhed beneath him, angling for more.

"Please. Please, Kurt." She looked into his eyes and thrust her hips against his.

"It'll be worth the wait. I promise." He pressed his cheek to hers again, smelling her scent, heightening his arousal. "I'm going to lick you." He kissed her cheek, then whispered again, "To suck you." He buried his hands in her hair and said in a guttural voice, "To devour you."

She whimpered a sweet, sexy, sensual noise, and he moved down her body again and spread her legs wide, then did just as he promised, holding her thighs open, her hips to the mattress, until she surrendered to the pleasure, her toes curled under, and she cried out his name.

"Oh God. Yes!"

She fought against his strength, trying to arch in to him. He knew she wanted more—needed more—as her juices flowed and her inner muscles pulsed with heat. Holding her thighs apart, he spread her lips with his thumbs and brought his mouth to her again, bringing her right up over the edge, until she was crying out again.

"Too...much." She tossed her head from side to side, breathing hard. "You. I need you. Oh God, Kurt. Please."

He captured her pleas with his mouth and drove into her. Hard. Over and over as another orgasm ripped through her body and she clawed his back, crying out as he moved his legs to the outside of hers, pressing her thighs together, thrusting into her tight, wet center, feeling her body grip him, swallow him.

"Oh God. Jesus." Her eyes sprang open. "Holy. Shit. Kur...Oh...My...Go—"

A bolt of heat shot from his thighs right through his groin and pierced his chest as he followed her into the depths of ecstasy.

Chapter Twenty-Seven

THURSDAY MORNING FOUND them, despite Leanna's wishes for a few more days with Kurt. She held Pepper's leash so tightly that her fingernails made moon-shaped crescents in her skin as she watched Kurt put his bags in the trunk of his car. She thought she'd prepared herself for his leaving. They were going to be apart for only a few days, and hell, she hadn't even known him a month ago. She should be fine.

She was the farthest thing from fine.

Lonesomeness coiled low in her belly, and her heart ached for him. She memorized the sound of his voice, the smell of him. She missed his touch, and he wasn't even gone yet.

Kurt closed the trunk and hugged her for the millionth time that morning. "You're going to do great. Daisy Chain's execs will love your products, and they'll love you, and...And I love you." He kissed her softly.

"I'm going to miss you so much."

"I'm..." *Oh God, really? Don't cry. Please don't cry.* She swallowed past the lump in her throat that had swallowed her voice. "I'm going to miss you, too. I'll call as soon as the meeting's over and let you know how it goes. Oh wait. I can't. You'll be at Jack's wedding. You should call me when you're done. When is the wedding? What time?" She ran her finger in circles along the door of his car as she spoke.

He pulled her close again and brought her hand to his lips, kissed it, then held it tightly in his. "Babe, take a breath."

She did. A deep one.

And then another.

Nope. Her throat still wanted to close, and those damn tears still wanted to fall.

"The wedding is Friday at ten, and I'll text as soon as I can break away. Then you can call when you're free. But today's only Thursday, so I assume we'll talk tonight once I'm in and settled, right?"

She nodded, still untrusting of her voice.

Bella, Amy, and Jenna walked out of Amy's cottage and joined them with solemn faces.

"Aw. It's so sad to see lovebirds part." Amy pulled at the hem of her sundress.

Leanna nodded.

"Don't worry. We'll take care of her," Amy continued. "We're all leaving Sunday, so you'll only have one night to be sad, Leanna, and Tony's here, so you can cry on his shoulder."

Kurt shot a curious look at Leanna.

"Don't worry. They're just friends," Jenna said as

she patted Kurt's arm. "Unfortunately, Tony would never fool around with a woman he's known as long as he's known us."

"Or with a woman who lives so close. Trust me. I've tried." Amy's cheeks flushed pink.

"You have?" Leanna's eyes widened.

"Once. Remember that night we each drank a bottle of Skinnygirl Margaritas?" Amy crossed her arms. "I wasn't exactly at my best that night. Or the next morning."

The memory of the morning after came back to Leanna, and she almost smiled, save for the sadness that gripped her emotions and tugged her smile back into a frown. "I remember."

Kurt squeezed Leanna's hand. "I want to grab some ice water. I'll be right back out. You ladies hug or reminisce about making moves on Tony, or whatever." He smiled at Amy.

Leanna watched him walk away in his jeans and white linen, button-down shirt hanging perfectly from his broad shoulders—the shoulders she'd clawed at so desperately the night before that she'd left scratches on his tanned skin.

Bella brushed against her shoulder. "Forget to close the windows last night?"

Leanna's eyes widened. Her hand flew to her mouth. "No. Oh my God! Shit." She spun around and saw Tony's curtains blowing in the breeze inside his cottage. "Oh my God, you guys!"

Jenna stifled a laugh. "Remind me to put a lock on the outside of your windows, and when we see Kurt's car in the driveway, the girls and I will be on mission control." She winked. "We'll have your back."

Leanna covered her face. "That's great, but. Oh. My. God. You know Tony heard us." She dropped her hands and searched her friends' amused faces. "Did you guys hear us?"

They shared a knowing glance.

"Everything?" Leanna asked with a thin voice.

Bella laughed. "Well, not everything. He must whisper or something, because we couldn't make out anything he said."

Leanna shook her head. "You were actually eavesdropping?"

"No!" The smile on Bella's lips betrayed her. "I was bringing ice cream to Jenna because she had a freak-out over a rock being out of place or something—"

"It was sand all over my floor." Jenna tucked her hair behind her ear. "I couldn't get it clean no matter how hard I tried. It was sticking to my feet."

Bella rolled her eyes. "Whatever. Anyway, we really just heard something like, *Holy shit. Kur...Oh...My...Go—*"

Kurt joined them with a wide smile. "Did I hear my name?"

"No!" they all said in unison.

Leanna's throat tightened again, and she pushed past the embarrassment. "So you're sure that guy will take your car back to your cottage and everything? I can do it for you."

"No. Don't be silly. I wouldn't waste your time on that. Besides, Savannah's brother Treat hooked me up with Smitty, his caretaker, a few months ago. He and his wife are wonderful, and they'll take care of it.

Enjoy your time with the girls, and..." He glanced down at Pepper, panting happily at his feet. He crouched and picked up Pepper, who made quick work of licking his cheeks. "And Pep."

He pulled Leanna close and kissed her again. "I love you, and I'm so proud of you for what you've already accomplished. Enjoy the next few days."

Leanna nodded, concentrating on keeping the tears burning her eyes at bay.

Kurt set Pepper down and embraced Leanna again. "I wish I wasn't leaving." He embraced Bella. "I'm so glad Leanna has you guys here with her."

"So are we," Amy said.

He hugged Amy. "Don't worry. You'll find your own Tony."

Then he moved to Jenna, who opened her arms wide and grinned. "I have been waiting to have this man against my body since Leanna first brought him home." She laughed.

Kurt shook his head and squeezed her tight. "Not so thrilling, is it?"

"Oh, I don't know about that," Jenna teased.

Amy swatted her.

He hugged Leanna again. "Don't cry, babe. It's only a few days, and we can do a few days. We can do anything knowing we'll be together at the end of it."

Ten minutes later, Leanna watched him drive away, and a single tear escaped down her cheek. She felt Bella's arm across her shoulder, then Jenna's around her back. Amy opened her arms and walked toward her. The group hug was exactly what she needed. If only it could last until Monday.

"Come on. You can tell us all about the *oh my God* moment." Bella took her hand and led her inside the cottage.

"I'll do no such thing, but...*oh my God*. That's all I'm saying." Pepper ran into the bedroom before Leanna could take his leash off, and she went after him. She stopped cold at the sight of a Shop Therapy bag in the center of her bed. She found a card inside with a picture of a big red heart on the front and pressed it to her chest.

"Hey, do you have any—" Amy came to her side. "Aw. He left you a card? What does it say?"

Bella and Jenna joined them in the bedroom.

Leanna eyed them, wondering if she needed privacy, in case he'd written something intimate inside the card.

"Open it," Jenna urged. She reached for the bag, and Leanna snagged it.

She'd never have privacy with her friends around, and that was okay. She needed them more than she needed privacy.

"One sec." She opened the card close to her chest and read the handwritten note.

My sweet, smart, not at all awkward Leanna,
I didn't realize that leaving you for a few days would mean leaving my heart behind, but apparently it is now tied so closely to yours (and Pepper's) that it refused to come with me. Keep it safe and warm until we're together again.
I love you,

Kurt

PS: Don't be nervous about Daisy Chain. You're perfect in every way, and if they don't see that as clearly as I do, then they don't deserve your Sweet Treats. I hope you feel as beautiful and confident in the dress as I know you'll look. Xox

Dress? She reached into the bag.

"What did the card say?" Bella took it from Leanna's fingertips and read it aloud.

"Aw, that is so sweet." Amy's hand covered her heart.

Leanna held up the aqua tie-dyed dress she'd admired while they were in Provincetown. "I can't believe he bought it. When did he even have time?"

"That is wicked cute!" Jenna rubbed the cotton between her fingers and thumb.

"When he told you he was writing, I bet," Bella said. "That man. Mm-mm-mm. He is something, Leanna."

Clutching the dress to her chest, she glanced at the bed, then the card, then Pepper. "Tell me something I don't know."

IT WAS ALMOST nine when Kurt finally arrived at Treat Braden's house in Weston, Colorado. Savannah's older brothers Treat and Rex lived on properties adjacent to her father's ranch, and Kurt's family would be staying with them. Kurt, Sage and Kate, and Siena and Cash were staying with Treat, and Dex and Ellie and Rush and Jayla were staying at Rex's house. Jack, Savannah, and Joanie and James Remington were staying with Hal, Savannah's father. Earlier in the day he'd confirmed with Blue that the renovations were progressing well, and he'd received several texts from Siena confirming his arrival time throughout the day, as if the plane might suddenly divert and take him to Timbuktu.

He sat in the rented Lexus in Treat's driveway and pulled out his cell phone. He and Leanna had texted throughout the afternoon, and she'd sent him a picture of her wearing the dress he'd bought her. He pulled it up before calling her. The aqua color and her wide smile lit up the screen. The scooped neckline exposed a sexy path of tanned skin, and the dress fit perfectly over her curves—not too tight, not too loose—and ended midthigh. *Luscious Leanna*. She sure as hell was, and he missed her so much his heart ached.

He pressed her speed-dial number, and she answered on the first ring.

"FaceTime. FaceTime," she said excitedly.

He laughed and pushed the FaceTime icon. Her beautiful smiling lips and hazel eyes filled the screen.

"There you are," he said.

"We all are. Look." She turned the phone, and on the screen he saw Bella, Jenna, and Amy waving. He could hear their laughter as if he were there with them.

He wished he were.

"This is Tony," Leanna said as she moved the phone toward a handsome man's face that filled the screen.

Kurt took stock of him in three seconds flat. Wide smile, dark tan, longish, sun-streaked, brownish blond hair that fell almost to his eyes, broad shoulders, and eyes that didn't hold a threat. Kurt had never been a jealous man. He assumed that not having a steady girlfriend helped in that regard. Despite the lack of threat in Tony's eyes, his gut clenched.

Tony waved. "Hey, man. Sorry we didn't get to meet while you were here. I slept for, like, two days. Jet lag, man, it's a killer. I was whipped."

"Nice to meet you. I'm sure we'll connect the next time Leanna and I are up." He couldn't help it; he had to claim her.

"Great. I'm looking forward to it. According to these goofballs, you're, like, Mr. Perfect. I'd be glad to break you of that nasty habit."

Tony laughed, and Kurt couldn't help but like his easy nature.

"I fear they have a limited stock of men to compare me to. I'm far from perfect, and trust me, they think the world of you, too."

Tony lifted his beer with a nod, and Leanna's face appeared on the screen again.

"Hey, babe. I just got to Treat's, and I just wanted to say hi before I went in. I don't know what they have planned for tonight, but I'll text you when I settle in for the night, and if you're still up, you can call me."

Three hard knocks on the car window drew his attention away from Leanna as she spoke.

"Sounds great. Thank you for the dress, and I love the card."

"Hold on, babe," he said as he stepped from the car, and Siena flew into his arms.

"Oh my God! I've missed you so much! I can't

believe you're finally here. I've waited all day to see you. Look how tan you are. Everyone's inside and—"

"Siena." He held up his phone and wiggled it.

"Hi, Siena!" Leanna said loudly.

"Oh my God! Leanna?" Siena's baby blues widened as she took the phone from Kurt's hand. "Hi. It's so nice to see you. Wow! You're really pretty." Siena wore a pair of white shorts and a pink T-shirt. She looked happy and full of life, reminding him of Leanna.

"Thank you. So are you. I'm sorry I didn't make it to the wedding, but I was honored to have been asked."

Kurt shook his head and smiled at the instant kinship between his sister and the woman he loved. He heard the smile in Leanna's voice, and despite wanting to give them time to talk, he was anxious to see her face. He grabbed his bags from the backseat and leaned against the car until Siena and Leanna paused to take a breath; then he reached for the phone.

"I'll give you back to Kurt, but I can't wait to meet you." Siena held a thumbs-up at Kurt.

"Me too." He heard the smile in Leanna's voice.

"I love her," Siena whispered when she handed him the phone. "I got your house all set up. She'll love it."

"Thanks, Siena. I'll be in as soon as I'm off." He turned his attention back to Leanna. "So, now you've met my sister."

Siena waved over her head as she hurried inside.

"And I love her. Oh my God, Kurt, she's so nice."

"Yeah, she's a pistol." Siena was nice, and funny,

and pushy—and he loved all of those qualities in her. She was also loving, sweet, and so in love with Cash that it practically dripped from her pores when she was around him. He wondered if his siblings would see something similar in him when he was around Leanna. He couldn't imagine how they could see anything else.

"I know you have to get inside with your family. I wish so much I was there with you. I feel like I'm missing out on such an important event, and I miss you like crazy. I can't imagine going to sleep alone tonight. I'm going to have to cuddle up to Pepper."

God, I love you. "At least you have Pepper. I'll have to be content thinking about you." He saw the front door open, and his younger brother Sage stepped onto the porch of the two-story, stone and cedar-sided home and waved. Kurt waved back, watching Sage approach in his cargo shorts and tank top. He was as religious about his exercise as Kurt was, and it showed in his powerful frame. "Sage just came out on the porch, which means he either wants a peek at you or he's anxious to see me, and since he's walking across the driveway, I have a feeling—"

Sage snagged the phone from his hand.

"Dude," Kurt snapped, although he knew his smile betrayed him. He was enjoying this new and different attention from his siblings, and he was proud to show off Leanna. He knew his family would love her as much as he did. She was easy to love.

"Leanna? Hi, I'm Sage. I wanted to meet you for myself, even if over FaceTime." Sage's dark hair had grown in thick and wavy over the summer.

"Hi, Sage. It's nice to meet you," Leanna said.

"You, too. Sorry to interrupt, but, well, what else are brothers for?"

Leanna laughed as Sage opened his arms and embraced Kurt. "Sorry, bro. Just wanted to say hi to you both. I won't let anyone else come out, but I couldn't resist." He picked up Kurt's bags and carried them inside.

"Sorry, babe."

"It's okay. Have fun with your family. They seem really nice."

He heard Bella shouting in the background. "Send one of those brothers over here for me."

He laughed. "Tell Bella they're all taken. I was the last of the available Remingtons, but I think Cash has a few single brothers." He thought of Blue working on the studio and debated telling Leanna about the work he was having done, then quickly decided to surprise her with a trip to the Cape once the renovations were complete. *A nice long weekend with no writing. Just us. And Pepper.* He couldn't even believe he was looking forward to not writing, but the thought stuck with him like glue.

"Ignore her." Leanna rolled her eyes. "I love you. Have fun with your family."

"I love you too. I'll text you later."

Kurt ended the call, and as he crossed the driveway, he braced himself for the razz of a lifetime.

Chapter Twenty-Eight

LEANNA WOULD GIVE her right arm to be an organized and efficient person for one day. Just today. Hell, she'd take a few hours if she could get it. Just long enough to gather her thoughts, the basket of jams and bread, the brochures and lists she'd picked up from the printer—which looked so professional that she didn't feel worthy of presenting them—and make it to her meeting on time. She was already late when a delivery truck blocked her driveway.

Great. The one time I actually park in my driveway. She closed the cottage door and shushed Pepper through the window. He'd been moping around all morning, running from room to room, as if he were trying to figure out where Kurt had gone, and now she felt guilty for leaving him alone. *Kurt wouldn't have left him alone.*

She put her supplies in the van and went around to the driver's side door of the delivery van. "I'm in a hurry. Can you please just pull your van up or back a little?"

Carey smiled down at her. "Hey there."

"What are you doing in this? Where's your van?" She stepped back and realized it was a fruit bouquet delivery service van.

He shrugged. "I'm doing deliveries to make a little extra money. That's why I wasn't at the flea market last Sunday. I've got a delivery for you." Carey climbed out of the van and walked leisurely to the back of the van in his khaki shorts and company polo shirt, complete with a logo over the breast pocket. She had a hard time reconciling his attire to the beach boy she knew.

"Me?" *What are you up to?*

He returned with an enormous fruit bouquet, complete with chocolate-dipped strawberries and a balloon that read, GOOD LUCK.

"My bet is that it's from Kurt, but what do I know?" He shrugged. "You look totally hot, by the way."

Leanna looked down at her dress. "Oh crap. I'm so late. Thanks, Carey. Hey, I've had a great time with you this summer. Will you be at the flea market next summer?"

Amy came out of her cabin. "Wow. What did you get?"

Leanna held up the fruit bouquet.

"I really need to go," Leanna reminded him.

"Oh, sorry." He climbed back into the van. "I'm not sure if I'll be here next summer or not." He shrugged. "Guess we'll find out next May. We can keep in touch over text."

"Sounds good. Thanks for all your help this summer, Carey." *I'm late. I'm late. I'm late.* She hated rushing their last conversation of the summer after he'd been so patient with her and watched her booth while she walked Pepper, but she would hate herself if she messed up her chance with Daisy Chain.

"No prob. And tell Kurt I'm sorry for kissing you." He waved to Amy.

"Oh gosh, wait!" Leanna ran to her van and retrieved the books Kurt had brought for Carey. "I almost forgot. He brought these to the flea market for you. They're signed."

"Awesome. That's so cool of him. Here's to a great summer."

As Carey drove off, Leanna handed the bouquet to Amy and opened the card.

"Kurt?" Amy asked.

"Who else would ever send me anything?" Leanna read the card, "*Go get 'em. I love you, K.*" She smiled at Amy. "He's the best, and I gotta run. Would you mind taking these in and maybe playing with Pepper a little? He's going a little nutty without Kurt."

"I don't blame him. Good luck, Lea. You'll do great."

She drove away with the card from Kurt on the passenger seat and she already felt better, late or not. Pepper had Amy, and in a few days, she'd be with Kurt.

HAL BRADEN'S RANCH encompassed a few hundred acres of rolling pastures set against the backdrop of the majestic Colorado Mountains. The air was crisper than at the Cape, fresher, cleaner. The grassy yard fell away to the east, ending at a large barn, and just beyond, there were more horse pastures, bordered on the far side by a thick forest.

The yard beside the house had been set up for Jack and Savannah's wedding, reminding Kurt of the last time he'd been at the Bradens' ranch, for Savannah and Jack's engagement party, and Hugh, one of Savannah's younger brothers, married Brianna. Brianna had a seven-year-old daughter, Layla. Kurt watched her running through the yard wearing a pretty white dress, her brown hair pinned up away from her face with barrettes. She'd grown at least two inches since he'd last seen her. His eyes slid to Hugh and Brianna, standing arm in arm by Hal. They were a handsome couple, Hugh in his dark suit and Brianna in a white lacy dress. Kurt wished Leanna were there with him.

White lilies and red roses adorned the hand-carved wooden gazebo that had been brought in for the wedding. Wooden chairs were lined up in neat rows with an aisle in between. The interior and exterior chairs were decorated with white satin bows and flowers. Kurt watched as everyone took their places in preparation for the wedding, and noticed, not for the first time, how similar the Braden family and the Remington family were. The men were tall and fit, with dark hair and, as he watched Treat with his arm slung over his younger brother Dane's shoulder, then caught a glimpse of Sage standing with Dex, both leaning in close, he realized that both families were also closely knit.

His father approached, looking important and imposing in his dark suit and starched collar, with a chin that could chisel granite and a serious look in his midnight-blue eyes.

"It's good to see you, son." James Remington wasn't an openly affectionate man, but over the past few months, since he and Jack had reconciled their differences and as each of his siblings had found their significant others, Kurt had noticed his father softening. Not just in his mannerisms, which included a smile more often than they used to, but also in the way he spoke to them. His father would always be a four-star general, retired or not. That stern, strict military skin was hard to shed. But he was also making strides at becoming more of an integral part of his children's lives, and Kurt was glad for that.

"Hi, Dad. I was just watching everyone. They all seem happy. Look at Mom. She looks beautiful, doesn't she?" His mother wore a long lavender skirt with a white blouse. Her gray hair flowed in natural waves down her back, and the smile on her lips hadn't faded for a second since he'd seen her last night.

"Yes, she does. How did your writing go at the Cape?"

Last night his brothers had ribbed him about Leanna, and it felt good to hang out with them again. His father and mother had been happy for him, and they were all looking forward to meeting her. Talking about the Cape only made him miss her more.

"It went well. I submitted the manuscript, and I actually think this one might be my best one yet."

His father smiled and nodded, then patted him on

the shoulder. "I'd say I expect nothing less from you, but you've heard that too many times in your life. So instead, thanks to your mother's late-in-life lessons, I'll say...I'm proud of you, Kurt. I always have been, and not just for your success."

Kurt and his father had enjoyed the least challenging relationship of all of his siblings. Kurt challenged his father only when his convictions were strong enough to be worth the battle, and as a quieter child growing up, he usually did what he was told. He followed the path of least resistance, except when it came to writing. He and his father had gone head-to-head about his pursuing a writing career, and Kurt hadn't backed down. In the years since, his father had grown accustomed to, and even taken pride in, Kurt's career and success. Kurt felt a little bad for his father. He'd wanted so badly for his sons to follow in his military footsteps, but they'd each gone their own way. After college, Jack had joined the Special Forces, but after he'd lost his first wife in a terrible accident, he'd left his military career behind.

"Thanks, Dad. I really have you to credit for how well I've done. At least on some level."

His father drew his thick, dark brows together.

"It's true," Kurt insisted. "You instilled in me the value of being one hundred percent focused on my goals, and in doing so, you taught me determination and drive. I worked every waking hour to be better than everyone else." He met his father's gaze. "And, hopefully, I'll use that same fortitude to be the best man that I can be for Leanna."

He was rewarded with a wide smile that

smoothed the creases across his father's forehead.

"Just don't make the same mistakes I did."

Kurt shook his head. "Mistakes?"

He followed his father's eyes as they shifted to his mother as she approached. He reached a hand out to her and pulled her close. His mother put a hand on his father's chest.

"Are you men ready?" she asked with a smile that Kurt had missed over the past few weeks.

"We are." His father kissed the top of his mother's head; then his voice turned serious again and he set his eyes on Kurt. "Be there for those who matter most. Not just with lessons, but with life, Kurt. It goes by far faster than you can imagine."

"Ah," his mother said with a smile. "I see I interrupted a moment."

"No, sweetheart," his father said as he pulled her close. "You *are* our moment."

Kurt was struck mute. Rooted to the ground. He'd never witnessed such intimacy initiated by his father, and as he watched his parents walk away arm in arm, he tried to send a message to his legs to move.

You are our moment.

Four words that changed the way he saw his father.

Four words that seeped into his heart and found Leanna.

You are my moment.

Chapter Twenty-Nine

FROM HIS PLACE by the gazebo, standing beside his brothers, Kurt watched as Jack took Savannah's hand in his and promised to love, honor, and cherish her for the rest of his life. Three words that resonated with Kurt when he thought of Leanna. *Love. Honor. Cherish.* He'd add a few of his own to that short list. *Trust. Desire. Protect.*

He noticed his brothers eyeing their girlfriends, who were seated together, each holding a fistful of tissues, their eyes playing between Jack and Savannah and his brothers. He wished Leanna were there, too, and longed to be with her again.

Ribbons of yellow and orange hovered over the mountains as the sun shone brightly and the day took on a romantic glow. Treat had become ordained to officiate at resorts he owned all over the world. His deep voice rang out in the silence.

"Jack, I invite you to kiss your bride."

Jack took Savannah in a deep, loving kiss that brought both families to their feet. When they drew apart, Jack wiped a tear from Savannah's cheek with the pad of his thumb.

"I love you, Savannah Remington." Pride and love coalesced in Jack's dark eyes, bringing a lump to Kurt's throat.

Savannah laughed and cried as Jack took her in his arms. She wore her auburn hair loose with a ring of white flowers at the crown. She looked beautiful and happy. They were a striking couple, both tall and fit. Jack's thick, jet-black hair against her long, auburn locks. Jack looked handsome in his black suit and tie, and Savannah's wedding dress was unlike anything Kurt had ever seen. Made of summery gauze with an overlay of lace, it was cut above the knee in the front and fell to the ground in the back, angling gracefully in between. The fitted waist had two strips of satin tied into dainty bows in the center, and lace sleeve caps covered Savannah's lean shoulders. The deep V-neck had a swatch of lace in between, giving Savannah a fresh, exotic, and almost daring appearance. It fit her feisty personality perfectly, and he began to wonder what type of dress Leanna might choose for herself.

Sage elbowed Rush. "You're next, bro."

Rush ran his hand through his short dark hair and nodded, eyeing his girlfriend, Jayla, as she headed his way. "Damn right."

"How do you know I won't be next?" Dex shook his head in an effort to clear his long, straight bangs from his eyes. They fell right back into place as he eyed their approaching girlfriends, three brunettes with wide smiles and dreamy looks in their eyes.

"Uh-oh," Kurt said. "Looks like all of your women want to be next." Weddings had never affected Kurt in the past, but as he listened to his brothers, he felt a tug of jealousy, and maybe desire, to be the next one to marry.

He went to congratulate Jack while his brothers embraced their girlfriends—which only made him miss Leanna more. He noticed each of the Braden men were arm in arm with their significant others as well.

Christ. He couldn't look in any direction without missing Leanna.

"Hi, Kurt!"

He crouched beside Brianna's brown-haired, wide-eyed daughter. "Hey there, Layla. You look beautiful."

"Thank you." She clasped her hands behind her back and turned her shoulders in half circles; her dress swished around her legs. "Josh made mine and Mommy's dresses. Aren't they pretty?"

He glanced at Brianna, wearing a sleeveless, knee-length, lacy shift.

"Gorgeous. Josh is pretty darn talented."

"I'm going to tell him you said that!" She ran off in Josh's direction.

Kurt opened his arms to Savannah. "Congratulations. You look gorgeous."

Savannah smoothed the front of her wedding gown. "Thank you, Kurt. You know I couldn't be happier. I adore Jack."

"That's evident in everything you say and do. Same with Jack. Transparent as glass." He nodded at her dress. "Did Josh or Riley design your gown? It's lovely."

"Josh designed it for me. Isn't it beautiful? I wanted something that didn't feel too formal."

"It's perfect, and so was the ceremony."

Jack pulled Savannah close. "She's perfect." Jack had an inch and seven years on Kurt.

Kurt draped his arm over his brother's broad shoulder. "Yes, she is. Congratulations, Jack."

"Thanks, man."

Jack had been so distraught after his first wife had died in a car accident that Kurt wasn't sure his brother would ever recover. For two years Jack had disappeared to a cabin in the Colorado Mountains that he hadn't even told his parents he'd bought. He'd spent those years alone, save for sporadic weekends teaching survival courses and flying clients around in his bush plane from time to time just to keep a modicum of income coming in. Savannah had attended one of his survival courses, and by some miracle, she'd seen through the angry, guilt-ridden shell that his brother had worn like armor and helped him heal.

"I'm really happy for you."

"I didn't get to talk with you much last night." Jack put a hand on Kurt's lower back. "Excuse us for a minute." He guided him away from the others and lowered his voice. "You doing okay? You look a little...something."

Something? Other than the two years when Jack had been dealing with his own loss, he'd always been in tune to his siblings' feelings. It didn't surprise Kurt that Jack would pick up on his missing Leanna. His emotions were a little rawer than he was used to or comfortable with. He tried to shift the conversation away from Leanna.

"You're a lucky guy, Jack. Savannah really loves you." He waved to Treat and Dane, who were heading their way.

"Don't want to talk about it, huh?" Jack asked.

Kurt shrugged. "It'll just make me miss her more."

"I've never heard or seen you like this. Ever."

"Tell me about it. She threw my whole world off balance; then she righted it with herself firmly lodged smack dab in the center of my heart." He was grinning so hard his cheeks hurt.

Jack threw his head back and laughed, a deep, hearty sound of joy. "Welcome to love, little brother."

"Another unsuspecting Remington falls prey to the love of a woman." Dane opened his arms and embraced Kurt, then Jack. "Too bad she missed the wedding. I'd have liked to meet the woman who got you away from your computer. From what I hear, that's not an easy feat." He waved to his girlfriend, Lacy Snow. Lacy was as blond as Dane was dark, with thick spiral curls and a slim figure. Dane was a marine researcher and shark tagger, and at over six feet tall, he was about two hundred pounds of lean muscle.

"She had a meeting today that she couldn't reschedule. She's just started a jam and jelly business. Luscious Leanna's Sweet Treats."

"She should call me. If her products are as good as the name, I'll carry it in my resorts." Treat owned luxury resorts all over the world. After living out of hotels for most of his adult life, he fell in love with Max

Armstrong, who was now just a few short weeks away from giving birth to their first baby. Max had lived and worked in Allure, Colorado, when they met, and Treat had given up his traveling lifestyle and put down roots in Weston to be with her.

"Seriously? That would be great, Treat. She doesn't know it yet, but I hired Cash's brother to renovate my studio at the Cape for her business. He's working on it now. I plan on surprising her with it in a few weeks."

"You hired Blue? I hear his work is excellent." Treat smacked Dane on the back. "Now that Savannah and Hugh are married off, I need to start working on getting my other brothers down the aisle. This one has yet to put a ring on Lacy's finger."

"Oh, the pressure. Work on Josh. He's already engaged, and from what I heard earlier, they're closing in on setting the date." Dane lifted his chin at Kurt. "When do we get to meet Leanna?"

"Get married, and I'll bring her along."

"I've got a better idea." Dane glanced at Treat. "Let's all crash one of Treat's resorts for a weekend."

"After the baby's born and Max is up to it, I think that's a great idea." Treat excused himself and went to join Max.

"That sounds great."

"I'll fly you out if you don't mind Savannah and me tagging along," Jack offered.

"Sounds perfect. Hey, I want to give Leanna a quick call. I'll be back in a minute." Kurt walked over by the fence at the edge of the yard and sent Leanna a text. *Miss you more than anything. Hope your meeting went well. Call me?*

OHMYGODOHMYGODOHMYGOD! Leanna had been driving for twenty minutes and her heart was still racing. She'd spent three hours with the executives of Daisy Chain, and though she was initially intimidated by the mere size of their offices, which took up the entire top floor of a four-story office building, the people had been down-to-earth and easy to talk to. They were smart, funny, and driven—and they wanted to carry Luscious Leanna's Sweet Treats in every store. *Every store!* The figures they discussed would allow Leanna to rent space on a full-time basis, which she'd need to keep up with orders. She would also need to commit to her business full-time if she wanted this contract—and she *wanted* this contract.

Leanna drove up Route 6 thinking about the opportunity and knowing that if Al were able to see her, he'd be proud. Her mind raced in a hundred different directions. She might need to hire a few trusted helpers, because while Leanna knew that she'd never want to dole out all of the day-to-day operations, she wasn't fooling herself. Wide distribution would take several sets of hands. Leanna also knew herself well enough to understand that there would be times when she wanted a few days off to spend with Kurt.

Kurt. Oh God. Kurt.

Therein lay the reason for the tightening in her stomach and the ache in her chest. Daisy Chain wanted her sweet treats not only because they were delicious, or because they liked and seemed to trust Leanna, but also because Luscious Leanna's Sweet Treats was a local business. Although Daisy Chain had stores throughout the East Coast, they were big on supporting local businesses. The owners, Arnold and Lilian Hayes, were both born on the Cape and had lived there for more than sixty years. Local to them was Cape Cod. Not New York.

She glanced at her phone on the passenger seat, and the muscles in her neck tightened. She'd seen the message from Kurt, and she needed to call him. She *wanted* to call him, but she was in such a quagmire about Daisy Chain that she felt sick to her stomach.

I want the Daisy Chain contract.
I want Kurt.
Why me? Why now? Why can't this be easy?

Leanna went off the main drag and took a residential road through Eastham toward Wellfleet. With her windows down, the breeze from the bay washed over her, settling her nerves a little. The smell of the damp sea air brought memories of the first night she met Kurt and the first time they made love on the beach. It made her long to be with him. The Cape had always soothed her in ways that no other town ever had. Her creativity flowed when she was here. She thought of her family's vacations at the cottage, arguing with her siblings over who got to sleep in the loft, playing in the surf, and when they all got a little older, scoping out the other teenagers. Summers with Bella, Amy, Jenna, and the other Seaside residents were irreplaceable. Those were memories she'd always cherish, and one day, she hoped to have her own family and create memories that were just as meaningful.

She wanted to create those memories with Kurt.

She knew he couldn't move to the Cape full-time. He'd made it pretty clear that his life was in New York and he had no intention of changing that. Why should he? It was Leanna who was changing the plans, not Kurt.

This is why I'm not a planner.

She pulled into Seaside and parked by the laundry room, then crossed the gravel road to Bella's cottage and walked right in. She kicked off her sandals by the door, dropped her keys on the floor, and headed into the bedroom. Bella's king-sized bed was always perfectly made. *Kurt would like that.* The fluffy pink comforter and lacy white pillows seemed out of place beside thoughts of Bella's brash personality. Pink and lace should be reserved for sweet Amy Maples. Leanna didn't have the emotional fortitude to figure out Bella at the moment. She was just thankful for their friendship. She knew Amy would have let Pepper out plenty of times and loved him up throughout the day, and right at the moment, she needed to disappear. She also needed to call Kurt. But the bed looked so inviting, and she couldn't call Kurt until she cleared her head. Just five minutes of escaping her worries; that's all she needed. Leanna lay facedown on the bed and closed her eyes with a heavy sigh.

Maybe she could just hide out here and everything would somehow be okay.

She heard the screen door open, and she grabbed a pillow and put it over her head.

"I told you I saw her van," Amy said as she came

into the bedroom. "Uh-oh. I guess it didn't go well. I'll get a bottle of wine and Pepper."

Leanna felt the mattress sink on her right side, and a hand landed on her lower back. The scent of Jenna's Hawaiian Tropic sunscreen gave her away. Bella's body landed heavily to her left, and when Leanna opened her eyes, Bella narrowed hers.

"Fuck 'em." Bella pressed her lips together. "You need Daisy Chain like you need a dickless male model. Fun to show off, but what are they bringing to the table?"

Leanna couldn't help but laugh.

Jenna stroked her back as the screen door opened again and Leanna heard Pepper's nails *click-clacking* on the hardwood floors. His paws and wet nose popped up by her head, and he barked.

Leanna reached out and petted his head, still sort of wishing she could close her eyes and everything would be okay.

"I've got wine and brownies that Pepper and I made together this afternoon. Oh, and we might have eaten a few of the fruits from your bouquet." Amy paused. "Okay, I might have eaten them, but Pepper didn't stop me, so he's sort of responsible, too."

Leanna flopped over onto her back and reached for Bella's and Jenna's hands.

"They want me," she said flatly.

"They *want* you?" Bella bolted upright and glared down at Leanna. "Then what the hell?"

Jenna's face came into view, head-to-head with Bella's above Leanna. "Isn't that what we worked so hard for? This is good, right?"

Amy's face joined the others, head tilting first one way, then the other. "Sweetie? Did something happen with Kurt? What's going on? What can we do?"

Leanna sat up, parting the wall of concerned faces like the Red Sea. Amy handed her a glass of wine, then handed one to each of the others. Leanna looked at the glass, hoping that somewhere in the sweet liquid was a remedy to her hurting heart—and knowing that all the wine in the world wouldn't help. She handed the glass back to Amy and fell back on the bed again—eyes slammed tight.

"Oh, no you don't," Bella said. "Ames, can you please take these?" They handed Amy their glasses.

Leanna felt her strong hand on her left arm, and Jenna's on her right, as they dragged her to an upright position. Pepper stood sentinel at Leanna's feet, barking at the others.

"Guess we're doing walk therapy, huh?" Amy took the glasses to the kitchen as Bella and Jenna brought Leanna to her feet and dragged her out to the deck.

They waited for Amy, who returned with Leanna's sandals, and she took ahold of Pepper's leash. They walked down the gravel road arm in arm.

"Spill," Bella directed.

Leanna let out a loud breath. "You know I'm supposed to move in with Kurt in New York on Monday." A lump formed in her throat.

"Right. Got it," Bella said. "And?"

"And Daisy Chain wants to carry my stuff everywhere, which is great, but they want me to remain local. To keep up with the distribution, I have to pretty much work year-round, but that means working here year-round, and if I do that, then I can't be with Kurt, and—" Her eyes filled with tears as they passed the pool and headed back up the hill toward her cottage. "And if I can't have Kurt..."

"Honey, why can't you have Kurt if you work?" Amy's voice was filled with compassion.

"Because. He's not going to upend his perfect, organized life in New York and live on the Cape. What's in the Cape during the winter? Snow? Ice? It's desolate, and he's a family guy. I told you about the interviews." Jenna made a *tsk* sound. "This is a dilemma. What does Kurt say?"

Leanna bit her lower lip. Jenna had spoken her worst fear. She'd said aloud what Leanna couldn't force herself to, because doing so would make the words—and the meaning of them—seem more real.

"You haven't told him?" Jenna exchanged a worried look with Bella. "Leanna, you have to tell him. Monday is only a few days away."

Leanna's gut clenched again. "Don't you think I know that?" She didn't mean to raise her voice. "I want to be there. And I want to be here."

Tony came out of his cottage wearing nothing but a pair of board shorts and a rich tan. "Hey, girls." He stood with his hands on his hips as they approached, taking in each of their worried faces. His smile faded quickly.

"Uh-oh. What's happened?" He fell in line beside Amy.

"She got the Daisy Chain contract," Amy explained.

"But she might lose Kurt because she needs to be here and he needs to be in New York," Jenna added.

Tony pressed his smiling lips into a firm line and cleared his throat while muffling a laugh. "She's not going to lose *Oh God, Kurt.*"

Leanna glared at each of the women.

"We didn't say anything. I swear it," Amy protested.

"Not a word," Jenna added.

"Your window was wide open, Leanna." Tony shook his head. "It's not like I haven't heard people having sex before."

"Oh my God." Leanna stopped walking and looked up at the sky. "Please, just shoot me down right here, right now. Spare me any more indignity. Please!"

"Don't worry. I deleted it from my memory banks just now," Tony assured her. "Although I was happy for you. I don't think I've ever heard your cottage rockin'. Now, Bella's, that's another story."

"A girl's gotta live," Bella quipped.

"You guys, this is serious. What should I do?" They arrived at Leanna's cottage and settled in around the table on her deck. Leanna buried her face in her hands. Pepper put his paws on her lap and panted at her until she reached down and stroked his fur. She couldn't even look at him without thinking of Kurt.

Who am I kidding? I can't breathe without thinking of Kurt.

Tony clasped his hands behind his head and leaned back. Amy's eyes slid to his broad chest and the waves of muscles covering his midsection. Jenna kicked her under the table.

"You're overthinking this, Leanna." Tony leaned across the table and touched her hand. "Call Kurt. Talk to him. You two will figure it out. Plenty of couples have long-distance relationships, and New York is a short flight from P-town."

"He has a point." Jenna brushed a few grains of sand from the table. "And you know, in many ways, seeing a guy on weekends might be better than living together. You won't get sick of each other."

"I highly doubt I'd ever get sick of Kurt. He's so..." She contemplated how to sum him up in one word.

"Hot?" Bella asked.

"Loving?" Amy suggested.

"Attentive? Good in bed? Intelligent?" Jenna bumped Leanna playfully with her shoulder.

"How about normal? Does a guy really have to be all those things all the time?" Tony set his eyes on Leanna's until she met his gaze. "He's a bestselling author, so yeah, he's probably pretty intelligent. He treats you well, from what I've heard, and he's definitely attentive in all the right places. Although I'm pretending that I didn't actually *hear* that. You all think he's handsome, so I take your word on that. He's not my type, as I like breasts and a vagina, but you know, hey, whatever." He held his palms up toward the sky. "Seriously, Leanna. If what I'm told is right, and you love Kurt the way you said you did the other night, then call him."

"Call him." Leanna set her palms on the table and used her most serious voice. "Okay. How would you react if your boyfriend—or girlfriend—committed to living with you, then called and said, *Hey, you know that promise? That plan we made? Guess what? I'm really sorry, but I got this great job offer to fulfill my* dream, and now you either have to change your entire life for me, or we're going to see each other on a once-in-a-while basis?" She sat back and crossed her arms. "See? Not exactly loving, is it?"

Bella rolled her eyes. "So you don't say it that way." She waved her hand in the air and spoke in a higher tone. "*Hey, babe. It's me. I got a great offer from Daisy Chain that's too good to pass up, but I'd have to be at the Cape full-time. Maybe we should talk about it?* Better?"

"Much," Amy said. "What about this? *I got this great offer, but I don't want to lose you, either. Maybe we can figure this out together?*"

Bella leaned across the table and pointed at Amy. "Even better. Nice addition."

Leanna shook her head. "Maybe you guys can make the call for me."

They talked for another twenty minutes, until they'd beaten the subject and hypothetical outcomes to death. Amy took Pepper back to her cottage to give Leanna privacy. Leanna gathered her belongings from Bella's and from her van, then went into her cottage with her heart in her throat and called Kurt.

Chapter Thirty

IT HAD BEEN almost two hours since Kurt texted Leanna, and he took that as a good sign that her meeting was going well. It was a cool, sunny day in Colorado, and Kurt was enjoying visiting with his family and the Bradens, even though seeing everyone paired off made him long for Leanna. Now he stood by the split-rail fence at the edge of the yard watching Hal Braden down by the barn with Treat and Max and his horse Hope.

Rex joined him and leaned his elbows on the fence, watching his father. Rex, like all of the men, had shed his suit coat and wore his dress shirt sleeves rolled up to his elbows. His bulging forearms twitched as he wrung his hands together.

"Dad and Hope," Rex said with a shake of his head. He looked up at Kurt. "I think we see them as a couple, like me and Jade, or Treat and Max."

"The horse?"

"Yeah. Dad bought that horse for my mom when she first became ill. She loved that horse so much, and after she died, I swear my dad began talking to Hope like my mom's inside her somewhere."

Kurt cocked his head in question.

"Yeah, I know." Rex pulled a necklace from beneath his shirt and rubbed it between his fingers and thumb. "I always thought Dad was a little *off* for doing that, but now? I'm not so sure. It sure feels like Mom's around, especially when I'm near Hope." Rex leaned his hip against the fence and crossed his arms. He wore his thick black hair longer than his brothers, like Sage preferred to wear his, brushing his collar. His powerful, broad frame reminded Kurt of Hal, and when he narrowed his dark eyes, the resemblance was uncanny.

"Do you miss Leanna?"

Kurt half smiled, half laughed. "Look around." He drew his eyes to Dex and Ellie, standing arm in arm, then slid them to Jack and Savannah, kissing by the buffet table. Jack ran his finger down Savannah's cheek, and she leaned forward and kissed him. "Hard not to miss her."

"Yeah, I can see that." Rex pointed to Jade standing beside Lacy and Riley, his brother's girlfriends. "I can't stand to be away from Jade for more than a few hours. Overnight? Forget it. That woman's got my heart wrapped around her so tightly that some days I worry about what I'd do if something happened to her." He clenched his jaw, then shifted positions and looked at his father by the barn again. "Then I understand where Dad's coming from. Have you ever felt that way? Do you feel that way about Leanna?"

Kurt mulled over the question. He'd been away from Leanna for a day, and he had no idea how he'd make it until tomorrow, much less Monday. He couldn't imagine his life without her. He leaned his arms on the fence and exhaled loudly. Talking about feelings wasn't something he was used to doing, but Rex made it look so easy, and feel so right, that the words came easily.

"To be honest, until Leanna, I never felt much for a woman. My life was about writing, and family of course, but that goes without saying. I don't know about the whole spiritual connection thing, mostly because I've never really thought about it. But as far as Leanna goes? I think about her every second." He smiled. "Boy, do I ever. She's gotten under my skin. I want her with me even when she talks incessantly and barely takes a breath." He looked at Rex. "So yeah, I guess I do feel that way. I'm going on thirty-one and have never lived with a woman, well, besides my sister, of course. I have no idea if I'll drive her crazy or what, but I do know that I can't wait to have her with me every day."

"That's love, man. It grabs you by the balls and doesn't let go." Rex stood up and put a hand on Kurt's back. "There's no greater feeling. Even when the shit hits the fan, it's still worth every blessed second."

Kurt's phone rang, and he pulled it from his pocket. "It's Leanna."

"Go ahead, man," Rex said. "Talk to her. We'll catch up later."

He watched Rex approach Jade from behind, place

his hands on her hips, and kiss her shoulder. Kurt walked toward the front yard as he answered Leanna's call.

"Hey, babe. How did it go?" He climbed the porch steps, thankful for the privacy.

"Hi. Wanna FaceTime?"

"Yeah, sure." A few seconds later, her lovely face—and worried eyes—filled the screen.

The look in her eyes tugged on his heart. He wished he were there with her, holding her, easing whatever disappointment she was feeling.

"Uh-oh. What happened?"

"Are you in a place where you can talk, or is your family right there?"

Something in her voice brought him to his feet and caused his gut to clench. He descended the porch steps and walked at a fast pace toward the driveway, feeling the need to move. He didn't know why his legs propelled him forward, and he didn't question it. He trusted his instincts and continued walking.

"I'm alone."

"Okay." She bit her lower lip, and he breathed a little harder.

"Babe? What is it?"

Her eyes filled with tears, and he froze. He stood on the side of the road staring at his phone and feeling completely impotent. "Leanna?"

She wiped her eyes. "I'm okay. I'm sorry."

"It's okay. Tell me what's going on." He held the phone in both hands and watched her wiping her eyes and taking deep breaths. He caught glimpses of her kitchen behind her as the phone shifted with her movements. At least she was home safely.

"Take your time, babe. Take a deep breath." What the hell was going on? His heart hammered against his ribs with worry. Every muscle tensed.

"The meeting went well." She wiped her eyes again.

"Okay. Good." *But?*

"They want to carry my products in all their stores."

"That's fantastic, so those are tears of joy?" *Why don't they feel like that?*

She shook her head.

Shit.

"They want me to remain local, and in order to fulfill the distribution to the stores, I'd really need to be here full-time." She pressed her lips together in a tight line.

"Full-time." His heart sank.

She nodded.

"Why? I don't understand. Can't you get another facility in New York and continue there in the fall and winter? Or work from my house? Our house?"

She shook her head. "They want to support local businesses, and they said if I prefer not to remain local, they'd rather not carry the products because they don't really need another jam distributor, but they would welcome another local business to support."

So it's me or your business. It was a shitty position for her to be in, and he could see from her watery eyes, the wrinkles along her forehead, and the way her lips turned down at the edges that the weight of it was too much for her to bear. Kurt had his career. He had his well-planned and enjoyable life that ran smooth as butter in New York. How could he ask her to give up the chance at having all of that herself?

He couldn't.

He wouldn't.

"Well, is this what you want?"

Tears tumbled down her cheeks as she shook her head. "I don't know. I finally found something that I really love doing, something that resonates with me on every level—and then I found you. I love you, Kurt, and *you* resonate with me on every level." She laughed through her tears and covered her face with her hand. "This is par for my crazy, fucked-up life." She lowered her hand and he studied her hooded, red-rimmed eyes.

All he wanted to do was ease her pain, and he knew there was only one way to do that. He knew how much she loved him. Every word she spoke was laced with love. Every glance of her hazel eyes bathed him in her warm emotions, and her heart—her glorious, generous heart—brought forth feelings he never knew he was capable of feeling. He had to do what she might not be strong enough to.

"Your life isn't crazy or fucked up." *This situation is.* "It's okay, Leanna. We can still make this work, if that's what you want."

"Yes. I want you. I want us." She nodded and swiped at her tears. "But how?"

"We do whatever it takes. This is your chance, Leanna. You've found the thing that you were searching for, and with you, I found what I never knew

I was missing. So, no matter how hard it is, we make it work. You'll stay at the Cape and do all the things you should be doing to build the business you've been working so hard to create. I'll stay in New York and commute to the Cape every chance I get. It'll take some coordinating, but we can do this."

Even if I hate it.

Even if I'll barely be able to think past the empty side of the bed where you should be.

Even if I miss you like a phantom limb.

"We can? You're sure?"

"Unless it's not what you want. You tell me, babe. I want you to be happy." *And I hope to hell you want me.*

The worry slipped from her eyes, and the edges of her lips curled up. "I want us on every level, so if that means weekends, then yes."

It had taken Kurt only a few days to fall head over heels in love with Leanna, and it took less than ten minutes for that love—and their new decision about their living arrangements—to rip his heart to shreds. He let out a breath and pressed his hand to the dull pain in his chest.

"I love you. We'll make it work." The sounds of laughter carried in the air. Laughter. He felt like his life was crashing down around him, and he couldn't lean on anyone for support. He wouldn't ruin their good time with his troubles. And there was no way he'd let Leanna feel bad at a time when she should be over the moon about her new endeavor. Weekends. Maybe it wouldn't be so bad. He could write without interruption during the week and make the best of his time with Leanna. He tried to convince himself that this was okay, that he could live with it.

"I don't want you to worry. Just...celebrate. This is your time, Leanna. Go out with the girls and know we'll be just fine. I'm not going anywhere." *Except, apparently, to Cape Cod every weekend.* Kurt began calculating drive times, flight times, and how much time they'd actually have together each weekend.

Not nearly enough.

It would never be enough.

Chapter Thirty-One

LEANNA DIDN'T GO out with the girls Friday night. She was too conflicted to celebrate. Instead they all went to Bella's cottage, ate too much pizza, finished the bouquet of fruit Kurt had sent, and watched *Say Anything*. She made the girls promise not to talk about Kurt or Daisy Chain so she could try to enjoy the movie. It didn't work. Even without mention of him, she'd thought about Kurt all evening. He had called again before she went to sleep, and he'd reiterated that they could make their relationship work, even if long distance. She thought she'd detected a hint of sadness in his voice that he was working hard to mask, but she tried to push the thought away and convince herself they really could make a long-distance relationship work. But she already missed him so damn much after two days that she had no idea how she'd get along seeing him only on weekends.

He'd called again this morning and reassured her

that they'd be just fine. He'd sounded surer, and she'd clung to his confidence like a security blanket as the day dragged on. The flea market was crowded, hot, and humid. Carey hadn't shown up, and without him to talk with, the afternoon seemed to last forever. By three thirty she was too distracted to concentrate, so she packed up her booth early and went home. She knew Kurt had plans with his family, and he was going to call her when he was settled back at Treat's for the evening, so she checked her email before going to help her friends pack.

The contract from Daisy Chain was waiting in her in-box. Her pulse kicked up as she read it, and her stomach clenched. The contract could not have brought on more bittersweet emotions. She still had a few days to make a final decision.

Leanna spent the rest of the evening helping Bella and Jenna close their cottages for the season, hoping to distract herself.

Bella came out of the bedroom in her T-shirt and shorts and wiped her face with her forearm. "Well, ladies, I think that about wraps it up. I can't believe another summer's over."

Jenna rebuttoned the buttons on her shirt that had come undone while she was scrubbing the bathroom, and one of the buttons popped right off and shot across the room.

Bella, Amy, and Leanna burst into fits of laughter.

"Maybe I shouldn't have had that pizza last night." Jenna stifled a laugh as she pushed her boobs together.

"I can't...I can't believe it flew off." Leanna covered her mouth, trying to regain control.

"I can!" Amy stood beside Jenna and arched her chest forward. They looked like a short-haired Sofía Vergara and Kate Hudson. Jenna swatted her.

"I can't help it if I was born with a killer body." Jenna wiggled her shoulders.

"Killer is right. You could knock someone out with those babies." Bella flopped onto the couch. "So what now? Amy's all packed. We're all boxed and ready to go. Except Leanna, of course, who has the luxury of living on the Cape—which makes me incredibly jealous."

"Don't be. Without you guys or Kurt, it's just me and Pepper, and as much as I love being with Pep…" She flopped onto the couch beside Bella and leaned her head on her shoulder. "I'm removing the ban on Kurt talk. I need to know. Am I making a huge mistake?"

"By building your dream job?" Bella asked.

"By not moving to New York with Kurt."

"Hey, if he loves you, he'll make it work. You can't change your life for a man. That's so…1950s." Bella patted Leanna's thigh. "I love Kurt, but I love you more. You've spent your whole life bouncing from thing to thing. Now you have something you love. It's time to allow yourself to do it."

"But I love Kurt, too."

"Yes, I know you do." Bella nodded. "And he loves you. This is a bump in the road. Fate will figure it out. Just don't you give up on following your dream. You're my inspiration, Leanna. You have tried a million things and you didn't settle. Don't settle now, or you'll crush my faith that women can have it all."

"Crush your faith? You aren't even religious." Jenna arched a brow.

"Faith in Leanna. Faith in ice cream. Whatever. You know what I mean. Global energy faith." Bella put her arm around Leanna and pulled her close. "Build your business; the rest will work itself out."

"And what if it doesn't?" Her voice was just above a whisper.

"Then you take that sexy little ass of yours to New York and get that man back full-time. But if it doesn't work out, that means that he didn't want it enough to make it work. See? I have this great double standard. We women get to progress as the years move on, but men?" Bella smiled and looked up at the ceiling with a sigh. "They still have to be chivalrous."

"I don't care about progressing. I care about Kurt." Leanna leaned her elbows on her knees.

"Do you care about your business?" Amy asked.

"Yes. Very much."

"Then you can't give it up. I agree with Bella."

Leanna closed her eyes. "I hate you both. Why aren't you telling me to pack my shit and go to New York right this very second? Do you think I'm making a mistake by being with Kurt?" She ran her eyes between them. "Wait. Before you answer that, you need to know that no matter what you say, I'm *with* him."

Amy knelt before Leanna and held her hands. "We love Kurt, and we love you. It's just that opportunities like this come once in a lifetime for some of us, and…" She glanced at Bella, then back at Leanna. "I agree with Bella. If Kurt wants this to work, he has to make it work."

"Then this should be easy, because he's already said he wants it to work, and he'll come to the Cape on weekends. So I guess I just need to get my act together, accept the offer with Daisy Chain, and live with a long-distance relationship. No matter how much it sucks being apart." Even as the words left her lips, she knew easy wasn't even in the realm of possibilities.

Amy pulled her to her feet and hugged her. "That's my girl."

Leanna took a step back. "And if you're wrong, I'll have to kill you. All of you."

THE EVENING SLIPPED seamlessly into night, bringing with it a cool breeze from the mountains. Kurt was enjoying a few minutes alone by the stone fire pit on Treat's patio, scrolling through the pictures of the studio that Blue had sent. The work was progressing much faster than either Blue or Kurt had anticipated. He heard the sliding glass door to the house open and recognized the heavy, determined steps of his brother Jack, followed by the slightly slower pace that could only be Hal Braden. He didn't recognize the third set of footsteps.

Jack pulled two chairs over to where Kurt sat. "How's it going?" Jack wore his typical outfit of Levi's, a black T-shirt, and heavy hiking boots.

"Oh, pretty well," Kurt lied.

"Mind if we join you?" Hal sighed as he sat beside Jack. He wore a white T-shirt beneath what must have been a favorite flannel shirt for the soft, worn appearance. It fit snugly across his broad shoulders and broad, strong chest. His jeans were dark and his cowboy boots black. At six foot six, Hal Braden was a bear of a man, with weathered cheeks, graying hair, and an easy disposition.

"Not at all." Kurt slid his phone into his pocket.

"It's nice out here tonight. You doing okay, Kurt?" Josh Braden was a few years older than Kurt, and like Kurt, he was the most reserved of his siblings. Josh wore a pair of dark slacks and a button-down shirt, and like his father, he exhaled as he settled into his seat.

"Yeah, thanks. I'm well." Kurt was anything but *well*. "The dresses you designed were gorgeous, Josh."

"The girls seemed to like them," Josh said. His eyes were dark and serious.

"Hal, this has been a very enjoyable weekend. Thank you for hosting the wedding and putting up with my family."

"Son, there's nothing to put up with. Family knows no boundaries, and you, Jack, and the rest of your family are my family now, too. You're always welcome here." Hal looked out over the mountains. "I'd like for you and your family to meet my sister, Catherine, and my niece and nephews at some point, too. Time goes by so quickly. It seems like just yesterday they were traipsing around the ranch. Catherine's youngest son, Luke, raises Gypsy horses over in Trusty, Colorado. He's had a love of horses since he was just a boy." Catherine had six children. Before her husband signed over his parental rights and took off with another woman, they'd lived in Weston, and after he left, Catherine and her children moved to Trusty. She changed her name back to Braden and gave her children the Braden name, too.

"Wes called me the other day. We're going to try to get together soon." Josh turned to Kurt. "Luke is your age, Kurt, and his older brother, Wes, owns a dude ranch just outside of Trusty."

"I look forward to meeting them," Kurt said. "I'd imagine it's hard to coordinate everyone's schedules."

"Life moves fast and changes often. It's hard to believe Treat and Max are having my first grandchild soon," Hal said. "And now I have three of my children married, too. Settled."

"And another around the corner, Dad." Josh slid a look at his father.

"Josh?" Hal leaned toward his son.

"We're close to setting a date. We want to wait until after Treat's baby is old enough to travel." Josh rubbed his chin. "I think we're going to get married either in New York or at one of Treat's resorts. We're not certain yet. We debated having it here, but you've had your fill of weddings here, Dad."

"Now, son, you know I won't have my *fill* until you're all settled." Hal smiled. "You could have the wedding in Treat's resort here in Colorado, but that'll be your big day, so whatever you decide, I'll proudly be there." Hal smacked his big hands on his thighs. "Yes, sir. When your children settle into their lives, it's a good feeling."

"Congratulations, Josh." Jack crossed his ankle over his knee. "It's a great feeling, Hal. I'm a lucky man to have met Savannah."

Hal set his dark eyes on Jack. "She's lucky, too,

Jack. You're a good man. Your father raised you boys right. And your sister, of course. She's a nice gal, that Siena. She and Savannah are like two peas in a pod."

"You can say that again," Kurt said.

Hal lifted his chin toward Kurt. "You're heading back to New York tomorrow?"

"Yes, that's right. I'm meeting with my agent Monday; then it's back to real life. I've been gone all summer, so there's a lot of catching up to do." *Catching up. With what?* Kurt usually craved getting back on schedule after spending time away from home. Now his muscles corded tight at the thought of returning home instead of going back to the Cape to be with Leanna.

"Did I hear a rumor that your little lady is moving in with you?" Hal crossed his thick arms over his chest and smiled.

Kurt's stomach clenched. "That was the plan, but she's been offered a contract for her business, and it looks like she'll be staying at the Cape." He tried to keep the disappointment from his voice, but even he could hear the thread of sorrow.

"Staying? When did this happen?" Jack narrowed his eyes.

"Yesterday." Kurt rubbed his hands on his thighs to try to calm his nerves.

"Yesterday? Why didn't you tell me? Are you okay with this?"

No. "Sure. I mean, I have to be. When I met Leanna, she told me she was trying to get this business off the ground. I'd have to be a pretty selfish guy to ask her not to do it." He scrubbed his face with his hand and sighed. "I want her to be happy."

"And what about you?" Hal asked.

"Me?"

"Yes, son. What about you? Are you happy with the woman you love miles away?" Hal held his gaze.

Kurt shook his head. "No, but I'm a big boy. Until I met Leanna, I wrote seven days a week. Now I'll write five days a week and I'll spend my weekends with her at the Cape."

"You're a better man than me," Josh said. "No way could I spend my weeks apart from Riley."

"If my Adriana were in another state when she was alive, I think I'd have lost my mind," Hal said with a serious shake of his head. "No sir. My heart wouldn't have been able to handle knowing she was living hours away when I could have been with her."

"I didn't even make it one night away from Savannah when we came back from the mountains after we first met," Jack reminded Kurt. "Have you considered moving there? To the Cape?"

"Sure. I've gone through all the options. I could move there, but you know my life is in New York. Our whole family is there, Jack, and my agent, my public relations rep, my friends." *Friends? More like acquaintances.* "What would I do with my house? What about Mom and Dad? They're getting older, and I'm the closest one to them. Since I work from home, I can be there in case of an emergency." He'd been going over this in his head for hours, and there was something that he wasn't admitting to Jack. He barely admitted it to himself. Kurt hated change. It was that simple. He lived his life in a methodical fashion, and that kept him focused and comfortable. Leanna had thrown his world off balance, and he'd found that it took him only opening his heart to her to find his balance once again, this time with Leanna by his side. But that was when she was coming into *his* world. Could he give up the safety net he'd created to be with her and leave his life behind?

Give up New York, where he'd worked so hard to put down roots?

Move away from his family?

Jack opened his mouth to speak, and Hal settled a hand on his arm, silencing him.

"You have a point, Kurt," Hal began. "The question is, where is your heart? Is what makes you whole in here"—he patted his chest—"in New York, or is it in Cape Cod?"

Chapter Thirty-Two

JENNA LEFT EARLY Sunday morning with her car packed to the hilt. Leanna and Bella waved to Amy as she drove out of the complex two hours later.

"I guess that just leaves you," Leanna said to Bella.

"Tony's here."

"No. He went out surfing this morning, and he's going to Nantucket for the week with friends. Once you leave, it'll be just me and Pepper." She crouched and pet Pepper. He panted up at her. "I'm going to miss you guys."

Bella had on a sundress and flip-flops. Her hair had lightened in the sun since she'd arrived earlier in the summer. She hugged Leanna and reassured her. "You're doing the right thing."

"It feels like the absolute wrong thing. Everything that I was so excited about feels empty now. It's like when Kurt left, he took a little—"

"Piece of you with him? I know. I can see it in your

eyes." Bella hugged her again. "Listen, we women are like ice cream. We're just fine without our freezers. Even melted, we still taste good. We're still sweet and delicious, but somehow when we have that freezer wrapped around us, we bloom into something more. Something better."

Leanna rolled her eyes. "What is it with you and ice cream this summer?"

Bella tapped her chin. "I'm not sure, but I think it's a good analogy. Without Kurt, you're still smart, fun, beautiful, capable, and…You're *you*. And we love you. But with Kurt, you're more." She shrugged.

"So why did you tell me to stay here? Why didn't you push me to go to New York? Jesus, Bella. Am I making the biggest mistake of my life?" It sure felt like it.

"Because you need both. You need this business and you need Kurt." They walked over to Bella's car. "And I have faith in ice cream. I told you that. Get this business going. Ice cream fate will take care of the rest." She kissed Leanna's cheek and hugged her one more time. "I gotta run before traffic is hell. I love you. Call me and text me. Let me know everything that happens."

"You know I will. Drive safely."

Bella pulled her car out of the driveway and waved. "Have faith in all things sweet, Leanna."

What does that even mean?

Leanna's phone vibrated with a text from Kurt on the way back to her cottage. *FaceTime?*

A few seconds later Kurt's face lit up the screen. She walked into her cottage, feeling the emptiness press in on her.

"Hey, babe." His low, gravelly voice raked a chill down her spine.

"You sound tired." His eyelids looked heavy, sleepy.

"A little. I didn't sleep much last night. How are you? How's Pepper?"

God, I love you. She crouched down and showed him Pepper.

"Hey, Pep!"

Pepper barked and whined. His tail wagged as he pressed his wet nose to Leanna's phone. Kurt laughed, and it chased the chill right back up to her heart. She turned the phone back toward her.

"I miss you so much." She could fall into those blue eyes of his. She wanted to fall into them. There was no way she could do this. *No way.* Her friends were wrong. She had to go to New York. She had to be with him. There would be other contracts, or maybe there wouldn't, but there could never be another Kurt.

"Me too. I had to see you. What are your plans today? Are you going to the flea market?"

"The girls just left, and I was considering skipping the last day at the flea market and taking Pepper to the beach. I haven't gone much this summer and..." She couldn't act like everything was okay. She couldn't talk about her day like she wasn't pining for him every second.

"And I miss you like crazy, Kurt. I can't help but feel like I've ruined everything. We had a plan, and you're a planner. You live by your schedules, and when you left, we had a schedule that we were both happy with, and now...Now it's all messed up because of me and my stupid business. And you know what? I'm just flighty enough to decide in two months that this business isn't what I want." That was a lie. That was who she thought she used to be, but Kurt helped her to see that she hadn't been that person at all. She just hadn't found her calling and there was nothing wrong with taking her time. After all, not settling had brought her to Kurt.

"Stupid business?" He shook his head.

"Wait. Don't say anything. That's not true. I won't change my mind about the business, but I did mess everything up, and I'm sorry."

"Leanna?"

She saw his lips move, but couldn't hear past her need to get her feelings out once and for all. "You're probably rethinking everything about us by now. I'm sorry I ruined our plans and upset your apple cart."

"Leanna. Take a deep breath. Please."

"Kurt—"

"No. It's my turn to talk."

His serious tone caught her off guard. She closed her mouth.

"You *are* my apple cart."

He said it so seriously that she thought she misunderstood him. What was it with food analogies all of a sudden?

"What?"

"You are my apple cart. You haven't ruined anything. You've made my life better in every way. I told you I'm not going anywhere, and I'm not."

"But being apart is hard." *So damn hard I can't*

stand it.

"Most things in life that are worth anything at all are hard."

She narrowed her eyes and couldn't suppress the dirty thought or the smile that accompanied it. "Well, I know at least one thing that is…"

"There's my dirty girl," he said in a seductive voice.

"Ugh! Not helping. Now I miss you even more. This is totally sucky." She drank in everything she could see. His dark eyes, so full of want and love she could practically taste it, the peppering of stubble along his jaw and above the swell of his upper lip. The way his dark brows knitted together—just a little—when he spoke. She wanted to touch his face, to feel his lips on hers. She wanted to hug him and sit beside him while he wrote. She wanted to see him plotting and creating, too deep in thought to look away from his computer.

"Leanna."

His voice pulled her from her thoughts.

"Right this very second I can see your face. I can hear your voice." His voice was sweet and patient. "This moment is anything but sucky. You know what's sucky? Losing the person you love."

"Yeah, that would really suck. I guess perspective is everything."

"You know what else?"

Pepper ran to the screen door and began pawing at it and barking.

"Pepper, shush." Leanna turned her attention back to Kurt. "Sorry. He's going bonkers. I don't know how you got him to listen." She turned her back to Pepper to try to hear Kurt better.

Pepper whined, scratching at the door.

"I've got to let him out. Pepp—" She spun around. Her eyes filled with tears at the sight of Kurt standing on the other side of the screen door, a bouquet of wild roses in one hand, the phone in the other.

"Hey, babe," he said casually, as if he'd just come back from walking Pepper and not just walked back into her life from halfway across the United States.

She burst through the door, jumped into his arms, and wrapped her legs around his waist. "You're here. You're rea—"

He dropped the phone and the flowers, cupped the back of her head and took her in the sweetest kiss she'd ever tasted. Pepper ran around them in circles, barking and whining and pawing at Kurt's legs.

"You are my moment, Leanna. If you're here, I want to be right here with you. Every minute of every day."

"Here?"

He kissed her again. "Here."

"But New York?" She couldn't believe he was there. He looked so tired, and he held her like she was light as air.

"Would be hell without you."

AN HOUR LATER Kurt lay on his back in Leanna's bed. Her head rested on his chest, her arm was draped over his stomach, and he'd never felt happier in all his life. A gentle breeze swept the curtains away from the window.

"Uh-oh," he whispered.

"What?"

"We left the window open again." He kissed the top of her head.

"Tony's not here. He went to Nantucket." She leaned up on her elbow. "So we can be as loud as we want."

"Does that mean we can chunky-dunk, too?"

"Only if you're very…" She kissed Kurt's chin. "Very." She kissed his lips. "Good."

"That sounds like an invitation to me." He lowered his mouth to hers again, intending to be far better than good. Again.

Chapter Thirty-Three

MONDAY MORNING GREETED them with sunshine, a warm breeze, and surety. Kurt felt invigorated. Alive. He knew without a shadow of a doubt that he'd made the right decision coming back to the Cape. *Coming back to Leanna.* He'd thought writing was everything, and he'd been so wrong that it was almost embarrassing. He had a lot to learn about life, and he looked forward to experiencing and learning it all with Leanna.

He called Jackie and scheduled a Skype meeting instead of a person-to-person meeting. Jackie told him he was the last of the holdouts, that she met with most of her clients via Skype, and not to worry about moving out of New York. It wouldn't have mattered what she said. He'd made up his mind, and his life was with Leanna, wherever that may lead them, and at the moment it was leading them to his cottage.

They walked along the dune overlooking the

beach. Leanna had on a pair of cutoff jeans shorts and a white tank top, and with the morning breeze blowing her hair off of her shoulders and the sun glistening against her silky skin, she couldn't have looked more beautiful. God, he'd missed her. His heart swelled with love as he took her hand and gazed lovingly into her eyes.

"I want a life with you. A whole life, Leanna. Not just part-time, and not just when things are good. I want to experience your world, and I want you to experience mine. You're my final chapter, Leanna. No revisions necessary. Live with me here, where we first met. Build a life with me."

Her forehead wrinkled and her lower lip trembled. She trapped it between her teeth and pressed her hands to his chest. "There's no place on earth I'd rather be."

He lowered his mouth to hers and kissed her softly; then, with Pepper at their heels, they crossed the lawn toward the studio.

"I forgot you even had a studio."

"It's not really a studio anymore. The renovations aren't yet complete, but soon..." He unlocked the arched wooden door and pushed it open.

Leanna took a step inside and drew in a deep breath. She reached for Kurt's hand as her gaze slid along the wall of custom cabinetry to their right. Blue was right; the warm bronze, beiges, and golds of the granite brought warmth to the hickory cabinets. There were still a number of cabinets to be hung, but the project was taking shape and the studio already felt homier, more like Leanna. She looked up at the exposed-beam ceiling, and finally, her eyes came to rest on the four stainless-steel ovens and stovetops that had yet to be installed, but he knew she could visualize the end result.

"Kurt," she said barely above a whisper. "You did this for me?" She walked farther into the room, one slow step at a time.

"We met on this property, so I thought you might want a place for your business that was meaningful."

Leanna ran her fingers along the granite countertop. She touched the fine wood finish of the cabinetry with both hands and turned damp eyes to Kurt.

"You took a big chance on me."

He folded her in his arms. "Did I? You didn't feel like a *chance* at all. You felt like fate."

"Fate," she whispered. Leanna pressed her hands to his chest and gazed up at him with a dreamy, loving gaze. "I can't believe you did this."

"There's nothing I wouldn't do for you. I've spent years living in the minds of fictional characters and wrapped up in fictional worlds. I want to spend the rest of my life wrapped up in you, Leanna Bray, living in the very real world that we create together."

The End

Recipes for Luscious Leanna's Sweet Treats are included at the end of this book

Please enjoy a preview of the next
Love in Bloom novel

Taken by Love

The Bradens

Love in Bloom Series

Melissa Foster

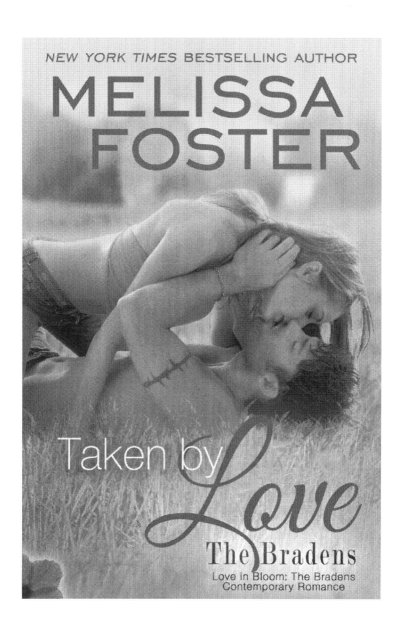

Chapter One

DAISY HONEY JUGGLED a cup of coffee, a cake she'd bought for her mother, a bag of two chocolate-dipped doughnuts—because a girl's gotta have something sweet in her life, and this was about all the sweetness she had time for at the moment—and her keys.

"You sure you got that, sugar?" Margie Holmes had worked at the Town Diner for as long as Daisy could remember. With her outdated feathered hairstyle and old-fashioned, pink waitress uniform, Margie was as much a landmark in Trusty, Colorado, as the backdrop of the Colorado Mountains and miles and miles of farms and ranches. Trusty was a far cry from Philly, where Daisy had just completed her medical residency in family practice, and it was the last place she wanted to be.

Daisy glanced at the clock. She had ten minutes to get to work. *Work.* If she could call working as a temporary doctor at the Trusty Urgent Care Clinic *work*. She'd worked damn hard to obtain her medical degree with the hopes of leaving the Podunk town behind, but the idea of relocating had been delayed when her father fell off the tractor and injured his back. She'd never turn her back on her family, even if she'd rather be starting her career elsewhere. She supposed it was good timing—if there was such a thing. Daisy had been offered permanent positions in Chicago and New York, and she had four weeks to accept or decline the offers. She hoped by then her father would either have hired someone to manage the farm or decided if he was going to sell—an idea she was having a difficult time stomaching, since the farm had been in her family for generations. Since the closest hospital or family physician was forty-five minutes away, and the urgent care clinic picked up the slack in the small town, Daisy was happy to have found temporary employment in her field even if it wasn't ideal.

"Yeah, I've got it. Thanks for the cake, Margie. Mom will love it." She pushed the door open with her butt—*thank you, doughnuts*—just as someone tugged it open, causing her to stumble. As if in slow motion, the cake tipped to the side. Daisy slammed her eyes shut to avoid seeing the beautiful triple-layer chocolate-almond cake crash to the ground.

There was no telltale *clunk!* of the box hitting the floor. She opened one eye and was met with a pair of muscled pecs attached to broad shoulders and six foot something of unadulterated male beefcake oozing pure male sexuality—and he was holding her mother's cake in one large hand, safe and sound.

She swallowed hard against the sizzling heat radiating off of Luke Braden, one of only two men in Trusty who had ever stood up for her—and the man whose face she pictured on lonely nights. When she'd decided to come back to Trusty, her mind had immediately raced back to Luke. She'd wondered—maybe even hoped—she'd run into him. Residency had been all-consuming and exhausting, with working right through thirty-six-hour shifts. She hadn't had time to even think about dating, much less had time for actual dating. Her body tingled in places that hadn't been touched by a man in a very long time.

"I think it's okay." With smoldering dark eyes and a wickedly naughty grin, he eyed the cake.

His deep voice shuddered through her. *Okay, Daisy. Get ahold of yourself. He might have saved you in high school, but that was eleven years ago.* He was no longer the cute boy with long bangs that covered perpetually hungry eyes. No, Luke Braden was anything but a boy, and by the look on his face, he had no recollection of who she was, making the torch she'd carried for him all these years heavy as lead.

"Thank you." She reached for the cake, and he pulled it just out of reach as his eyes took a slow stroll down her body, which was enough to weaken her knees *and* wake her up. She'd left Trusty after high school and had purposely found work near her college and med school during summers and breaks, so her memory of the people she'd gone to school with was sketchy at best after eleven years, but his was a face she'd never forget.

"You've got your hands full. Why don't I carry it to

your car?" His dark hair was cut short on the sides. The top was longer, thick and windblown in that sexy way that only happened in magazines. His square jaw was peppered with rough stubble, and Daisy had the urge to reach out and stroke it. *His stubble, that is.*

Luke looked like one of those guys who took what they wanted and left a trail of women craving more in their wake, and in high school his reputation had been just that. *Carry the cake to my car? Like that won't end up with you trying to carry me to your bed?* The idea sent another little shudder through her. It was exactly what she'd been hoping—and waiting—for.

He had been two years ahead of Daisy in school, and because she'd spent her high school years fighting a reputation she didn't deserve, she'd kept a low profile. She'd darkened her hair in medical school to combat the stereotypical harassment that went along with having blond hair, blue eyes, and a body that she took care of. Now, thanks to a six-dollar box of dye every few weeks, it was a medium shade of brown. She'd never forget the time in her sophomore year when Luke had stood up for her. She'd carried a fantasy of him thinking of her for all these years. *Was I really that invisible to you?* Apparently, she was, because by the look on his face, he didn't recognize her, which stung like salt in a wound.

Her eyes caught on a flash of silver on his arm. Duct tape? She squinted to be sure. Yes, the wide strip of silver on his bulging biceps was indeed duct tape, and there was blood dripping from beneath it.

He followed her gaze to his arm with a shrug. "Scraped it on some wire at my ranch."

She should take her cake and walk right out the door, but the medical professional in her took over—and the hurt woman in her refused to believe he could have forgotten her that easily. She took a step back into the diner. "Margie, can I borrow your first aid kit?"

Luke's brows knitted together as he followed her inside. "If that's for me, I don't need it. Really."

Margie handed Daisy the first aid kit from beneath the counter. "Here you go, sugar." She eyed the tall, dark man, and her green eyes warmed. "Luke, are you causing trouble again?"

He arched a thick, dark brow. "Hardly. I'm meeting Emily here, but I'm a little early."

"Good, because the last thing you need is more trouble." Margie gave him a stern look as she came around the counter, and he flashed a warm smile, the kind a person reserved for those he cared about.

Daisy felt a stab of jealousy and quickly chided herself for it. She'd been back in town for only two weeks, and she had kept as far away from gossip as she could, but she couldn't help wondering what type of trouble Luke had gotten into. Her life was crazy enough without a guy in it. Especially a guy with enticing eyes and a sexy smile who deserved the reputation she didn't. She focused on his arm and slipped into doctor mode, which she was, thankfully, very good at. In doctor mode she could separate the injured patient from the hot guy.

Luke shot a look at Daisy, then back to Margie. "Can't believe everything you hear."

I bet.

"Glad to hear that." Margie touched his arm like she might her son. "I have to help the customers, but it's good to see you, Luke."

He flashed that killer smile again, then shifted his eyes back to Daisy, who was armed and ready with antiseptic. "I don't allow strangers to undress my wounds." He held out a hand. "Luke."

"You really don't remember me." Even though she'd seen it in his eyes, it still burned. "Daisy Honey?"

His sexy smile morphed into an amused one, and that amusement reached his eyes. "Was that Daisy, honey, or Daisy Honey, as in your full name?"

She bit back the ache of reality that he didn't even remember her name and passed it off with an eye roll. She turned his arm so she could inspect his duct-tape bandage. "Daisy Honey, as in my given name."

He laughed at that, a deep, hearty, friendly laugh.

She ripped the tape off fast, exposing a nasty gash in his upper arm.

"Hey." He wrenched his arm away. "With a name like Daisy Honey, I thought you'd be sweet."

She blinked several times, and with her sweetest voice she said, "With a name like Luke Braden, I thought you'd be more manly." *Shit. I can't believe I said that.*

"Ouch. You don't mince words, do you?" He rubbed his arm. "I was kidding. I know who you are. I get my hay from your dad. I just didn't recognize you. The last time I saw you, your hair was blond." He ran his eyes down her body again, and damn if it didn't make her hot all over. "And you sure as hell didn't look like that."

You do remember me! She ignored Luke's comment about her looks, secretly tucking it away with delight, and went to work cleaning his cut. "How'd you do this, anyway?" She felt his eyes on her as she swabbed the dried blood from his skin.

"I was walking past a fence and didn't see the wire sticking out. Tore right through my shirt." He rolled down the edge of his torn sleeve just above his cut.

"Barbed wire, like your tattoo?" *Your hot, sexy, badass tattoo that wraps around your incredibly hard muscle?*

He eyed his tattoo with a half-cocked smile. "Regular fence wire."

"Was it rusty?" She tried to ignore the heat of his assessing gaze.

He shrugged again, which seemed to be a common answer for him.

"When was your last tetanus shot?" She finished cleaning the cut and placed a fresh bandage over it before wrapping the dirty swabs in a napkin.

He shrugged. "I'm fine."

"You won't be if you get tetanus. You should stop by the medical clinic for a shot. Any of the nurses can administer it for you." She tucked her hair behind her ear and checked the time. She was definitely late, and he was definitely checking her out. Her stomach did a little flip.

"Are you a nurse?" He rolled up his torn sleeve again.

"Doctor, actually," she said with pride. She wondered if seeing her helping *him* stirred the memory of when he stood up for her all those years ago. By the look in his eyes, she doubted it. He had that first-meeting look, the one that read, *I wonder if I have a shot,* rather than the look of, *You're that girl everyone said was a slut.*

He nodded, and his eyes turned serious. "Well, thank you, Dr. Daisy Honey. I appreciate the care and attention you've given to my flesh."

He said *my flesh* with a sensual and evocative tone that tripped her up. She opened her mouth to respond and no words came.

Margie returned to the counter. "Can I get you something, Luke?"

Thankful for the distraction, Daisy pushed the first aid kit across the counter, then gathered her things. "Thanks, Margie."

"I'd love coffee and two eggs over easy with toast," Luke said.

Daisy felt his eyes on her as she struggled to handle the cake, bag, and coffee again.

"Coming right up, sugar." Margie disappeared into the kitchen, and Daisy headed for the door.

He touched her arm and batted his long, dark lashes. "You're just going to dress my wound and leave? I feel so cheap."

Despite herself, she had to laugh. "That was actually kind of cute."

He narrowed his eyes, and it about stole her breath. "Cute? Not at all what I was going for."

Then you hit your mark, because it wasn't cute that's making my pulse race.

He held the door open for her. "I hope to see you around Daisy, honey."

"Tetanus isn't fun. You should get the shot." She forced her legs to carry her away from his heated gaze.

LUKE THOUGHT ABOUT Daisy as he sat in a booth drinking coffee and waiting for his sister to arrive. Luke bought hay from Daisy's father, and he'd known David Honey's daughter was coming back into town for a few weeks, but he'd never have connect the Daisy Honey he met today, with her entrancing blue eyes and way-too-sexy body, with the white-blond girl who used to walk through the halls of school with her head down, trying desperately to be invisible. Daisy's eyes were sharper and wiser than they'd been all those years ago, and there was something else about this new, grown-up Daisy that had captivated him. When she touched him, the air between them sizzled. She'd done everything possible to keep him from seeing that she'd felt it too, and for some strange reason, that intrigued him.

He was still thinking about her when Emily slapped an armful of drawings and folders down on the table.

"You are such a pain. I can't believe after I asked you a dozen times if you were sure you wanted the bed and bath separate, and I begged you—*begged you*—not to do it that way, that now you want to change it." She tossed her straight dark hair over her shoulder and straightened her white silk blouse and black pencil skirt before sitting down. Emily was an architect and owned a design build company. She was also becoming an expert in the field of sustainable energy. "This would have been much easier if you'd listened to me at the beginning—but..." She narrowed her eyes and pointed a finger at him. "Then again, if you had listened to me, I could have built you a passive house, and you could have saved seventy percent on your energy bills—"

"Okay, okay. I get it. Sit down and chill." Emily was fourteen months older than Luke, and at the moment she was giving him the same narrow-eyed, knitted-brow stare he'd seen too many times growing up. "Maybe you should skip the coffee this morning."

"Ha-ha." She flagged down Margie and ordered coffee. Black. Emily had always been feisty, and Luke supposed she had to be, growing up with five brothers. "So, are we just modifying the bed and bath in the apartment above the barn, or did you decide to move the kitchen to the other side of the apartment as well?"

He knew moving the plumbing and the framing was going to be a pain in the ass for Emily and her staff. He'd never ask another builder to move the plumbing; he'd have left it as it was originally designed. But just as Emily had no issue calling him at three a.m. to discuss a dream she'd had or to show up unannounced with a bottle of wine when she needed to vent with someone she trusted, he knew she probably had expected his changes and was relieved he'd made them before the walls were erected.

She ran her eyes down his arm. "Hey, what happened?"

Margie brought Emily her coffee as Wes walked into the diner. "And then there were three."

"Hey, Margie." Wes slid into the booth beside Emily. Each of the Bradens were blessed with thick dark hair, though Emily's was straight and shiny, Luke's was coarse and wavy, and Wes's was a shade lighter and he kept it cropped much shorter than his brothers'. His cargo shorts and tank top were streaked with dirt, as was his forehead.

"Hey, sugar. I'll bring your usual over in just a sec." With her hand on her hip, she looked Wes over and shook her head. "Were you out on the trails already today?"

Wes raised his hand. "Guilty as charged. Checking out new trails. Tough life, but someone has to do it." Wes ran a dude ranch and spent his time teaching well-paying clients how to rope and run cattle, ride horses, skeet shoot, and fish. He also took them on overnight pioneering adventures. Wes eyed Luke and Emily, then the pile of drawings on the table. "Did I miss anything?"

"What are you doing here?" Luke had recently helped Wes on a pioneering trip with a group of clients. He'd wound up going head-to-head with one of them and was arrested for assault. Even though the charges against Luke had been dropped, Luke was still dealing with what it said about him. He'd been thinking of nothing but ever since.

"Em said she was meeting you for breakfast." Wes shrugged. "I was hungry."

"I was just asking Luke what happened to his arm." Emily arched a finely manicured brow.

Luke shrugged. "It's nothing. I cut it on a fence, but I did just run into Daisy Honey, who cleaned it up for me. You guys remember her?" He thought of the way she'd ripped the tape from his arm and her snarky comment. She was feisty, and he liked it.

"Isn't she the girl who had that horrible rep about sleeping around in high school?" Emily drank her coffee and opened one of her folders. "God, I felt so bad for her." Trusty was like any other small town, where gossip spread faster than weeds.

"Hot little blond number?" Wes asked.

"Not anymore. I mean, hot yes, but she dyed her hair darker. I guess she got tired of dealing with all the crap, and just for the record, I don't think those rumors were true." Luke could relate to dealing with crap, and a memory was snaking its way into his mind. He couldn't quite grasp it, but he had the distinct feeling that it had something to do with Daisy.

"I see that look in your eye, Luke. Careful. You're the last thing a woman dodging a prickly past needs." Wes held his gaze a beat too long. One of his key employees, Ray Mulligan, had quit a few weeks earlier, leaving Wes and his business partner, Chip, to lead every group that came to the ranch. Wes had been snappy and short-tempered ever since.

Luke was all too aware of his own reputation, and the arrest didn't help much. He wasn't big on lasting relationships. Or rather, he didn't connect well on deeper levels with people. Give him a horse and he could practically tell what they were thinking, but people? Women? Whole different ball game. It was only recently that he'd begun to wonder why that was.

"Dude, what's that supposed to mean?" Luke held his brother's gaze. Having been raised by their mother after their father, Buddy Walsh, took off with a dime-store clerk from another town while their mother was still pregnant with Luke, all of his siblings were protective of one another. Luke was the same, and usually their fierce family loyalty served them well, but at times like this, the last thing he needed was to be judged by Wes.

"She's had enough of a bad rep. She doesn't need yours following her around."

"Shit, Wes. You know damn well that arrest wasn't my fault. You saw what went down." The muscles in his jaw twitched.

"I wasn't talking about the arrest."

Emily slid a folder across the table to Luke; then she unfurled a set of architectural drawings, her eyes darting between them. "Can we not play Neanderthal today? Please? I have client meetings to attend to."

Margie brought Luke and Wes their breakfasts, and Emily slid the drawings to the side. "There you are, boys. Em? You want anything else?"

"No, thanks, Margie. I'm good." Emily watched Luke skim the file. "Want me to explain it?"

Luke set the file down. "Nope. I just want you to do it. I don't need to decipher the details. I want the bathroom and bedroom attached. It was shortsighted of me not to do that in the first place. I just didn't like the idea of there not being a guest bath."

Wes shook his head.

"What?" He knew damn well what Wes was thinking. His brother was a planner. He mulled over every detail of his life, which was a good thing in his profession, and he thought Luke was impetuous, that he didn't think things through. The truth was, Luke was a pantser—hard and fast. He ran from planning too far ahead or in too much detail like a rebellious teenager. Most of the time, his gut instincts were right, but sometimes, where they might have been right at the time, after thinking things through, he realized that the next idea he had was better.

In Luke's eyes, those changes would have come after his decision was made even if he'd planned things out first, like Wes did. That thought process was so far from Wes's that they often butted heads.

"Don't you want to go over the specifications?" Wes asked.

"Hell no. What I want is to get home and check on my new foal. I trust Emily's judgment, and she knows my budget. She's banging out a few walls, moving some plumbing around."

"Hey. Nice to know you value my job so much, you ass." Emily took a piece of toast from his plate and bit it, then smirked at him. "It's a one-bedroom apartment for a ranch hand. Why on earth would it need a guest bath? If you'd only listened..."

"Sorry, Em. You know I value what you do, and yeah, maybe I should have listened." Luke shoveled his food into his mouth and lifted his chin in Wes's direction. "Don't you have a playdate?"

"Yeah," Wes said with a sly grin. "With a petite little brunette and a set of books."

"Clarissa?" Emily pointed at Wes. "I knew you two would hook up."

"She's my bookkeeper, not my girlfriend, and we've never hooked up." He put his arm around Emily with a sigh. "If you put as much energy into your own love life as you do mine, then maybe you wouldn't be alone."

"I'm not alone. I'm dating." She scrunched her nose. "Sort of. I think. Ugh. Do you have any idea how hard it is to date in this town?"

Luke and Wes both laughed, deep, loud, knowing laughs.

"Right. I guess you do, but it's easier for guys. You guys have dated half the women in Trusty and it just makes the women you haven't dated want you more. It's not like that for girls."

"It sure as hell better not be," Luke said. He might be her younger brother, but he'd learned from the best four older brothers a guy could have how to protect his sister. Part of protecting her meant making sure she didn't put herself in a position to become the talk of the town. That was better suited for the men in the Braden family—or at least it had been. Luke had changed. He'd always been restless, and that included being unable to settle down with just one woman, but since buying the ranch two years ago, that restless itch had calmed, and he'd become far more focused. He liked working with his hands, being around animals, and not being told what to do. The ranch was a perfect fit, and he was finally ready to make changes in his personal life, too. He wanted to be with one woman, a woman who would understand him, love him for who he was—his inability to plan and all. Someone who valued family, loved animals, and wasn't looking for something more than he could give. But that took opening himself in ways he didn't even understand himself, and he had no clue how to go about any of it.

Wes finished his food and locked his eyes on Luke.

"I've got to run. Bro, just tread carefully with Daisy, that's all. You know what she's been through."

Twenty minutes later Luke climbed onto his Harley and headed back toward his ranch, thinking about Daisy and what she'd gone through in high school. Maybe they weren't so different after all.

(End of Sneak Peek)
To continue reading, be sure to pick up the next
LOVE IN BLOOM release:

TAKEN BY LOVE, *The Bradens*
Love in Bloom series, Book Fifteen

Please enjoy a preview of the next
Love in Bloom novel

SEASIDE DREAMS

Seaside Summers, Book One

Love in Bloom Series

Melissa Foster

Chapter One

BELLA ABBASCIA STRUGGLED to keep her grip on a ceramic toilet as she crossed the gravel road in Seaside, the community where she spent her summers. It was one o'clock in the morning, and Bella had a prank in store for Theresa Ottoline, a straitlaced Seaside resident and the elected property manager for the community. Bella and two of her besties, Amy Maples and Jenna Ward, had polished off two bottles of Middle Sister wine while they waited for the other cottage owners to turn in for the night. Now, dressed in their nighties and a bit tipsy, they struggled to keep their grip on a toilet that Bella had spent two days painting bright blue, planting flowers in, and adorning with seashells. They were carrying the toilet to Theresa's driveway to break rule number fourteen of the Community Homeowners Association Guidelines: *No tacky displays allowed in the front of the cottages.*

"You're sure she's asleep?" Bella asked as they

came to the grass in front of the cottage of their fourth bestie, Leanna Bray.

"Yes. She turned off her lights at eleven. We should have hidden it someplace other than my backyard. It's so far. Can we stop for a minute? This sucker is heavy." Amy drew her thinly manicured brows together.

"Oh, come on. Really? We only have a little ways to go." Bella nodded toward Theresa's driveway, which was across the road from her cottage, about a hundred feet away.

Amy glanced at Jenna for support. Jenna nodded, and the two lowered their end to the ground, causing Bella to nearly drop hers.

"That's so much better." Jenna tucked her stick-straight brown hair behind her ear and shook her arms out to her sides. "Not all of us lift weights for breakfast."

"Oh, please. The most exercise I get during the summer is lifting a bottle of wine," Bella said. "Carrying around those boobs of yours is more of a workout."

Jenna was just under five feet tall with breasts the size of bowling balls and a tiny waist. She could have been the model for the modern-day Barbie doll, while Bella's figure was more typical for an almost thirty-year-old woman. Although she was tall, strong, and relatively lean, she refused to give up her comfort foods, which left her a little soft in places, with a figure similar to Julia Roberts or Jennifer Lawrence.

"I don't carry them with my arms." Jenna looked down at her chest and cupped a breast in each hand.

"But yeah, that would be great exercise."

Amy rolled her eyes. Pin-thin and nearly flat chested, Amy was the most modest of the group, and in her long T-shirt and underwear, she looked like a teenager next to curvy Jenna. "We only need a sec, Bella."

They turned at the sound of a passionate moan coming from Leanna's cottage.

"She forgot to close the window again," Jenna whispered as she tiptoed around the side of Leanna's cottage. "Typical Leanna. I'm just going to close it."

Leanna had fallen in love with bestselling author Kurt Remington the previous summer, and although they had a house on the bay, they often stayed in the two-bedroom cottage so Leanna could enjoy her summer friends. The Seaside cottages in Wellfleet, Massachusetts, had been in the girls' families for years, and they had spent summers together since they were kids.

"Wait, Jenna. Let's get the toilet to Theresa's first." Bella placed her hands on her hips so they knew she meant business. Jenna stopped before she reached for the window, and Bella realized it would have been a futile effort anyway. Jenna would need a stepstool to pull that window down.

"Oh…Kurt." Leanna's voice split the night air.

Amy covered her mouth to stifle a laugh. "Fine, but let's hurry. Poor Leanna will be mortified to find out she left the window open again."

"I'm the last one who wants to hear her having sex. I'm done with men, or at least with commitments, until my life is back on track." Ever since last summer, when Leanna had met Kurt, started her own jam-making business, and moved to the Cape full-time, Bella had been thinking of making a change of her own. Leanna's success had inspired her to finally go for it. Well, that and the fact that she'd made the mistake of dating a fellow teacher, Jay Cook. It had been months since they broke up, but they'd taught at the same Connecticut high school, and until she left for the summer, she couldn't avoid running in to him on a daily basis. It was just the nudge she needed to take the plunge and finally quit her job and start over. *New job, new life, new location.* She just hadn't told her friends yet. She'd thought she would tell them the minute she arrived at Seaside and they were all together, maybe over a bottle of wine or on the beach. But Leanna had been spending a lot of time with Kurt, and every time it was just the four of them, she hadn't been ready to come clean. She knew they'd worry and ask questions, and she wanted to have some of the transition sorted out before answering them.

"Bella, you can't give up on men. Jay was just a jerk." Amy touched her arm.

She really needed to fill them in on the whole Jay and quitting her job thing. She was beyond over Jay, but they knew Bella to be the stable one of the group, and learning of her sudden change was a conversation that needed to be handled when they weren't wrestling a fifty-pound toilet.

"Fine. You're right. But I'm going to make all of my future decisions separate from any man. So...until my life is in order, no commitments for me."

"Not me. I'd give anything to have what Kurt and

Leanna have," Amy said.

Bella lifted her end of the toilet easily as Jenna and Amy struggled to lift theirs. "Got it?"

"Yeah. Go quick. This damn thing is heavy," Jenna said as they shuffled along the grass.

"More..." Leanna pleaded.

Amy stumbled and lost her grip. The toilet dropped to the ground, and Jenna yelped.

"Shh. You're going to wake up the whole complex!" Bella stalked over to them.

"Oh, Kurt!" Jenna rocked her hips. "More, baby, more!"

"Really?" Bella tried to keep a straight face, but when Leanna cried out again, she doubled over with laughter.

Amy, always the voice of reason, whispered, "Come on. We *need* to close her window."

"Yes!" Leanna cried.

They fell against one another in a fit of laughter, stumbling beside Leanna's cottage.

"I could make popcorn." Jenna said, struggling to keep a straight face.

Amy scowled at her. "She got pissed the last time you did that." She grabbed Bella's hand and whispered through gritted teeth, "Take out the screen so you can shut the window, please."

"I told you we should have put a lock on the outside of her window," Jenna reminded them. Last summer, when Leanna and Kurt had first begun dating, they often forgot to close the window. To save Leanna embarrassment, Jenna had offered to be on sex-noise mission control and close the window if

Leanna ever forgot to. A few drinks later, she'd mistakenly abandoned the idea for the summer.

"While you close the window, I'll get the sign for the toilet." Amy hurried back toward Bella's deck in her boy-shorts underwear and a T-shirt.

Bella tossed the screen to the side so she could reach inside and close the window. The side of Leanna's cottage was on a slight incline, and although Bella was tall, she needed to stand on her tiptoes to get a good grip on the window. The hem of the nightie caught on her underwear, exposing her ample derriere.

"Cute satin skivvies." Jenna reached out to tug Bella's shirt down and Bella swatted her.

Bella pushed as hard as she could on the top of the window, trying to ignore the sensuous moans and the creaking of bedsprings coming from inside the cottage.

"The darn thing's stuck," she whispered.

Jenna moved beside her and reached for the window. Her fingertips barely grazed the bottom edge.

Amy ran toward them, waving a long stick with a paper sign taped to the top that read, WELCOME BACK.

Leanna moaned, and Jenna laughed and lost her footing. Bella reached for her, and the window slammed shut, catching Bella's hair. Leanna's dog, Pepper, barked, sending Amy and Jenna into more fits of laughter.

With her hair caught in the window and her head plastered to the sill, Bella put a finger to her lips. "Shh!"

Headlights flashed across Leanna's cottage as a car turned up the gravel road.

"Shit!" Bella went up on her toes, struggled to lift the window and free her hair, which felt like it was being ripped from her skull. The curtains flew open and Leanna peered through the glass. Bella lifted a hand and waved. *Crap.* She heard Leanna's front door open, and Pepper bolted around the corner, barking a blue streak and knocking Jenna to the ground just as a police car rolled up next to them and shined a spotlight on Bella's ass.

CADEN GRANT HAD been with the Wellfleet Police Department for only three months, having moved after his partner of nine years was killed in the line of duty. He'd relocated to the small town with his teenage son, Evan, in hopes of working in a safer location. So far, he'd found the people of Wellfleet to be respectful and thankful for the efforts of the local law enforcement officers, a welcome change after dealing with rebellion on every corner in Boston. Wellfleet had recently experienced a rash of small thefts—cars being broken into, cottages being ransacked, and the police had begun patrolling the private communities along Route 6, communities that in the past had taken care of their own security. Caden rolled up the gravel road in the Seaside Cottage community and spotted a dog running circles around a person rolling on the ground.

He flicked on the spotlight as he rolled to a stop. *Holy Christ. What is going on?* He quickly assessed the situation. A blond woman was banging on a window with both hands. Her shirt was bunched at her waist, and a pair of black satin panties barely covered the most magnificent ass he'd seen in a long time.

"Open the effing window!" she hollered.

Caden stepped from the car. "What's going on here?" He walked around the dark-haired woman, who was rolling from side to side on the ground while laughing hysterically, and the fluffy white dog, who was barking as though his life depended on it, and he quickly realized that the blond woman's hair was caught in the window. Behind him another blonde crouched on the ground, laughing so hard she kept snorting. *Why the hell aren't any of you wearing pants?*

"Leanna! I'm stuck!" the blonde by the window yelled.

"Officer, we're sorry." The blonde behind him rose to her feet, tugging her shirt down to cover her underwear; then she covered her mouth with her hand as more laughter escaped. The dog barked and clawed at Caden's shoes.

"Someone want to tell me what's going on here?" Caden didn't even want to try to guess.

"We're..." The brunette laughed again as she rose to her knees and tried to straighten her camisole, which barely contained her enormous breasts. She ran her eyes down Caden's body. "Well, *hello* there, handsome." She fell backward, laughing again.

Christ. Just what he needed, three drunk women.

The brunette inside the cottage lifted the window, freeing the blonde's hair, which sent her stumbling backward and crashing into his chest. There was no ignoring the feel of her seductive curves beneath the thin layer of fabric. Her hair was a thick, tangled mess. She looked up at him with eyes the color of rich cocoa and lips sweet enough to taste. The air around them pulsed with heat. Christ, she was beautiful.

"Whoa. You okay?" he asked. He told his arms to let her go, but there was a disconnect, and his hands remained stuck to her waist.

"It's...It's not what it looks like." She dropped her eyes to her hands, clutching his forearms, and she released him fast, as if she'd been burned. She took a step back and helped the brunette to her feet. "We were..."

"They were trying to close our window, Officer." A tall, dark-haired man came around the side of the cottage, wearing a pair of jeans and no shirt. "Kurt Remington." He held a hand out in greeting and shook his head at the women, now holding on to each other, giggling and whispering.

"Officer Caden Grant." He shook Kurt's hand. "We've had some trouble with break-ins lately. Do you know these women?" His eyes swept over the tall blonde. He followed the curve of her thighs to where they disappeared beneath her nightshirt, then drifted up to her full breasts, finally coming to rest on her beautiful dark eyes. It had been a damn long time since he'd been this attracted to a woman.

"Of course he knows us." The hot blonde stepped forward, arms crossed, eyes no longer wide and warm, but narrow and angry.

He hated men who leered at women, but he was powerless to refrain from drinking her in for one last second. The other two women were lovely in their own right, but they didn't compare to the tall blonde with fire in her eyes and a body made for loving.

Kurt nodded. "Yes, Officer. We know them."

"God, you guys. What the heck?" the dark-haired woman asked through the open window.

"You were waking the dead," the tall blonde answered.

"Oh, gosh. I'm sorry, Officer," the brunette said through the window. Her cheeks flushed, and she slipped back inside and closed the window.

"I assure you, everything is okay here." Kurt glared at the hot blonde.

"Okay, well, if you see any suspicious activity, we're only a phone call away." He took a step toward his car.

The tall blonde hurried into his path. "Did someone from Seaside call the police?"

"No. I was just patrolling the area."

She held his gaze. "Just patrolling the area? No one *patrols* Seaside."

"Bella," the other blonde hissed.

Bella.

"Seriously. No one patrols our community. They never have." She lifted her chin in a way that he assumed was meant as a challenge, but it had the opposite effect. She looked cuter than hell.

Caden stepped closer and tried to keep a straight face. "Your name is Bella?"

"Maybe."

Feisty, too. He liked that. "Well, Maybe Bella, you're right. We haven't patrolled your community in the past, but things have changed. We'll be patrolling more often to keep you safe until we catch the people who have been burglarizing the area." He leaned in close and whispered, "But you might consider wearing pants for your window-closing evening strolls. Never know who's traipsing around out here."

(End of Sneak Peek)

Check online retailers for the Seaside Summers series

Coming Late Summer 2014

SEASIDE DREAMS, Seaside Summers, Book One
Love in Bloom Series

Full LOVE IN BLOOM SERIES order

Love in Bloom books may be read as stand alones. For more enjoyment, read them in series order. Characters from each series carry forward to the next.

SNOW SISTERS

Sisters in Love (Book 1)
Sisters in Bloom (Book 2)
Sisters in White (Book 3)

THE BRADENS

Lovers at Heart (Book 4)
Destined for Love (Book 5)
Friendship on Fire (Book 6)
Sea of Love (Book 7)
Bursting with Love (Book 8)
Hearts at Play (Book 9)

THE REMINGTONS

Game of Love (Book 10)
Stroke of Love (Book 11)
Flames of Love (Book 12)
Slope of Love (Book 13)
Read, Write, Love (Book 14)

THE BRADENS (coming soon)

Taken by Love (Book 15)
Fated for Love (Book 16)
Romancing my Love (Book 17)
Flirting with Love (Book 18)
Dreaming of Love (Book 19)
Crashing into Love (Book 20)

Read, Write, Love

SEASIDE SUMMERS (coming soon)

Seaside Dreams
Seaside Hearts
Seaside Sunsets
Seaside Secrets

THE RYDERS (coming soon)

Duke Ryder
Blue Ryder
Trish Ryder
Jake Ryder
Gage Ryder

Specialty Jam Recipes*

Frangelico Peach
Makes 10 to 12 eight-ounce jars
Caution: Frangelico product contains nuts

3 lbs. peaches
2 tablespoons lemon juice
2-1.75oz packages of store-bought powdered pectin
7 cups sugar
1/4 cup Frangelico Liqueur

Place peaches in blender and blend until they are finely chopped.
Place peaches and lemon juice in an 8-quart saucepan and bring to a boil.
Add pectin and return to a boil. Continue stirring slowly so as not to let it burn to the bottom of the pan.
Add sugar slowly; bring to a boil.
Add 1/4 cup Frangelico; bring to boil for 2 minutes.
Fill jars.

Apricot with Lime
Makes 10 to 12 eight-ounce jars

3 lbs. apricots
2 tablespoons lemon juice
2-1.75oz packages of store-bought powdered pectin
3/4 cup lime pulp
7 cups sugar

Blend the apricots until they are finely chopped.
Place in 8-quart saucepan, add lemon juice and lime pulp, then bring to boil. Continue stirring slowly.
Add pectin and return to boil.
Add sugar slowly; bring to boil for 1 minute
Fill jars.

Strawberry-Apricot
Makes 10 to 12 eight-ounce jars

2 lbs. strawberries
1 lbs. apricots
2-1.75oz packages of store-bought powdered pectin
2 tablespoons of lemon juice
7 cups sugar
1/4 cup white wine

Place strawberries and apricots into blender and mix until finely chopped.
Place the fruit into 8-quart saucepan and bring to boil while stirring slowly.

Add lemon juice and pectin; bring to boil for 1 minute.
Add sugar slowly, continue stirring and bring to boil.
Add wine of your choice; boil for 1 minute.
Fill jars.

*Recipes compliments of Al Chisholm, Al's Backwoods Berries. www.alsbackwoodsberries.com.

Acknowledgments

Coming from a family of seven children, the closeness and importance of family is a subject that is always near and dear to my heart. I've received so many emails and social media messages from readers who enjoy the family aspect of my books, and I enjoy every one of them. As always, my fans have inspired, supported, and encouraged me. Thank you for reaching out. I'm delighted that the Remingtons and my writing has touched you, and I'd like to thank you for insisting that I write more books about the Bradens. I'm thrilled that the Bradens have stolen your hearts as they have stolen mine and look forward to more stories about the Bradens, the Remingtons, and the Snow Sisters.

In this book you've also met several of the characters who will be in the Seaside Summers series, and I hope you enjoyed them as well. If you follow me on social media, then you know Cape Cod is my favorite place on earth, and writing about it fills me with joy.

Congratulations to Denise Smith, who won a contest to name a character in this book. Thank you for giving me Leanna, and a special shout-out to your daughter Olivia. Thank you to all of my supportive friends and family who encourage me, talk me off the ledge, and indulge my obsessive writing endeavors.

There's not enough gratitude in the world to cover what I owe to my editorial team: Kristen Weber, Penina Lopez, Jenna Bagnini, Juliette Hill, and Marlene Engel. Thank you, Natasha Brown and Clare Ayala, for your endless patience and expertise.

Melissa Foster

Many thanks to Al Chisholm of Al's Backwoods Berries, my partner in the creation of Luscious Leanna's Sweet Treats and the best damn jam maker around. If you're ever in Wellfleet during the summer, you can find Al and Luscious Leanna's Sweet Treats at the flea market, or visit his website noted on the recipe page in this book.

Last but never least, thank you to my supportive husband and family, who make my writing possible.

Melissa Foster is a *New York Times* and *USA Today* bestselling and award-winning author. Her books have been recommended by *USA Today's* book blog, *Hagerstown* magazine, *The Patriot*, and several other print venues. She is the founder of the Women's Nest, a social and support community for women, and the World Literary Café. When she's not writing, Melissa helps authors navigate the publishing industry through her author training programs on Fostering Success. Melissa also hosts Aspiring Authors contests for children and has painted and donated several murals to the Hospital for Sick Children in Washington, DC.

Visit Melissa on her website or chat with her on The Women's Nest or social media. Melissa enjoys discussing her books with book clubs and reader groups and welcomes an invitation to your event.

Melissa's books are available through most online retailers in paperback and digital formats.

Made in the USA
Charleston, SC
08 June 2014